Salmo....

A Cornish Crime
Comedy Caper

By MG Mason

If history were taught
in the form of stories,
it would never be forgotten –

Rudyard Kipling

Salmonweir Tourist Board: A Guide to the Non-Living Residents

Event Sponsor: Afterlife PLC: **"Your Death, Is Our Life"**

Salmonweir has 500 residents, so not everybody you see is listed here. As you wander through the village, you may wish to use this list to encourage your children's interest in the people you see from our history, and ask if they can identify anybody noted here. Feel free to ask us for autographs; we're friendly and probably the least scary ghosts you are ever likely to meet! If you see anyone not listed here, please don't be afraid to talk to them.

The first five are permanent members of the village council

DI Karl Blackman: The village's only living resident (at present). A retired Detective Inspector from Cambridge who left the leafy streets of the university city for the sleepy village of Salmonweir and what he hoped would be a quiet retirement. Little did he know what an exciting retirement he would have in store on his arrival in Cornwall!

Hook Hand Harry: Salmonweir's most famous son! He is an 18th century pirate, captain of the galleon known as *The Lady Catherine*. You will nearly always see him aboard or around the ship. If he's not there, try *The King's Head* pub. We advise against accepting a rum drinking challenge. Ghosts can't get drunk and even if they could, Harry spent most of his life building up a tolerance to rum.

Kensa: Our very own Iron Age Warrior Queen! She was a chieftain of Dumnonia in life around the time of the Roman invasion. Salmonweir was not founded until centuries after her death and it's possible the village of which she was in charge lies beneath our village or nearby. Nevertheless, Kensa has come to see Salmonweir as home. **Caution: do not ask her about Boudicca.**

Brother Jowan: A Benedictine Monk from St. Michael's Mount at Marazion who visited Salmonweir in the late 1340s as part of the effort to provide medical relief for the victims of The Black Death. His medical training consists of chantry, herbs and dispersing miasma with incense. You will often find him in or around the church.

Pastor Eli: A Civil War Era Puritan preacher who visited Salmonweir as part of Lord High Protector Oliver Cromwell's efforts to subdue the pro-royalists in Cornwall. He assumed primacy over the village church. Although he stayed in our village just a short while before his death, his essence remains and he has become rather fond of our village. It is rare you will see Jowan and Eli together. If you do, run away, quickly.

Other people you might encounter

Ebrel Penrose: Daughter of Corin Penrose – the village shop owner. She certainly has *not* struggled to adjust. She can't wait for the day her father permits her to have a mobile phone even though nobody else in Salmonweir has one and not knowing anyone outside the village.

Dora Wilson: Wife of a war hero who died aboard HMS Hood during World War II. You will mostly see her on a bench overlooking the sea on the western side of the village. She doesn't interact with people much but has a friendly disposition.

Morwenna: Wife of a former innkeeper who, upon her reappearance in the 21st century, decided she fancied the job once performed by her husband. Morwenna is now landlady of *The King's Head* – a free house. She pulls a good pint! Incidentally, *The King's Head* has one of the largest ranges of cider anywhere in Cornwall.

Babajide: In life, he was a slave for Morwenna and her husband. Now, he is a barman and administrator for the village's tourist board. Babajide is rather quiet, but once you engage him in conversation at the bar, he is always willing to offer some anecdotes.

Cato: A Roman Naval officer who was part of a scouting mission along the coast of Dumnonia when his trireme sank when it encountered a storm. Cato was second in command of the ship and we know that he was born in what would be modern Syria.

Corin Penrose: An early 19th century shopkeeper. He hasn't quite got to grips with modern life and can't understand describing a person as both "cool" and "hot" are not contradictory. He runs the shop and stocks a range of local produce and big-name brands.

Wilhelmina Yorke: Miss Yorke is our local poet and spends most of her time in the pub compiling sonnets. For a small fee, she may write you a poem! Proceeds are split between Miss Yorke and the Salmonweir Tourist Board.

Chapter 1

Hello, my name is Karl, I'm a retired detective, the only living human in the village, and I have a murder to solve.

Was that a dramatic enough opening? My editor friend told me I need to be dramatic to make sure you keep reading. And now you've reached this point, I'm guessing I already have you hooked. You're intrigued to know how I could be the only person in a village and yet must solve a murder that took place here.

I said I was the only living human. I never said I was the only person.

I live in a pretty little village called Salmonweir. It's on the south Cornish coast, about halfway between Treen and Lamorna Cove. It's small, unassuming and completely untouched by the tourists from up country making the trek to Land's End. We're on the AONB (Area of Outstanding Natural Beauty for those who don't know) which is the least developed part of this sparsely populated county – and that's just the way I like it. It's the reason I came here in the first place.

There is craggy coast to our west and our east, and the village sits in a dip carved by a lazy, meandering river –

these days only a river – that leads to an ancient wooden quay cut square and sharp into the rock.

We have a pub and a shop next to each other on the quay, a teashop a little farther upstream next to the public car park (which can hold two coaches and about twenty cars – but I have never seen it full). On the eastern hillside is a 950-year-old church overlooking the quay and the village; it is the highest point of Salmonweir. From the top of the spire on a clear day, you can easily see Land's End.

We aren't normally affected by the summer tourist season here in Salmonweir despite that the place is so idyllic. The only thing to bring people in is the spectacular scenery and dramatic view of the village. There's nothing to keep people here, hence the tiny car park which is still too large to ever fill up even at the height of tourist season.

The worst we ever get is a few coach loads of ramblers on the way down to Land's End or back up, or day-trippers from Mousehole or Penzance. They take a few photos including the obligatory "selfie" with a statue of Hook Hand Harry, a pirate and the most famous person ever to come from this village.

They might then go in the village's only tea shop, turn their noses up and leave because it's so small and then go to the pub for some cider, and they leave again. Incidentally, the pub is a Free House and serves mostly cider – four of the regulars on tap have won the country's most prestigious awards. We're the Cider Capital of Britain and nobody knows it, and that's just the way I like it too.

We do, however, get quite a few walkers stopping off here along the Southwest Coast Path. They don't stay long and they're happy to keep our little village's charm quiet as a trade secret to be shared only with fellow serious hikers.

You may have realised that I'm not from here, but I already feel fully part of the village and its history. Two years ago, I took early retirement from Cambridgeshire Constabulary to live the dream down here in deepest, darkest pirate country. We bought a house on the west rim with a great view of the sea and a birds-eye view of Salmonweir.

We get the brunt of the wind in the autumn and the worst of the rain in winter, but my God we have a fantastic view on a clear day all the way up here! The view from the back bedroom would rival that from the church spire if it wasn't for the hill to the west blocking our view of Land's End.

Ah yes, the murder. Please hold your rum glass. I'm coming to that and there's something else you need to know first.

My wife – sorry, my soon to be *ex* wife, hates it here, but I didn't find that out until six months ago when she walked out and returned to Cambridge.

It was too much for her to be away from her family, especially since our kids settled where they went to university – Claire in Bristol, and the twins (Paul and Cassie) in Cardiff. Inseparable those two, even now – they even went to the same uni, fancy that! They never planned it, but Cardiff was the best place for each of their respective degree choices. Now, Paul is engaged to Cassie's best friend and Cassie is dating a friend of a friend of Paul's.

I kind of like it here – those were the last words I ever said to my wife face to face before she walked out on me for good, away from this weird village, away from what happened here. The incident was what broke the camel's back, but it was only a matter of time before she upped and left anyway.

This is what came to be. This is what made Salmonweir the talk of the tabloids and this is what made my soon to be ex-wife leave me and return to Cambridge.

11

It was a Sunday morning in April, unusually warm for the time of year and clear too. I had just popped to the local shop to get the newspaper and some milk so we could have tea. The last lot had gone off, probably because of the small power failure we'd had in the early hours lasting slightly too long.

We usually have breakfast in bed on a Sunday, every Sunday without fail – honey on toast and a pot of tea. But breakfast in bed without tea is just not breakfast and neither of us take our tea black. On the really good days, we sat on the veranda, but that was rare in April. We'd planned our first breakfast on the veranda for that particular morning, but everything changed.

When I got back to the quayside, I saw a few of the young lads from around the village were up already and basking in the sunshine; some brave souls had even gone for a dip – it couldn't have been all that warm, not in April. This is Cornwall, but there are cold months.

'Good morning Mister Blackman!' called one of the lads. I recognised him as the youngest son from the family a few doors away.

I bid him good morning in return and turned up the path leading to my home when he shouted the most horrific string of expletives. It was unbecoming a nine-year-old boy. When I was nine, I hadn't heard even half of those words.

I turned around to chastise him for breaking the sanctity of this pleasant Sunday morning when my jaw hit the floor so fast it made speech virtually impossible. If I had tried to speak, I'm sure it would have come out something like "whaaaaouswernaaa".

When I composed myself, I finally managed to ask him a question. 'Where did *that* come from?'

"F##k knows. I was just f###ing sat here drinking my f###king can of cola" ok, I'll leave out the swear words now you get the idea.

The boy told me that "it" had appeared from nowhere. One moment, he was admiring the view and enjoying the sunshine on his face, sipping his ice-cold coke for breakfast when a wooden ship flying the Jolly Roger appeared at the quayside.

His swearing ascended to a whole new level when a pirate hopped onto the harbour wall, crossed it and stopped in front of us. 'Greetins' landlubbers!' (I didn't say the pirate was not stereotypical). 'Please direct me at the nearest tavern. I be wanting some rum and maybe be enjoying meself with some local wenches?'

A young lad appeared from behind a large crate on the deck. He vaulted over the side of the ship, onto the dock and immediately went to the side of the pirate.

'There's no need to talk to us like that,' I snapped, 'we're not tourists.' I smiled at the boy who nodded in return and looked straight to the elder man like a puppy would its master.

The pirate ignored my comment and went on acting pirate-y, 'where be the nearest tavern landlubber?'

I cringed at the thought that he might add har-har-har at any point. 'You probably want *The King's Head*. It's just up the slope.'

He blinked at me. 'They keepin' the King's Head in there? Christ alive! King George be only on the throne this twelve month!'

I rolled my eyes; I'd never had the patience for foolishness from suspects. Now it seems I had no patience for over-zealous costume actors either. I gave him a smile and pointed along the road 'It's just up there and no, it's just the name of the tavern. They don't actually have a king's head.'

'This "King's Head". Does it serve rum?'

'Yes, but only the trendy big-name labels, I think. There's not much call for it around here. Plenty of cider though.'

'Bleddy cider? That might have to do, I suppose.' He gave me a queer look and then charged up the road. He stopped after four paces and turned back to me, noticing the boy staring curiously up to the buildings of the village and pointing. 'Come on Eddie!' he called, 'before the rum all be gone!' The boy did a half skip and ran up the road to catch his captain up.

I watched in disbelief as the man swung his sword about him and started singing *The Coast of High Barbary* at the boy, prompting the lad to join in.

I never knew the song before I came down here and now I hear it a dozen times every summer, usually when some tourist event is on in Padstow, Penzance or Falmouth. His rendition was certainly not the best I had heard but it had a certain quaint charm nonetheless.

At the quayside, the children were trying – and failing – to climb aboard the pirate ship. I watched them curiously; they couldn't get a hand grip on any part of the ship, no matter where they tried to climb aboard.

A few pirates were on deck and egging them on, encouraging them to take a long jump. Finally, the neighbour's boy marched away from the quayside for a run up, turned around and sprinted towards it.

His friends and the pirates cheered him on as he leapt into the air, legs flailing as he catapulted off the quayside and towards the ship. He appeared to make it and two of the pirates stepped forward to catch him – but inexplicably (then) he fell through their arms, through the decks, and into the water, leading to uproarious laughter from the pirates and from his friends. It wasn't dignified and he swore again as his head bobbed back up to the surface.

Leaving the boys and the pirate with the hammy acting, I continued my journey along the coast path until I got to the steps that lead to the small group of houses overlooking the bay. This is where we bought our dream home – or what I thought back then was our dream home.

There is a bench about halfway up and I sometimes stop to admire the view in the mornings. You can see a lot of water here, and it's the best view of the eastern crags too. I tend to think of it as my bench because I'd never seen anyone else use it.

That morning was different; I was surprised to see a woman in her late twenties or early thirties sat there. She gave the impression of being willowy and elegant, the sort of person who'd be typecast in costume dramas based purely on her appearance if she had chosen acting as a career.

I intended to bid her good morning and keep moving but as I passed, I heard a sob and could see she was crying into a handkerchief.

She wore old-fashioned clothes, even by my limited knowledge of modern women's fashion – a long, plain grey skirt, a white long-sleeved blouse and – get this – blue ribbons in her hair.

'Are you all right, my love?' Please don't see that term as sexist, I know people have turned against it in recent years. Maybe I'm old-fashioned, but I call every young lady that – and it nearly always worked to put female crime victims or witnesses at ease.

Besides which, this is the West Country, and everybody calls everyone else "my love" here irrespective of gender, age, or anything else. If I'm to blend it properly, I need to start getting used to it, right? Hey at least I didn't offer her an awkward "wazzon?".

'No,' she replied in a soft local accent, 'nothing will be all right again, good sir.'

Cautiously, I took my place on the bench next to her but kept my distance. She moved away from me, though whether in politeness to make sure I had enough space or to keep her distance from a stranger, I wouldn't like to hazard a guess.

'Whatever is the matter?'

'He's gone. He died at sea just as I knew he would.'

I frowned; I certainly hadn't heard of a fishing accident overnight, so I pressed her for more.

'I got the telegram this morning,' she said, 'He was on The Mighty Hood, we were so proud when he got that commission. Now sir, I trust there is no more else that needs to be said. It's all over the newspapers by now and on the wireless.'

'HMS Hood?'

She nodded. 'They said she were invincible, didn't they? But God thought otherwise. Now sir, if you don't mind, I want to remember my sailor husband alone and in peace. He done his duty for King and Country, and God saw fit not to spare him.' She turned away from me and I respected her wishes, leaving her alone on the bench and returning to my home.

Above our heads, a mean herring gull cawed a long mournful song and that seemed to set her off again.

This was most peculiar. Who were these people? Was there a history festival going on and nobody told the village? Was it some kind of weird history flash mob?

I carried on up the slope, enjoying the wind on my face and the cawing gulls serving as a permanent reminder that I live on the coast now. I went through the kissing gate and was back on top of the hill. As I neared our house, I heard an almighty scream from inside. From the bedroom, it was the unmistakeable shriek of my wife Valarie.

My legs had never been good at running, in fact my only attempt at a charity 10K brought me in at an embarrassing 1hr 50 mins where I struggled to stay ahead of the power walkers. I couldn't walk for days afterwards, but at that moment I ran with a pace that would have made Usain Bolt reconsider his career options.

I barged in through the open door and took the stairs two at a time. By the time I got to the top, I was already out of breath. I rounded the bannister and went crashing through the closed bedroom door, thinking to myself that I would be angry with her and feeling stupid at myself if it was only another spider she wanted me to throw out of the window.

What met me was the most curious sight. Wrapped in two towels – one around her body and another around her head and standing on the bed cowering, was my wife Valarie.

At the foot of the bed was a man dressed in black robes and waving what looked to me like a thurible... Oh hang on, if you're not Catholic you won't know what that is, will you? I'm a lapsed Catholic and for those who've never been inside a popish institution, it's the thing that the priest swings in the church with smoke coming from it; eventually it fills the building with incense smoke. It's kind of pleasant and reassuring, or so non-Catholic friends commenting later on its appearance have been eager to tell me.

Anyway, this monk reacted to my wife's screaming with complete indifference, continuing to wave the bloody thing all about our bedroom.

Valarie pointed at the monk with one hand and protected her modesty with the other. 'Get him out, get him out, Karl!'

'Calm yourself woman!' the monk chastised as though he had an open invitation to enter our bedroom and ruin the breakfast I should have been enjoying about now. 'This house is infested with plague!'

'Plague?' I asked incredulously.

'If the woman continues to disturb me, I might have to have her removed from my presence. This will not do.' He went on, 'I have important work.'

'Right, that's it.' I slammed the newspaper and milk on the bedside table. 'Get out of my house!'

'I was sent here at the owners' request. I'm here to disperse the miasma.' Finally, he stopped swinging the thurible. 'You can't send me away now! I came all the way from St. Michael's Mount. More are coming here; we must begin the chantry as soon as possible if we're to-'

'No chantry, no miasma and no bloody incense. Get out!' I pointed to the door. He gave us both a solemn look before silently gliding out of the room and down the stairs. I closed the door behind him.

I returned to the bedroom to see my wife Valarie sobbing on the bed. I put my arm around her and she flinched – not, I must add, for the first time.

'Valarie, talk to me. This isn't about that... monk, is it? Where the hell did he come from, anyway?'

'He appeared in the room while I was drying. I can't even have a bloody *shower* in peace now.' She complained.

'Something strange is going on in the village.' I explained the pirate ship and the war widow on the bench. 'Do you know of a history festival?'

She shook her head as though I'd just told her we'd been hit with a nuclear bomb. ''No, nothing ever happens here,' she sighed. 'What a horrible, horrible place this is!'

'Hey, that's a bit strong.' I put my arm around her wet shoulder.

This time she didn't flinch, instead she shrugged me off and pulled away. 'I was upset before he turned up and you *know* why. I can't do this. I can't stay here. I never wanted to come.'

'Woah, that's the first you've ever said *that!*' I did not reach out for her again. What I said was true. We both wanted this move.

'Yes well, there's a lot of stuff I should have said but didn't before we came down. I thought things would be better, but I was wrong. I'm leaving. Today.'

I couldn't believe what I was hearing and told her as much. 'Don't be daft! The kids are in Bristol and Cardiff.'

'I'll stay with dad for a while then get my own place. He needs help since his operation. Mum can't do it alone. It will be ideal for all of us in the short term. Sorry, I've decided. This is no whim; I've been contemplating it for days, weeks even.'

She stood up, grabbed some clothes, and retreated into the bathroom to dry and dress, sobbing the whole time.

And that was that. Within the hour, she had packed a suitcase full of clothes and essentials and left, driving first to Bristol to stay with Claire and then going on to her dad's place in Cambridge.

She never kissed me, hugged me, or even wanted to touch me. That moment felt like the end of our marriage. In some ways, I felt I learnt more about her in that hour-long conversation than I had in the nearly thirty-five years of our marriage.

If you haven't figured it out by now, Salmonweir (or "Salmonweird" as it is now called by the rest of the country) is home to just one *living* human – me. Everyone else is dead. One living human among 500 or more ghosts.

You've met three already: Hook Hand Harry the pirate, Dora Wilson the war widow, and Brother Jowan, the monk. You might be wondering what happened to Hook Hand Harry at the pub. He didn't like the rum and threatened to run the barman through – which he promptly did. His sword and his hand ran through the barman and nothing happened – much to everyone's amusement. It seems that the ghosts can interact with inanimate objects, and with each other, but not with living material.

Why did I choose to stay in this Cornish village with no salmon and no weir? Well, I *do* like it here. I admit this wasn't quite how I pictured my retirement going and I *certainly* never pictured being the only living human in the village, but I get to experience history every day; I get to meet weird and wonderful people.

New arrivals have now slowed to a trickle. Most turned up on that first day (about 300 by my reckoning) and we haven't had a new arrival in around three weeks. The last but one human resident left on the fifth day.

Now, some six months later, things are about to take an even stranger turn and I'm glad I stayed. I'm about to come out of retirement for these ghosts I have come to call friends and acquaintances.

Yes, the murder I mentioned at the start. There is a killer in Salmonweir, and because Devon & Cornwall Police Service (naturally) don't believe that people who are already dead can actually be murdered, I am all this village has.

DI Karl Blackman (retired and unretired) at your service.

Chapter 2

Let me tell you something else about Salmonweir. If it doesn't sound Cornish to your ears, then well done for spotting that small piece of trivia. It isn't Cornish and there has *never* been salmon around here. The weir is long gone, probably robbed of its components when the river became a stream sometime in the Tudor period.

We know that a monk founded it around the early 13th century as a monastic grange. The excitable young man travelled all the way from Glastonbury... so we are told. Now, this young man came from somewhere in the midlands and had (apparently) never seen a fish. His father, not knowing what else to do with him, presumably as his inability to identify a fish was the last straw, packed him away to Somerset to become a monk.

When he first saw a strange scaly creature with fins but no legs, he asked one of the elder monks what it was. The monk told him it was a salmon. We have no reason to doubt the elder monk's piscine identification skills. But to this young man who had never seen a fish – anything vaguely fish shaped was henceforth "salmon".

Delighted by his new discovery, he volunteered to be part of the building of a Grange funded by the convenient discovery of King Arthur's grave at the abbey. They ended up all the way down here in a gentle valley with a stream running through it and built the grange in which the young man swore he had seen salmon.

It wasn't to be.

Within 6 months, the young man and the rest of the team returned to Somerset in shame. The shallow river was home to eels, not salmon, and there wasn't many of those either. Word is, they couldn't even catch enough to feed all the monks at least one meal a day on the things. Not that the affluent monks up country would have stomached eel with their new-found A-list culinary expectations.

It was reported that the departing monks told the nearby Cornish villagers "the salmon weir is yours" and the name stuck. It didn't take much brain power for a 21st century hack journalist to add the "d" and now we're "Salmonweird".

I was thinking about this amusing story, and whether the clueless young monk would ever turn up in

Salmonweir, when the tree outside my window rattled against it.

That wasn't what woke me up on that October morning. Not that it was particularly cold for October, the slow decline of summer, and autumn finally waking up sometime in November was something about Cornwall I loved. It was cold compared to the mild day we'd had the day before and the good weather we'd been promised all week. The wind and the threat of rain this morning was most unwelcome. No, what woke me was the landline.

I grunted, rolled over, saw the name on the digital display and answered immediately. Nobody ever calls the landline except the kids and the media.

'Hello dad, it's Cass.'

I rubbed my eyes to clear the morning fog. 'Yes, I know. I've finally figured out how to make your names appear on the little screen.' I injected a smile into my voice. 'Good morning, sweetheart.'

'Sorry, did I wake you?'

'Just a little,' I lied, 'but it's about time I got my backside out of bed and had some tea. How are you, love?'

'I'm fine thanks, dad. Just going off to the airport with Charlie for our mini break.' I heard the distinct sound of traffic in the background.

'You're not on the phone and driving, are you?' I frowned.

'No, no. We've got an Uber. Parking costs are a nightmare and it's still not the easiest airport to get to.' She sighed.

'Where is it you're going, again?'

'Edinburgh, for a long weekend. It's Charlie's 30th birthday and I thought I'd treat him.'

'Make sure you have a good time. Send him my best wishes and remind him I've yet to meet this man who is making my daughter so happy.'

'We're coming at Christmas, remember. I'm curious to see Salmonweir. Must be the only person in the country who is though.' There was a sigh and a pause. She always did this when she wanted to say something important but didn't know how to say it. 'Dad?'

'Yes, love?'

'Paul and I. In fact, *Claire*, Paul and I think you should talk to mum. Try to sort things out and make it-.'

29

The line momentarily cut; they probably went under a bridge. My heart sank because I knew what was coming.

'Cass...'

'Dad, I know it's over, we all accept that. I know what mum is like but try to keep this amicable? Hang on a minute, dad.' she covered the speaker.

'Sorry, we're almost at the airport. Talk to her, please, if only so the divorce goes as smoothly as possible. She's too stubborn to phone you and I think this is one of those occasions where *you* need to offer the olive branch. Phone her or something; just reach out. for our sake and for the sake of not letting some shithead of a solicitor drag it out for you both.'

I know what you're thinking. This is a bit cliché, retired cop down on his luck facing a divorce that was his fault because he hit the bottle or hit the wife – or both. No, that's not what happened. I'm not and have never been an alcoholic, nor did I ever hit her though she threatened to punch me more than once over something she imagined I had done or not done but hadn't actually done or not done.

'Cass, I spent thirty years reaching out and trying to make your mum happy. I can honestly say she never gave me the same courtesy in return. When it came to something I wanted-'

'Dad, please. I love you and I love mum. Believe me, I _know_ what she's like. Whenever she had a go at you for nothing, nobody defended you more than I did, and you know I've never had any trouble telling mum when she's being a bitch, even though I've never used that word to her face. So please don't think I'm taking her side.'

She was right about all of that.

'But for both of your sakes and for ours, please talk to her. Phone her or something. Don't let the bitterness fester. Remember you loved each other once; let that guide you through a smooth divorce. That's all we want. We're all here for you and, well, you know we'll mediate where we can.'

A lump formed in my throat. 'I'll do my best, Cass.'

'Thanks, dad. We have to go now, we're at the airport.' Her voice went silent as she moved the phone away slightly. 'About here is good, thanks.'

'Have a good time in Edinburgh, Cass. I love you.'

'Got to go. Love you too.' She hung up.

31

I sighed heavily and quickly decided I wasn't going to let that ruin my day, even though Blighty weather was doing its best to ruin it for me. Of course, I would eventually phone Valarie, but not today.

After a breakfast of bacon and eggs and a strong cup of coffee (I decided I need that rather than tea), I stepped outside of the house.

It was warmer than I thought it was going to be, but the October wind was bringing the temperature down. Not quite scarf and gloves weather, not for at least another six weeks anyway.

I looked out to sea; there were a few ships on the horizon, but they looked modern – not ghost ships, possibly tankers and cargo vessels making their way to North America and down the African coast. We've had more than our fair share of those, but Hook Hand Harry's ship *The Lady Catherine* was the only one that ever docked here these days. Not even the occasional pleasure boat.

I walked down the slope and saw without surprise that Dora was on "her" bench. She still cried every morning about her husband who died with the sinking of *HMS Hood*, but at least I could get conversation out of her these days. Sometimes she even managed to work up a smile.

'Good morning Mrs Wilson.' I waved.

'Good morning DI Blackman. Lovely day for it!'

'Not to my liking,' I grumbled, 'I prefer spring, myself.'

'Oh "A good bracing wind invigorates the soul" as grandma used to say.' In response, a cool wind passed over us both. 'Like that one.'

She laughed and I chuckled with her. 'That's alright for you to say, you can't get a cold, flu or pneumonia. In fact, can you even *feel* the weather?'

'I can feel the cold and the heat yes. Don't be such a child, Mister Blackman,' and she gave me one of her rare smiles.

'You seem in a good mood this morning, Dora. Would you care to join me for some tea later?' I asked this at least once a week and her answer was always the same.

Her face dropped and she shook her head. 'No, I must not, wouldn't be right. But thank you. You do me a great kindness in offering.'

'Think nothing of it, you don't tend to mix much.'

She offered me a sad smile. 'Just like to keep to meself.'

I guarantee she would be crying again by the time I reached the foot of the hill.

It occurred to me that Dora Wilson, had she still been alive, would be around the century old mark. By the standards of Salmonweir, she is the baby of the village and certainly the youngest in terms of having been born last – of those that I knew of, anyway.

The "eldest" of the village is Kensa – I will come to her, she's quite the character. Another of the ancients is a Viking, but nobody has ever been able to get any sense out of him and nobody knows his name. He keeps to himself on the other side of the village and sometimes wanders to the quay to stare out to sea for a few hours. I once caught him digging in the sand. When I asked what he was doing he simply shouted "Saxon Silver" and carried on.

I have always wanted to find out what happened to Dora but never had the heart to ask her directly. I fear sometimes that it didn't end well for her, but part of me hopes she found happiness to a ripe old age despite being a widowed single mother. Part of me hopes she only died last year as a happy old woman surrounded by about a thousand grandchildren who adored her, but then even for a cop who had to have a heart of iron sometimes, I can be a big softie.

I suspect that each and every ghost here came back the age they were at their death. That means Dora was hovering around her 30th birthday, maybe a year or two either side, when she passed on.

There was nearly always somebody at the quayside admiring *The Lady Catherine* or asking for somebody to spare the time to show them around. Usually, it was one of the older ghosts for whom the galleon represented advanced technology or one of the younger ones for whom it was a chance to see real history rather than a dressed up and sanitised version.

The pirates waved their good mornings and I hastened my step towards the shop on the other side of the quay as the wind picked up behind me. I slipped inside and closed the door quickly. The bell tinkled as it closed. The new owner insisted on replacing the electronic version because he couldn't get used to it and wanted the shop more in keeping with the 19th century: the time in which he lived.

Let me tell you something about the economy of Salmonweir. As I said before, the ghosts here can interact with inanimate objects. That means they can accept food deliveries, hand me my newspaper, take money from me, bank it and operate business accounts.

Nobody wants to come here, but they're more than willing to trade. Suppliers are willing to sell to anyone with the means to pay and the means to receive delivery of stock – no questions asked. So, I still get to enjoy my honey on toast and pot of tea on a Sunday morning.

The ghosts here who work for businesses that operate outside Salmonweir are officially employees too. It's good for PR, you see, to show that death is never a hindrance to employment equality or career development – plus there is the celebrity factor. Oh, and everyone is paid, which mean there's money to keep everyone in business.

This village continues to function despite that every piece of real estate is valueless because the hope that things might change, and the property becomes *priceless*, keeps those suppliers and owners keen to keep an eye on their investment and not risk losing something that isn't presently worth anything. Confused? I admit it sounds completely insane, but so long as it works for me and I get what I need, I don't really care.

'Good morning DI Blackman,' said the stocky, balding ghost who was now the proprietor of the village shop. 'What'll it be this morning?'

'Just the usual please!' I replied.

He nodded. Corin Penrose had owned this shop sometime in the early 1830s. I suspect, but do not know for certain, that he and his daughter Ebrel both died of cholera in '32. As for his wife and three sons, nobody knows. Whatever happened to them, only these two came back. Perhaps they survived and moved away.

'Will you please talk to that daughter of mine, DI Blackman?' he said as he handed me my newspaper and I gave him the money.

My heart sank. I was often called on as mediator between warring village factions. Ebrel and her father were not the most frequent, but barely a week went by without friction. 'About what?'

'She's a wilful young lady,' he replied gruffly, operating the ancient till – it was one of the few pieces of technology he had come to accept and learn to use. 'Now she's decided she wants one of those infernal machines you call a "mobile phone".'

I looked at him blankly. 'What on Earth for? Nobody else here has one and she doesn't know anyone outside the village.'

'She wants to connect to something called "the internet" and "social media". She wants to talk to other young ghosts over the world and feel a connection.'

I nodded thoughtfully. 'That would make sense. Social media is great for that sort of thing, I've heard.'

He raised his hands in exasperation. 'I keep telling it's no good and won't help her, yet still she wants one. Apparently "all the cool kids have them". Ridiculous use of a perfectly good word – "cool" should only be used to describe autumn mornings like this. How can young people be "cool" unless they're not wearing enough clothing?'

'These days, "cool" refers to something fashionable or modern, something that people appreciate.'

He nodded thoughtfully. 'I thought so but it's an absurd use of the term.' He leaned forward on the counter and looked at me quizzically. 'If she describes one of the local boys as "hot", this means he is uncool? She feels he is unfashionable, yes? She does not like him, or finds him foolish?'

I pursed my lips. 'No, um, it also means good – just in a different way. It means she thinks he is handsome and eligible, the sort of young man she would not mind being courted by.'

Corin Penrose frowned in confusion. 'Are you quite sure? I'm not sure how that could apply to the boys to whom she refers.' He frowned and then shook his head in despair. 'But who decides such things? Who corrupts our language?'

'Well, from the colonies mostly. Especially, um, the Americans and Australians. And I think the Indies.' I cringed.

'Like Mohammedians and pagans?' he screwed his nose up. 'How strange.'

'Some people feel it is part of the beauty of English.' I shrugged my shoulders. 'I'm sure you will come to learn more of them in time.'

The bell above the door tinkled again and we both turned to see the new arrival; it was his daughter Ebrel.

Before I met her, from her father's description of her temperament, I assumed Ebrel was a 13-year-old tearaway. Yet Ebrel was 19, mostly gentle in nature, kind, polite, and always respectful towards me.

'Good morning, Karl,' She said and gave me a friendly wave along with a big smile. She had her father's blonde hair but obviously more of it.

'*Mister* or *Detective* Blackman to you, young lady!' her father mildly rebuked.

Despite being "of that age", I had no problem being addressed by my forename. Sometimes, I hated people using my title, especially when off duty.

'Good morning, Miss Ebrel. How are you this fine morning?'

'Good, thanks.' She took a step towards me, forming a neat triangle between the three of us.

She gave her father the sweetest smile and then turned it on me. 'Father, may I go to the public house tonight with some of the boys?'

'Which boys?'

'From the village.' She looked at me and smiled again.

'I know your game, young lady. *Which* boys? Ebrel, I want names.'

She paused then gave me a quick glance, 'Philip and his friends.'

Her father looked disapprovingly at her. 'I refuse. Those boys are no good.'

That was probably what Ebrel was waiting for; I felt compelled to defend Philip for his own sake. 'That is not entirely fair, Corin. I've met Philip and most of his friends.

They are boisterous at times, but Ebrel will be in good company. They are gentlemanly and know how to treat a lady.'

He slammed the newspapers onto the counter and straightened up a pile that was already as straight as they could be. 'It is not the done thing for a young lady to be cavorting like that with boys, no matter how good their breeding! My answer is still no.'

'Father!' She crossed her arms like a scolded child. I was only surprised she didn't stamp her feet. 'Mother would have let me.' Then she looked at me again.

'Your mother is not here. I am and you will abide by my rules.'

I cast a quick glance at Ebrel then. A moment of pain passed over her at the mention of her mother. It was gone as soon as it appeared.

Going against my training of not challenging a parent's authority on stuff that doesn't concern the Police, I threw caution to the wind and interjected again. 'Perhaps this decision has been a little too hasty. I will make myself available as Miss Ebrel's chaperone for the evening if you would kindly reconsider, Corin.'

'You would do this?' he asked.

'It would be my honour.'

'I don't need a chaperone!' she snapped.

I sighed heavily. 'I understand that you've embraced the new age, Ebrel. Nobody else in the village has done so quite so passionately as you. However, you should also respect your father's wishes. I am offering a compromise and I think this is the best solution for both of you.'

'But you can't help her if those boys try to hurt her.'

'True, *I* can't. But I *know* those boys. They are good-hearted and unlikely to cause her harm. If they did act ungentlemanly towards Miss Ebrel, I can ask the other patrons to interject. One flick of Harry's sword or a strong word from Kensa and they'll scarper. Each of them is terrifying alone, but together? It would take an incredibly stupid person to think they could handle both at once.'

I'm not sure if I had mentioned that whereas I cannot physically interact with the ghosts, they can interact with each other.

'Let me think about it.' He turned on his heel and retreated into the back room.

Ebrel went to say something. 'It's best you do not force a decision with spiteful words,' I said, pre-empting whatever retort was about to leave her lips, 'or you may not like his response.'

I lowered my voice to a whisper. 'He's thinking about it; that means it's more of a possibility than it was two minutes ago.'

Her face sank. 'But I don't *need* a chaperone, Karl,' she reiterated.

'I know you don't *need* an escort, but your father worries for your safety. I know those boys are nice, and you know those boys are nice, but he doesn't. He's still struggling to adjust and I'm sure he misses your mother just as much as you miss her. You've done remarkably well, Ebrel and I am so proud of you. Not everybody has coped as well as you. Just, cut him some slack.'

She frowned at me.

'Sorry, another modern term you will get used to. It means try to understand his position and realise there's no malice intended. Allow him some leeway. He may yet surprise you.'

She nodded thoughtfully. 'I'll let you buy me a small glass of wine, then.'

'If your father agrees, *you* owe *me* a beer.'

I collected my things from the counter. As I went to leave the shop, she called me back. 'Oh, Karl?'

I stopped in my tracks, holding the door. 'Yes?'

'I came past the church. Eli was in the graveyard pacing around. He asked if I had seen you. He looked and sounded outraged to say the least.'

My heart sank. I believed I already knew why *he* would want to see me – and I wasn't wrong.

Chapter 3

Eli had been the village's Minister in the mid to late 17th century, which means he lived through England's Civil War. He wasn't actually a village native but had been sent to Cornwall in 1652 following Parliamentarian victory. He never wanted to come here but was sent – probably by Cromwell directly or one of his immediate inner circle – because he had no family ties up country.

The job to do The Lord's Work was offered around to others first, but each found a reason to refuse – a sickly child, a demanding elderly parent, too many business interests. I learnt that Eli's father had just died and there was no Mrs Eli in life. No family ties meant no excuses.

Cornwall had been a Royalist region during the Civil Wars. Cromwell, keen not to see face a repeat of the riots and uprisings of elsewhere, sent many of his own men to the peninsula to subdue the locals. He needed to do so both spiritually and temporally.

Eli was strongly and unsurprisingly anti-Catholic. When he turned up month after the first arrivals to see Brother Jowan had already claimed the 800-year-old church for himself, it put his nose severely out of joint. I had been acting as mediator between them both ever since.

The church sat on the brow of the eastern hill and provided the best view of the village and the coast. Just a handful of the few annual Salmonweir tourists made their way up here on their brief stops. It's a shame or a plus depending on how you look at it because it's an attractive building that has maintained most of its original fabric. It had initially been the chapel for the ill-fated Benedictine grange of Glastonbury Abbey but soon became a parish church.

During the plague years, Jowan said he had wanted the job of village priest but "the situation meant that was not possible". He came on a flying visit to help with the relief efforts. He wouldn't elaborate and for a while I assumed he died of plague. Later, I determined that Jowan had spent several years *after* the end of The Black Death back at St. Michael's Mount.

I am fond of Brother Jowan. He is a passionate and sometimes thoughtful man. Initially saddened to see the interior colour and decoration removed from the walls and ceiling during the Civil War, he was pleased that the Rood Screen installed before he was born survived intact to the 21st century.

It was like watching a child with a new toy, or one of those academics we regularly see on television getting excited at a new discovery.

All was peaceful until Eli arrived.

I'm not entirely sure what happened, but I was out for an evening stroll when I heard shouting inside the church. The shouting came from just one man – Eli. He screamed a number of what I believe to be 17th century insults but wouldn't translate well even if I could remember all of them. The only one I remember was "papist cumberworld" (I admit I had to look that term up – it still makes me chuckle). Another one may have alluded to a certain pope accused of having sex with animals, and how all Catholics probably did it too.

In stark contrast, Brother Jowan remained calm and unmoved by the screaming man who was around half his weight, a clear foot taller and ten years his junior (if I had to guess at their ages at time of death, for Jowan it would be 50, for Eli maybe closer to 40). The only words the Benedictine Monk spoke was to ask from which particular reformist group Eli originated. He wasn't anywhere hear that polite, but it was the gist of the line of questioning.

This only angered Eli further who screamed his membership and role of pastor in The One True Church. Their relationship had not improved since then.

I met Eli at the gate, halfway up the slope that led to the church. Yes, there's a lot of hills to climb here and it keeps me fit! The churchyard is the least flat I have ever seen; the tombstones peppering the hill made it look like a giant hedgehog.

'DI Blackman,' Eli growled.

'Good Morning, Eli. What can I help you with?'

'Brother Jowan.' He waved a finger at me as though it was my fault. 'I knew it would come to this; the man is quite unreasonable!'

'I might have guessed. What's the problem this time?'

'Not content with assuming primacy over this church, now he has locked himself in and refusing me any entry whatsoever!'

'Why? What did you say?'

'Nothing.' To hide his discomfort, he turned his back to me and walked up the hill, beckoning me forward.

'Did you threaten to hang him again?' I asked, trying to keep up with his pace.

He pushed through the gate and held it open for me to step through behind him. 'No! I simply-'

48

'And why don't you just Pop in there?'

'You know I feel that is rude.'

Popping is what we call how the ghosts teleport. Not all of them can do it – I know of only about five or six and Eli is one of them. All can walk through walls too but not many choose to do it while there is a door to open or a window to vault through. Both Harry and Eli separately told me it was an unpleasant feeling, so they generally choose not to do it.

Sorry to disappoint all your beliefs and stereotypes about corporeal beings, but reality is nearly always more mundane than fantasy.

'Will you please talk to him?' urged Eli.

'Yes, but you need to tell me why he's upset with you. If I don't know, I can't help.'

He pursed his lips and let out a sentence without pausing for breath.

'I heard "burn him" and "bonfire". I guess I don't need you to go back and fill in the gaps?' Without waiting for an answer, I marched into the porch and banged heavily upon the old oak doors. 'Jowan, it's Karl. Open up please.'

For some minutes, I could hear only silence from inside. I raised my first to bang again but Jowan opened the door. 'The answer is "no",' he snapped.

'I'm not here to convince you to be burnt at the stake on Bonfire Night.' I turned to face the Puritan. 'Eli, go to the pub or something. I'll handle this.'

'I don't indulge, you know that.'

'Then ask for a plain tap water, maybe really push the boat out today and ask for ice and a slice of lemon?'

His gaze flicked from me to Jowan and back again before he walked off down the path.

When he had gone, Jowan stepped back and opened the door, allowing me entry. It had really warmed up outside, but I didn't notice until I stepped in through the church door.

I followed him into the church, and we sat on the front pew. A musky smell of old incense hung in the air. I knew Eli didn't like it but to Jowan, it was an important part of the ritual of his faith. I was pleased to see the Rood Screen looking clean and fresh; Jowan must have cleaned it again. I often wondered what he felt about the other Protestant icons in here – the tombstones inside the church and the war memorial in English.

'I won't do it,' he said. 'It doesn't matter if I won't be harmed. It doesn't matter that I'm the village's most prominent Catholic. He only asked it to ridicule me. He has done all he can to make a mockery of me and God's Church in Rome.'

'I'm not going to ask you to be the Guy on Bonfire Night; I think you know me better than that, Jowan.' I pleaded.

'Yes, but to even suggest such a thing in jest? It's hideous! Utterly horrifying of him! I would never have made such a suggestion to him.'

'While he went overboard, you're not always innocent in all this, Jowan. You seem to take pleasure in antagonising him. You know precisely how to push him to breaking point with only a few words.'

He looked at me taken aback as if I could suggest that his actions towards Eli had been anything less than perfect. He went to protest but I interrupted before he could get a word out.

'He's doing it to get at you, nothing more. I think this Bonfire Night celebration will be good for us. I think it may even bring in some tourists. We've been talking for weeks about how to get people coming back here and I have a suggestion for the village meeting later today.'

51

'I won't be in the same room as *that man*.'

'That's tough, Jowan. You're on the Village Council, a permanent member at your own insistence and your presence is required. Today of all days, you know why this one is important.'

I hated taking this hard line with either man, but if one refused to turn up to meetings every time the other said something out of turn, neither man would ever go to a meeting. 'Today is an opportunity to move forward for the good of the village.'

He nodded. 'Yes, you are right. I realise I have no choice. Perhaps if I can engage him in the right way, we can find some common ground over this? Perhaps he might find a place in his heart that enjoys a little frivolity?'

'He's a Puritan, I doubt that.' I raised my hand for a high five, a moment that was lost on Jowan so I dropped it immediately.

'You're doing well in sharing the church with him. Really, you have both been more reasonable than I'd hoped,' (ok, that was a bit of a lie). 'Events like today set things back a little. This church belonged to both of you in different ways at different times. It's his as much as it is yours and you can't lock him out whenever he says something upsetting.'

'I quite agree. I must be better. But you must understand why I feel his presence-'

'Right now, I don't care.' I snapped. 'To my knowledge, at no point has he stopped you from entering the church. You must pay him the same courtesy.'

'I may not agree with sharing this church with such a man, and I am sure he feels the same way.' He sighed. 'However, you are most certainly correct on one matter. He has never prevented my entry. I believe he would never do so. I must, despite my reservations, permit him to use it.'

'Good. I'm glad we see eye to eye, my friend.' I stood to leave. 'I will see you later at the meeting?'

'Yes, DI Blackman, you certainly will.'

I had to go home and get some more coffee, today was already wearing me out and it had barely started. As I made my way down Church Hill, I kept my fingers crossed that I wouldn't face any further interruptions.

Thankfully, the world decided that I deserved a few nanoseconds of peace. That second morning coffee went down a treat and after reading my book for a bit, I was ready to face the day again. Nothing much had happened in the world, though there was still ongoing speculation about Salmonweir in the nationals, and whether "the swarm of ghosts" would eventually spread to other parts of the country.

Let me give you a brief summary of what the papers are saying: In the first few days, some paranoid right-wing politician blamed gay marriage. An equally paranoid far left politician blamed Mossad. I don't know if any paper published "Will Visiting Salmonweird Give You Cancer?" or "Ghosts coming over here to steal our jobs and our benefits" because I stopped reading the nationals at that point. The less in the way of that nonsense, the better, methinks.

I decided to sit in the garden, put my feet up and read a book for the next few hours. The good weather continued, and I decided to make the most of the warming autumn morning. When I heard a gentle rap on the front door, I knew it was time.

I opened the door to see Kensa standing before me. She looked fierce and striking in her leather armour in ways I imagine only Celtic warrior queens could look. She had flame red curls and more freckles than I could count stars in the sky when all the village lights are out. She was not the big muscled brute you might imagine as portrayed on the screen but she clearly had physical strength in life. I could quite easily imagine her going toe to toe with a cohort of Roman soldiers, towering over the shortest members. I wouldn't be surprised if she'd died in battle.

'Good morning DI Blackman,' she said in a strange accent. Though undoubtedly Cornish, even I struggled with it at times. 'Are you ready for the meeting?'

We walked to the hall, mostly in silence though she did ask about the situation between Eli and Jowan. I explained it to her the best I could, and she was amused that Eli felt asking Jowan if he would be the Guy on Bonfire Night was a reasonable request.

'Christians eh? I'm still learning about their god of peace who seems to enjoy war so much.' She shook her head. 'I'm even more surprised the Romans chose to adopt him when they had so many others to choose. If I ever meet one, perhaps I will ask – shortly before I run him down with my chariot.'

I smiled. 'What are you planning for the Bonfire Night event, Kensa?'

'I had an idea of what I would like to do, but I'm afraid the modern world is not quite up to standard so I must think of something else.'

'What was that?'

'Something called "replica armour". I looked on your internet. Most of it is poor quality. I was going to give a talk and a demonstration on how my people made swords and armour before the Roman slugs came to

55

Dumnonia, but I have to rethink it now. I used to make armour, you know. I wasn't good at it, but I *was* good at killing Romans with it.' She turned to me and offered me a rare smile.

'Maybe you can make your own?'

She nodded. 'Yes, I have thought of this as something to do for the future. It is too late for Bonfire Night. For the spectacular, I have been negotiating with another resident to do something else though. You'll find out in the meeting. Morwenna has made a poster.' Her face betrayed a small smile. Whatever it was, she was clearly excited and struggling to hold it in until then.

We were the last to arrive. The other council members, Eli and Jowan and Morwenna the Innkeeper were already waiting in the pub. I call Morwenna Brewer "The Innkeeper", but in the 18th century when she was alive, she was the wife of the village's innkeeper. She knew how to pull a pint, she was good with the customers and the books, and she relished the chance to step into her husband's shoes. She proved a natural from the start, so now she's Morwenna The Innkeeper, not Morwenna The Innkeeper's Wife.

The final person in the room wasn't part of the council, but our volunteer administrator and transcriber. In life, Babajide was the slave of Morwenna and her husband and had been their administrator, bookkeeper and odd job boy. All accounts he was exceptional at it and relished the chance to act on behalf of the village.

Some of the modern ghosts – and I for that matter – were not comfortable with a former slave taking up a role he'd previously been pressed into doing, but he was more than happy to show us his skills, for pay and with no obligation.

At the last meeting, Morwenna had come up with the idea of turning Salmonweir (with or without the "d") into a viable tourist destination for *living* people. If we could show the world that we're all just normal people – just dead – they'd come flooding back.

'I had some posters made,' said Morwenna, gesturing to Babajide. 'Would you be so kind, Baba, as to show them?'

The slender, dark-skinned young man stood up carefully and lifted the first poster. It was an attractive aerial photograph of the village including striking imagery of the rugged cliffs to the east. It would have made for the perfect promotional poster had it not been for the wording. I'd seen better headlines in the average tabloid than *Come and See Plague and Cholera Victims in the Flesh (Rotting)!*

'What do you think?' asked Morwenna.

Uncomfortable murmurs passed over the crowd.

She forced a smile. 'Perhaps it's not quite right. Maybe this would be more to your liking.' She gestured to Babajide who put down the first poster and picked up another. It was an image of a Hook Hand Harry and Kensa sword duelling. So that was Kensa's secret. No wonder she was so excited.

The image was fine, in itself; it was fun and would certainly excite kids with a taste for cartoon gore.

The caption let it down. No, the caption killed it.

'Oh my,' I exclaimed. 'No, trust me you really can't use that one.'

'Why ever not?' Morwenna asked sharply.

'Because asking visitors which of the two they'd like to see dismembered is sending the wrong message entirely. One of the big heritage charities might get away with that because kids will love it, but here we need to play it a bit safer. People are terrified of us; let's not give them further justification.'

'Baba, he doesn't like our slogans.' She crossed her arms; Babajide just gave me an apologetic smile. 'What do you suggest then?' She asked accusingly.

'We need something a bit more positive than playing up to the nonsense of tabloid media. Why don't we ask Wilhelmina to come up with something?'

Four jaws hit the floor; even Babajide looked bemused and startled. When I looked at him quizzically, he took on a stony expression and directed his gaze at the floor.

'Well, why not?' I asked. 'Anybody?'

'She's a poet,' said Jowan.

'And?'

'Have you read her work?' asked Eli.

'Yes,' I responded.

'I rest my case,' said Eli.

Jowan nodded enthusiastically – it was the first time, to my knowledge, they had agreed on anything. I suggest you make a note of this, as it may never happen again.

'If you can find anyone who can do better,' Morwenna's tone stopped short of venomous, 'then please do so. Remember that Bonfire Night is less than a month away. These were Babajide's suggestions by the way. He worked *very* hard on them.'

I looked at him apologetically but was surprised to see him shake his head and gesture at Morwenna. I winked in acknowledgement.

'Now, I believe DI Blackman has a suggestion?' Brother Jowan egged on, looking at me eagerly.

'Yes, I do.' I cleared my throat. 'Now, we've all been wondering about what to do for the Guy.' I looked quickly at Eli who looked down, embarrassed.

'I think we should get the children involved. Maybe have a competition on who can design the best Guy.' I looked to Eli and Jowan in turn. 'What does everybody think of that?'

A few murmurs passed around and each looked to his or her neighbour to nod in agreement.

'That is a wonderful idea!' Eli clapped his hands. 'Perhaps Brother Jowan could-'

I cleared my throat.

But he went on, '… ask the youngest at his children's sermon tomorrow? Most village residents go to church and this would be the easiest way to organise it. The more, the merrier perhaps. It would give visitors some understanding of our art and way of life. I will also ask those who attend my own service.'

'Very gracious of you, Eli,' I commended, 'I'm pleased you are willing to work together on this competition.'

A firm hand knocked at the door.

One of the pub regulars stuck his head in. I knew him only as "Antony" and he lived during the reign of Henry VI. We had not interacted beyond slight pleasantries, and that is where my knowledge of the man ended. Nevertheless, he addressed me first. 'Mister Blackman and gentlemen and ladies, apologies for my interruption. We have a new arrival down at the quay.'

Chapter 4

Face down on the strip of brown, mucky sand beneath the elevated quay, I could tell from his attire precisely which era he came from. World War II history was about my limit, but there was no mistaking the military uniform of a Roman soldier. Even the average four-year-old could have told you that.

As I knelt to tend to the man, I heard the unmistakeable sound of a sword being drawn from its scabbard. 'Put it away, Kensa.'

She muttered as she begrudgingly re-sheathed her sword.

'Atticus Justus Cato,' the Roman finally spoke, rising to his knees. 'Where am I?'

He was darker than I expected, maybe Middle Eastern or North African. Either way, it's a curious thing and it still shocks me every time. No matter where and when these ghosts come from, they always seem to speak English with crystal clarity.

I would later learn that this man – Cato – was Syrian by birth and drafted into the military as the fourth son of a minor government official.

At the time, Cato was the third arrival to turn up in Salmonweir *not* born in the British Isles; Babajide and the Viking were the other two.

'Cornwall, England.'

'Dumnonia!' Kensa snapped and stepped forward to help me lift the Roman to his feet. 'How did you get here?'

'We were scouting the far reaches of the Dumnonii lands when a storm hit our ship. We sank, I made it to shore obviously. What is this place? This is no village of the Dumnonii I know.'

'Atticus Justus Cato, it is going to be a little difficult to explain. It is best that you come with me.'

I took him to my house and spent the next half an hour bringing him up to speed as best I could. I didn't want to overload the poor lad with information; I never wanted to overload them at all but there are some things they need to know straight away.

Firstly, it's common courtesy to let them know they are already dead. Get the shock out of the way first, then gently fill them in on the other details.

He looked around curiously at the building and the décor of my house. To that Roman, this must have been the most alien of places.

Kensa went off to fetch Jowan; though the two men would not have shared religious beliefs, the monk had proven himself more than capable of accepting this weird world and engaging with most people in it. Jowan arrived promptly, but Kensa did not return; I was relieved, I'd hate to think she'd pick a fight with this Roman just for *being* Roman.

Cato looked Jowan up and down. 'What are you, a druid?'

'I most certainly am not, young man; I am a Christian Priest.' Jowan sat on the couch next to him. 'This is all going to be peculiar to you, but you are no longer in the time you were born.'

'That much is quite apparent.' Cato gave Jowan a suspicious look. '*When* am I?'

Despite having only sat for a few seconds, Jowan stood and gestured to the door. 'Perhaps we should go for a walk and have a talk? Perhaps a visit to the inn for refreshment?'

'Do they serve mulsum?'

'That is similar to mead, isn't it?' Jowan gently touched his shoulder. 'I believe they do.'

I banged heavily on the door of the Penrose shop.

The sun had almost completely set, leaving a pleasant early-Autumn glow in the air of gold and amber against light purple clouds. The cold wind coming in from the sea reminded me of the actual season after what had turned out to be a pleasant spring-like day.

I don't like the cold, as you have probably already guessed, and that's why I moved to sub-tropical Cornwall, to make the best of the good weather for as much of the year as possible.

'Come back tomorrow. We're closed,' Corin called from just behind the door.

'It's me,' I said, 'I've come to collect Miss Ebrel for the evening.'

'Ah.' There was a clunk as Corin Penrose unlocked the door before swinging it open. 'Do come in DI Blackman, Ebrel will be just a moment.'

I nodded and stepped in through the door to a sensation only slightly warmer than the outside. I could feel a growing sense of heat warming the building. The ghosts did not feel the heat, but some lit fires in the evenings as a reminder of the comfort of the past and to create the illusion of normality.

'I appreciate you doing this, Detective. I know my daughter is in safe hands with you. Now, I agree to this evening out with those boys, but there are rules. I trust you, as an elder and responsible gentleman, to enforce them upon my daughter in my absence. She may be wilful, but she clearly respects you, and likes you, and will therefore listen to you. Besides, sometimes I think you have a better way of expressing yourself than I.'

I nodded again. 'Certainly. What time would you like her back here?'

'Ten-thirty, tell her no later than that, but five minutes will be acceptable in case of any delay saying her goodbyes. I also know how much she enjoys talking with you. She is *not* under any circumstances to drink alcohol. I know it will not affect her, but I *am* worried about what the boys of the village with think of an unmarried woman without the supervision of a male relative.'

'I agree and I don't think she is interested in alcohol. If she attempts to buy some, I *will* stop her.' It would have been pointless, at this point, explaining that alcohol and the unmarried maiden was not the taboo it once was.

'Thank you.'

The internal door opened and Ebrel stepped through, giving me the sweetest smile. 'Hi Karl!'

'Good evening, Miss Ebrel.' One of the other "skills" of certain ghosts was that they could change their attire to anything they may have worn while alive. I had no idea that Ebrel was one of those ghosts until she stepped through the door. She wore a plain long skirt with a simple yet pretty blouse, an outfit right out of a period drama. Her hair – usually straight with no styling – was now woven into complex braids and adorned with pale blue ribbons.

'Do you like the new outfit?'

'You look beautiful, Miss Ebrel. I'm sure Philip will not be able to remove his gaze from you.'

She blushed.

'Remember,' Corin Penrose reminded us, 'ten-thirty and no later.'

'Miss Ebrel, shall we?' I offered her my arm and she hooked her own through it. Naturally, I couldn't feel it.

When we got outside, she surprisingly tried to hug me, which felt weird embracing someone I could only see and hear but not feel. 'Thank you, so much!'

'I didn't talk your father into it, he decided of his own volition. Be sure to show him your gratitude at the end of the night, hmm?'

'You're right,' she sighed, 'he didn't have to allow this. It's all about compromise, isn't it?'

We began walking up the road towards the pub. 'He may not be a "cool dad" but he *is* trying. He struggles to accept that you two have returned to a time so different from your own, and without your mother and brothers.'

A painful expression briefly passed over Ebrel's face.

'Not everybody here has adjusted as well as you have, Ebrel. For some it is especially difficult.'

'I know.' She offered me a sweet smile. 'Tell me about this Roman soldier? Is he handsome?'

I shrugged. 'His name is Atticus Justus Cato. Handsome? I suppose so if you like the rough, rugged yet swarthy military type. Don't forget, young lady, you already have a date this evening before you set your sights on the next!'

'I know, but an eligible lady shouldn't put all her hopes in one man.'

We soon arrived at the pub – it's just a five-minute walk from the shop at a steady pace, and uphill so can sometimes take longer. I opened the door and ushered her through, grateful for the warmth that greeted me on entry. The pub is wide and open, square shaped with a bar at the back.

A 19th century extension once served as a small restaurant but that was no longer viable as a use, at least, not under the current circumstances. Morwenna and Babajide converted it for more bar space, adding a pool table and a dartboard.

We didn't have to look far. The young man in question (one Philip Latimer) and several of his friends congregated at the table nearest the door. Tragically, they had all died around the same time during the reign of Henry VIII, probably of the mysterious Sweating Sickness.

When they first arrived two months ago, they all appeared together, a group of five of them in the space of about sixty seconds and were delighted to have returned together.

'Miss Ebrel!' he exclaimed, lifting her hand to kiss it. 'May I say how beautiful you look this fine evening?'

She slapped him gently on the arm. 'Drop the act, Philip. Karl isn't stupid.'

He visibly relaxed. 'Oh, that's all right then. Would you like a drink, sir?'

'Thank you kindly. I'll have a small glass of the dry cider. I am under strict instructions that Miss Ebrel is not to consume alcohol tonight though. Cider, wine, beer and spirits are all off limits.'

'Lemonade for me,' she said, 'I don't want alcohol anyway.'

'Harry is trying to catch my attention so I will leave you to it.' As we entered, I'd noticed the pirate captain furiously waving at me. He sat at a table near the bar with the Elizabethan poet Wilhelmina Yorke and the wiry cabin boy who I had met on the day the ship arrived and only twice since.

I say "boy", but I would guess he was around 15 or 16. Harry waved at me as I turned away from Ebrel, Philip and his friends.

As I got close to the table, he leapt to his feet. 'Ah, Mister Blackman. Let me buy you that drink I owe ya.'

'Actually, Philip is-'

'No, no. I insist. A man must always pay his debt. It's a rule of my ship.' Had he been physically capable, I'm sure he would have dragged me by the hook to the bar. As we leaned against the bar, I tried to explain again that I already had a drink on order, but he muttered just one word at me.

'Help.'

'What's wrong?' I asked, concerned.

'Wilhelmina. I can't stand to listen to it – it's hideous!'

'What is?'

'That blasted poem of hers about the man she loved. You know I'm uncultured, I'm a pirate who can barely read, but even I can tell when poetry is a load of shi-'

'Quiet, she might hear you!' I waved him down into silence.

'Come and sit with us and maybe you can try to help her?'

'Me?! What on Earth do you think I know about romantic poetry?' The closest I ever got was a variation of

71

"Roses are red, violets are blue…" in a Valentine's Card for my ex-wife.'

'I've no idea what you're talking about but by the sound of it you know more than what I know, I guarantee that. Please help us?'

Philip passed me my half pint of cider and I joined the three of them at the table, grateful for the company if nothing else.

Wilhelmina Yorke looked perturbed but no less pleased to see me. 'Ah, Mister Blackman! I wondered if you would help me with some modern language so I may correct my poem?' She waved a quill at me.

'I'll try but I have the poetic talent of-' I paused (a failed Elizabethan poet?), ' of a three-year-old.'

'"My love, when I look at you my eyes get stuck!"' she said then looked at me anxiously.

I cocked my head curiously, 'Is "stuck" the word you are looking for? Doesn't strike up notions of romance to me, more like a medical problem?'

She slumped in her chair. 'That's the only line I like so far.'

'Trust me, it's the best line at the moment,' said Harry bluntly.

'So, what *do* you mean?' I asked her.

'When I look at the man I love, I cannot avert my gaze, it is as though my eyes are intoxicated by his beauty.' She shrugged. 'Is that not obvious?'

'Yes, but the wording is not quite right. It's hard to use the word "stuck" in a romantic context. Make it flowery and sweet. Could you perhaps find a comparison in nature? How you are drawn to – I don't know, what are you drawn to in nature?'

'Trees, grass, a summer's day. But I also like the gusts and the colours of autumn.'

I smiled. 'Then try finding a comparison that works for you and would conjure up the right image for the reader.'

'My love, I compare thy skin to that of a thistle,' she began.

My heart sank and clearly, so did Harry's. I took a long sip of my cider. 'Not sure a thistle sends the right image. They're not exactly pleasant to touch.'

'This is true. What about "My love, let me fall into the brambles of thine arms"?'

'Not much better, if I'm honest. I get the imagery but there must be something better?'

She shot me an evil glance.

Harry used the moment to conveniently "remember" why he had gone to the pub in the first place. 'I see Babajide has gone out back. Should probably pick up the barrel for the boys, young Eddie. They'll be as parched as a nun's- as a dry dock! I'll be along in a moment.'

The Cabin Boy looked visibly relieved and scampered off behind the unoccupied bar. Morwenna and Babajide did that from time to time, there was no crime here – and these dead people won't get far with ill-gotten gains anyway.

' "Thine beard is akin to a floor brush. When will thou sweep me away?"' Wilhelmina looked at me. 'That's quite romantic, isn't it? Is that the sort of thing men want to hear?'

I cringed and squirmed and did many other things that people do when about to be uncomfortably left alone by a friend who was waiting for the right moment to scarper and leave you there. I glared at Harry and thought *you're my friend, but I could go off you*.

'You don't like it?' She put her quill down and heaved a big sigh. I'm not sure how long Wilhelmina Yorke had been plying her trade as a poet when alive, but if she had been doing it all her life, she had never seen fit to give it up as a lost cause. I would guess she was approaching 40 at her death so would hardly have been new to creative writing as she breathed her last.

My cheeks went bright red. 'Well, umm. I'm not *really* the best person to ask anyway.'

'It's *him* isn't it? Everyone loves *him*! When William Shakespeare became famous, there was no room for anyone else to get their poetry published. Least of all a mere *woman* like me.'

If I had heard this once from her, I'd heard it a thousand times. Harry and I exchanged glances and returned quickly to our drinks as her rant about Shakespeare went on.

When she finally finished, she calmed down and went back to thinking up more lines for her poem, paying Harry and me little attention except for the occasional query of whether this or that word was suitable in a poem about love.

Harry and I conversed between ourselves, commenting on the fabulous range of drinks and the décor of the pub. He enquired about the afternoon's meeting and I told him what I could but pointed out that without the official motion, this was all merely suggestion.

'Come back here you little bastard!' a voice bellowed from behind me, interrupting our conversation. As usually happens, everyone turned to the source of the voice. It was Philip. When I turned to look, he was racing across the pub towards a retreating Eddie the Cabin Boy who was hastily making his way toward the exit door with a barrel about half his size.

Ebrel reached for Philip and grabbed him by the arm but he shook her off. 'No, he shouldn't talk to you like that.'

'I knew that boy's mouth would get him into trouble one of these days,' said Harry.

We both stood and followed the pair outside into the dark and cool evening. Ebrel decided to come with us too, offering me an apologetic smile. 'What happened?' I asked her as I stepped through the door, turning my head to look at her.

'It was nothing. Philip over-reacted.'

Outside, we saw Philip holding Eddie by the throat up against the wall of the pub. The barrel of rum was on the floor next to them. 'Apologise now before I make you regret it, boy.'

'Philip!' Ebrel threw herself at her date and pushed him off the Cabin Boy. 'Get off him *now*.'

'He should not have spoken to a lady like that!' he argued, letting go of the boy.

'And there was no need for you to over-react!' Ebrel said. 'Philip, look at what you're doing!'

'What's going on here?' I put on my best "Copper Voice" and looked at each of the young men in turn.

Despite the dark, I could see the fury in Philip's face as it was momentarily lit up by the light from the door opening. Philip looked at Eddie and stepped away from the cabin boy. 'He was rude to Ebrel. I shan't repeat it — disgusting!'

'It's fine,' Ebrel said softly, 'he didn't know what he was saying. He probably learnt a few words from the ruffians aboard Captain Harry's ship. Isn't that right, Eddie?'

Eddie looked sheepishly at me and then to Harry and quickly to Ebrel.

Harry grabbed him by the collar. 'What did ye say, boy? Ye know how to properly speak to a lady and how not to, so what did ye say?'

'For pity's sake, it was nothing. It doesn't matter, Harry! Philip, come back into the pub *now* or I will instruct Karl to take me home.' Then she grabbed him by the arm and pulled him back towards the pub entrance.

Finally, Philip relented and followed Ebrel back into the pub. We waited for the pair to leave before Harry once again pressed Eddie for an answer.

'She was right. I repeated something I heard on the ship. Something the men say about Ebrel. Well, not just Ebrel, but some of the other village girls too.'

'What was it? Tell me boy or I'll clip you 'round the ear.' I'd never seen Harry so furious.

'I said "you should come to the ship tonight. I have a rope I want you to tug on".'

Harry clipped Eddie around the ear anyway. 'Ye no right to talk *to* a lady like that, ye understand? Talk like that stays on the ship, lad! The Lady Catherine can take it, but no other lady. I said *do ye understand me*?'

He looked down at his feet. 'Yes, captain. Sorry captain.'

'Now go apologise to Miss Ebrel *and* Master Philip and get your skinny arse back to the ship with that barrel or you're on crow's nest duty for the next three months.'

We followed him back into the pub to witness the apology – after which, Harry sent Eddie on his way and offered to buy us all a drink. Everything was cordial after that and after a few hours of conversation, Harry invited both Philip and Ebrel for a tour of the ship with the promise that the boys would be on their best behaviour. They gladly accepted and all was right with the world once again.

At ten twenty, I reminded Ebrel of her curfew and the need to say goodbyes. She shared a (very) quick kiss with Philip. He kissed her hand and she kissed his cheek. It was all very sweet and we were soon on our way back down the rise towards her home.

Our silent journey was a contrast to excited conversation of the walk up the hill that evening. I wanted to make sure she was ok after what Eddie said to her, but she seemed unfazed. The only thing Ebrel said to me was how she was looking forward to a tour of the ship.

I checked my watch when we reached the door of the shop; it was ten thirty-one. Our pace had been slow. Corin must have been waiting behind the door as it opened fractions of a second after my third knock.

'A good evening?' he asked us both.

'Pleasant,' I replied.

'Ebrel?'

'Lovely. Philip was the perfect gentleman just as I knew he would be.' She turned to me. 'Thank you, Karl for your conversation and company, and good night.' And with that, she was gone.

I listened to the sound of silence for a few minutes, the gentle lapping of the waves against the wooden posts of the dock. Faintly, I could hear singing from the berthed ship.

As I made my way along the quay, I could hear the large group of men singing "What shall we do with a drunken sailor?" and had to stop myself joining in.

Chapter 5

Ominous rain clouds welcomed in the next morning.

I had become used to rain moving sideways blowing in from off the water and it no longer fascinated or surprised me. Autumn was well and truly here, and when the sheet rain from the sea began pounding my windows, I vowed not to go out today – to read a book, finally start my memoir (hah, fat chance of that!) or just spend the day reorganising, tidying and cleaning the house.

I even considered boxing up what was left of Valarie's things, but the idea pained me a little too much. Not today, another time.

Fate, however, conspired against me. At just gone nine, while enjoying a cup of coffee and some political programme on the radio, I heard a frantic voice bellow through my letterbox. It was the unmistakeable thick Cornish accent of Hook Hand Harry.

I groaned and rubbed my head. It wasn't unusual that one of the previously deceased residents woke me with some urgent news. What was unusual about it was the person banging on my door and waking me up.

I would normally expect it to be Jowan or Eli complaining about the other. Sometimes, it would be Kensa wanting to discuss something that happened in the most recent village meeting, or help with doing on the internet. Or it was Ebrel wanting to talk to me about her father's unreasonable behaviour or to show me something in a magazine and ask where she could get one.

It had never been the pirate captain before today.

I opened the door wrapped in my winter dressing gown and woolly slippers. It wasn't quite cold enough for them, but for a Brit I am averse to cold rain like this and here at the end of this peninsula, we get a lot of it.

Harry gave me a startled look and gave me the once over. 'Is that what you call a smoking jacket?' he asked.

'What? No! I don't smoke. It's just something comfortable that keeps me warm on cold days like this. What's wrong, Harry?'

He rubbed his face; the scrubbing of hand against ginger stubble would have made a noise had it been real skin. It's amazing the things I take for granted and the things I notice about these ghosts. 'Well, I wonder if you'd been out late last night or early today.'

'In this? There's no way I would voluntarily go out of the house today.'

He rubbed his face again. 'Ah, you see. I may need you to come out. It's our Eddie. Nobody knows where he is and I – we –was wondering if you'd seen him.'

I thought back to the altercation the previous night when Philip lost it with Eddie over something the Cabin Boy said to Ebrel. 'No, I haven't seen him, and he certainly hasn't been here.'

He looked downcast for a moment, clearly believing I could and would help him.

I softened up a bit. This was what I did for a job before I retired and here was a friend asking for my help to find a young lad – one that had been dead since the early 1700s and could not possibly have come to any harm whatsoever. But help him I should as a friend and as a former copper.

'Right, let me get dressed and we'll go and see Ebrel to see if-'

'No. Miss Ebrel is at the ship. She came down this morning to see him, to talk to him all nice like, not to have a go at him or nothing. But he wasn't there. He wasn't in the Crow's Nest and the lads said they hadn't seen him after he went to his bunk looking all sheepish like. She didn't come aboard, wanted to give the lad some space. Will you come see?'

I smiled at him. 'Of course I will, Harry.'

I dressed in minutes and soon stepped out into the bracing cold with my trench coat on; some might have said I really looked the part but that was not the idea – I am not *that* pretentious.

We made our way quickly to the ship, the biting rain coming at me from the south, still moving sideways. This led to the peculiar situation that my right side got wet while my left side remained dry. I wished I could actually get on board *The Lady Catherine* – not just to take shelter, but also that I could see the inner workings of a real pirate ship instead of a sanitised version presented to the tourists. The rain eased off a little as I made my way down the hill, but not by much, not nearly enough.

Ebrel and Philip were no longer there. Only the First Mate remained on the quayside; the rest of the lads were presumably back aboard without giving the boy a second thought.

'Sorry for dragging you down here Mister Blackman.' His Cornish brogue was heavier than Harry's – something I didn't think possible.

'That's alright. Ben, isn't it?'

'Benjamin sir, if ye don't mind.'

I nodded and got out my notebook. 'So tell me, Benjamin, when did *you* last see Eddie?' I asked.

'He came back last night to give us the rum. I asked him what was wrong and he said nothing was wrong. But that's the look we all gets when the Captain gives us a scolding. I wasn't surprised when Cap'n told me later that was what happened. Anyway, I assume Eddie, he went to his little sleeping bay, and I never saw him again.'

'What time was that?'

Benjamin only blinked at me. Why for one moment did I think he would possess something as useless as a watch?

'We reckons,' interrupted Harry, 'he came straight back here and went to bed after I clipped his ear. He got on the ship and went into hiding. Benjamin was the last person to see him and nobody seen him after that. That's what we reckons.'

'Is that true?' I asked the First Mate.

'Yeah, that be right. I've asked the lads and nobody's seen him after he got back. He put the barrel in the hold and went to his bed never to surface again.'

'And *you* never went to see him after you returned to the ship?' I asked Harry.

Harry hesitated. 'No, no I did not.'

'Are you *sure* about that, Harry? You took a while to answer. Either you did or you didn't,' I pressed.

'Yes,' he answered almost too immediately.

'At any point this morning, has anybody been to check on where he sleeps?'

The First Mate and Harry looked to each other before finally the former spoke. 'Yes.'

'And?' I asked, marginally irritated when his only response was to give me a blank look. I had no idea if ghost people could leave marks in ghost blankets. So much of this still didn't make sense to me and probably never would.

'As we said, he's not there and nobody saw him there all night. He might been there, might not.'

'But Benjamin said he went to his bunk?' I turned to the First Mate. 'So he probably was there at some point, no?'

'He told me he was going there. I didn't actually see him there. Neither did anyone else.'

86

'Ah I see.' I nodded thoughtfully. 'If nobody saw him, it's safe to assume he spent last night somewhere else then, despite saying he was going to bed when he got back, and maybe even started to go to bed but decided to go somewhere else to keep out of everybody's way. Is there anywhere he goes?'

Harry and his First Mate both shrugged. 'He shouldn't leave the ship without our permission.'

'That might be. But it isn't what I asked, Harry.'

'Cap'n,' the First Mate nudged his captain, 'we should tell him.'

'Tell me what?'

Harry looked at *The Lady Catherine*. 'Prying ears in there, let's get away from the good lady for few minutes.'

We didn't travel far, just to the car park. 'What would you like to tell me what's making you so anxious, Harry?'

'It's the sweet little lady of his. Well, I say "his" but I know she's not his. Just, he's sweet on her if you know what I mean. That girl in the shop, that girl in the pub last night, y'see.'

'Ebrel Penrose?'

Harry nodded.

'What about her?' I shook my head in confusion.

'Well, not her really. She can't help what he said, and she can't help what he been doing. She can't help that Eddie's sweet on her, can she?'

Ah, the vague bush-beating witness, how I had missed them! '*What* has Eddie been doing?'

'Well, ah, you see,' Harry cleared his throat and I resisted losing my rag, 'they got a little building, like a storage shed and it overlooks the back of the shop there.' He pointed in the general direction of the shop; we couldn't see it from our position.

I could see where this was going.

'And he goes there at night to watch her do stuff.' Harry scratched his neck uncomfortably.

' "Do stuff?" He can't really watch her get undressed or watch her sleep seeing as she doesn't do either. As far as I'm aware, nobody else but me in this village can sleep or undress.'

Harry looked horrified. 'No! And if I thought he were watching a lady get undressed without her saying it was alright, he'd get more'n a clip round the ear from his captain! No, he watches her do stuff like sittin' in the garden, taking out the rubbish, accepting deliveries, reading her magazines and things.'

'Soppy idiot told me she sings to herself opening the shop and what an angelic voice she got. Lads joke him about it. It's all innocent! Nothing more'n that. He likes her but he aint no peeper over ladies, DI Blackman!'

'Any of you thought to go to this shed to see if he's there?' I looked to both of them, but they shared only a blank look.

'No,' said Benjamin, 'Miss Ebrel only left a few minutes before you got here. Didn't think it a good idea to tell her about that.'

'Right then lads, who's going to show me where it is?'

Benjamin asked if he could do any more to help and I asked him if he would talk to the lads again to jolt a few memories as to where Eddie might be. Harry and I went to the shop, but didn't make our presence known to Ebrel or her father, taking care to sneak around the back. By now, the rain had died down to a light drizzle. I pulled my waterproof tight around me.

The building looked like a wood fuel storage shed by the last human owners, but it seemed the Penroses had no present use for it. This made it an ideal hiding place for somebody wanting to keep a close watch on the shop.

The door was loose on its hinges, open and not locked – clearly for an unused building, it had regular visitors. It was musky and silent inside, Sunlight poured in through the cracks, beams of light illuminating dancing dust. 'Are you in here, Eddie?'

If the boy *was* there, he did not respond.

'You're not in trouble lad, we just want to talk to ye,' Harry offered.

Still there was no response from inside the small building. We did see signs of his presence though – several blankets (real ones) which he had forged into a makeshift hammock behind a large piece of wood he'd used as a lean-to propped against the side wall but shielding the interior from the door. 'Well, he's not here,' I said, 'is this the only place he comes?'

'That we know of, yes,' replied Harry.

'Who's there?' The unmistakable voice of Ebrel came from behind us. 'What are you doing in that building? Oh Harry, what are you doing here?' her tone quizzical as he turned to face her.

I poked my head outside the building so Ebrel could see me too and gave her a friendly wave. When she saw me, she immediately rushed to us and started gabbling about how sorry she was, how Philip over-reacted and she just wanted to make things up with Eddie. More than once, she asked how the lad was.

'We're here about Eddie,' I informed her, 'nobody has seen him since last night. Have you?'

She cocked her head to one side. 'No, what makes you think I would have? And what are you doing all the way over *here*?'

I explained that he used this outbuilding as a hideaway when things got too difficult on the ship; I left out the bit about using it to spy on her.

'I've never seen him here. He must keep very quiet. Dad and I don't use this shed, it wasn't here when we were alive. Dad thinks it's ugly and wants to knock it down to grow more vegetables.'

'Your dad has not mentioned seeing him?'

She shook her head slowly. 'You can come in and ask him if you want. He's getting ready to open the shop.'

We entered through the back door, seeing for the first time how the Penroses had attempted to convert the living space back to something that would have been familiar to them. Corin was only happy to help but knew nothing. We went through the formalities; after a brief exchange, I learnt nothing new.

Corin had never entered the shed, didn't know that Eddie had used it as a bolthole, and had never seen anyone coming or going. All he could confirm was that he knew who Eddie was; the lad bought supplies for the ship more than once.

After this, Harry made his excuses and told me he had to get back to the ship but would let me know if Eddie turned up.

So much about this did not make sense: where would Eddie go? It was possible he had another bolthole, possible, but unlikely. I returned to the shed behind the shop to see if there was any other clue.

In life, Eddie had few possessions; that carried through in death too. There was nothing here except the blankets.

I checked every corner, behind every bit of debris, under the hammock and finally to the hammock itself. I gave it a good shake, plunged my hands into the folds and found something wrapped up inside.

It was small, oblong in shape, no more than three inches long and wrapped loosely. When I pulled it out, I was surprised to see half a bar of chocolate with clear bite marks pressed into the chocolate and caramel.

'Messy sod.' I examined the chocolate. It lacked the dryness or the white powdery texture of older chocolate, so it hadn't been there long. The instinct would not go away, the more I thought about this, the more uneasy I felt and the more convinced that this was a crime scene. The boy may turn up in a few hours, but I had to scratch the itch a little more today.

The day had brightened a little over the next hour, but angry grey clouds threatened to drench the village again. When I was satisfied that the weather had turned for the better, I made my way to *The Lady Catherine* to have another word with Harry.

'Is Harry aboard?' I shouted up at Benjamin who was lecturing a few of the younger pirates about something.

'Aye,' he replied and disappeared below, returning with Harry.

'Harry, my friend, would you mind coming down here so I can show you something? If you're not busy?'

'Certainly not busy!' he said with a cheery smile. 'What can I do for ye?

'Do you know what this is?' I produced an electronic device from the pocket of my waterproof.

He looked at the object curiously. 'No. What be that thing?'

Of course he hadn't seen one before. This was the first time in about a year I had used mine and I doubt anyone else here owned one. Dora would have seen one, might even have used one, and the most likely candidate in the village to have ever owned one, but nobody else. 'It's called a "camera".'

'Very interesting if you don't mind me saying so, now what does it do?'

'From this position here where we're standing, what would you say is the prettiest view of the village?'

'It got to be that road there.' He gestured to the main road out of the village, an otherwise unremarkable tarmac strip leading up a gentle slope towards the hills.

Bemused, I asked him what it was about the potholed, narrow tarmac road that he most liked.

'It leads to the rum!' and he gave a hearty laugh.

'Of course, now let me show you something.' I took a picture of the road, the pub in the background and the view of the road out of the village towards the moor. Then I showed Harry the display screen.

'Well strike me! How does it paint a picture so quick?'

'Just technology; I don't really know how it works, all I know is that this captures images. Now, would you like to try it out? All you do is bring it up to your face like this,' I demonstrated, 'and capture the image on this thing – it's called a "screen". When you are happy with what you see, press this button.'

Harry tried it out and showed me a picture of the sky with a bit of mast from *The Lady Catherine*.

'Er, no, sorry. I should have explained. You need to keep the camera steady, hold it on the image you want to capture and *then* press the button.' I demonstrated it for him. 'When it makes a noise, you can safely move again.'

His second effort was much better; he managed to capture the side of *The Lady Catherine* and Benjamin talking to the young deckhands. Harry clapped his hands in delight. 'That be Benjamin!'

The First Mate must have heard his Captain because he turned around to nod at us.

'Benjamin, me old mate! I got you that portrait of yourself what I always promised you. Ha ha ha ha ha ha!'

'That's great, well done Harry. Now, I need you to do something for me. I can't go aboard the ship as you know, so I need you to take photographs of where Eddie sleeps.

'We don't sleep. We just pretend, really. Helps us feel normal like.'

'I see. Either way, I need pictures of his bed, the area, any furniture, anything that specifically belongs to him or that he uses. Can you do that for me? The place *where* he sleeps and all around it if you can. Photograph anything that looks unusual. I suspect there won't be anything, but I need to eliminate- I need to check that nothing is out of place.'

'Yes sir!' he proclaimed. 'Betting I could make money out of these little portrait thingies!'

I waited patiently; after some ten minutes, Harry returned proudly waving my little camera above his head.

I had a quick look through, everything seemed fine on the viewfinder, but I would have to check them on the computer for finer detail.

'Thank you, Harry. These look really good. Can I ask that nobody disturbs Eddie's space?'

'Course! Nobody goes there anyway, and they know better than to mess around with each other's things. That's one of the rules of *The Lady Catherine* – what's yours is sacred.'

'Wonderful, I really appreciate your help, Harry. I might need to come back for more if you're happy to help me. It won't be long before Eddie turns up I'm sure, but let's do all we can to speed it up a bit?'

I bid him a good day and returned to the small shed at the back of the shop to take some photos of my own, looking for anything that might suggest where Eddie was or what might have happened to him.

I photographed the hammock, how it was attached, the ground beneath it, the shelf next to it (and noted it was empty aside from the half bar of chocolate I'd put there) and around the place where I had found the chocolate. Finally, I opened the makeshift hammock. I stopped dead, frozen to the spot.

In the middle of the large wrapped blanket was what, to my trained eye, looked like cuts in the fabric, like it had been slashed and stabbed repeatedly and not with anything approaching panache.

In that moment, a half-eaten bar of chocolate had stopped being a young boy's messy habits and seemed to become potentially a crucial piece of evidence – so had the whole shed and everything in it. I felt it best to talk again to Corin Penrose in case anything jogged his memory and that's where I went right away.

The shop was now open and I was surprised to see it was so late, it was approaching midday when I stepped through the door. Corin was at the shop front restocking bags of flour. 'Twice in one morning?' he asked me. 'Of course, it's always good so see you Detective Blackman.'

'Yes, sorry, I won't take up too much of your time. I need to talk to you again about last night. If there is anything you remember, anything unusual even if it seems insignificant, it might help. I don't know what's going on, but I think we have more than a missing boy now.'

Corin stopped what he was doing and looked thoughtfully at the ceiling. 'No, it was a night like any other aside from the fact I was waiting for you to bring my daughter back.'

'When I returned last night with Ebrel, you were in the shop and close to the door; it was long after closing time. You weren't stocking up that late, surely? Were you waiting there for us?'

'No on both counts, I had actually just turned away a customer.'

'What, that late?'

'Yes. That new fellow, the Roman. He knocked on the door minutes before the two of you came back. I sent him away again.'

I frowned. 'What did he want?'

'He asked if I had rope and a knife he could buy. I told him not and even if we did, we were closed and he should come back in the morning so I could order it for him. There is nothing unusual about that. Nearly every returnee has come by my shop after hours asking for *something*.'

I should probably talk to Cato anyway just in case he saw anything. I thanked him for his time and went back to the ship to tell Harry about the knife.

'Problem is,' he said, 'I can't be sure it weren't already there. We're pirates, we make do with what we got. We don't replace blankets just because some idiot drops a fish-gutting knife on his bed, even if it really stinks!'

'That may be, but because of the place where the cut is on the blanket, I can't yet rule anything out. Besides, this has been cut and sliced repeatedly. This damage is not accidental.'

I was at a loss and I had to talk to Cato but I was already growing a little tired of chasing a boy who still might turn up at this point. Expect the unexpected, as they say, and sometimes the unexpected is the most mundane possible solution. 'Apparently, Cato went to the shop last night and asked Corin if he had some rope and a knife. Did you see the Roman last night?'

'Aye, that I did when I got back from the pub.'

'Where? When?'

'Well ye see, he was a navy officer for the Romans weren't he?' He ain't no land lubber I can tell that. He were on the ship last night learning how to tie some knots – been here for hours learning some of our seamanship. I think he got himself a mind to become part of my crew. Would be pleased to have him aboard.'

'So why did he go to the shop for rope and a knife? Surely you have plenty of that on board?'

'Aye, that we do so I have no answer for why he wants some of his own.'

No answers yet, only more questions.

Chapter 6

On the fifth day of the saga of the missing cabin boy (and I had made no further advance to my enquiries), the sound of a tooting car horn pierced my peaceful afternoon. That was my cue to put the kettle on. I set out two cups – put a teabag in each and retrieved the sugar from the cupboard, placed them on the breakfast bar and then went to the door.

I opened it to see my only son Paul walking up the cobbled path of my front garden with a small holdall and a briefcase. He looked rather swish in the suit and I told him so. 'Look at you, quite the businessman!'

Paul grinned at me. He looked most like Cassie when he smiled. 'My income doesn't really reflect being a successful businessman, but I suppose that's the joy of being self-employed. Hello dad, how are you?' He placed his baggage on the floor and gave me a big hug.

'Did you have a good drive?' I ushered him in and closed the door against the cool breeze.

'Yes, but it's quite the trek from Plymouth.'

I tutted. 'I did tell you it was farther than it looked! Nice easy drive, stunning views, but quite the distance if you're not used to it.'

'As I said on the phone – I had today free because my other client cancelled on me. She's hoping to reschedule for tomorrow and as I still have the hotel booked until the morning, why not come down and see dad?'

'Of course! Tea?'

'I'd love one.'

'Scone?'

He shrugged his shoulders. 'How could I come to Cornwall and not have a scone?'

'They eat them in Devon too.'

'Got to sample them in both counties, dad. Rude not to.'

I poured our teas, adding just half a sugar to Paul's which is the way he liked it, and served up the jam and clotted cream from the fridge. 'The jam is made right here in Salmonweir by the way – it was the local shopkeeper's wife's old recipe and now he makes it himself, so this a real piece of history. Where are you staying in Plymouth, again?'

'It's called *The Royal Mayflower*, I think. It's about a stone's throw from the aquarium.' He took a sip of his tea and prepared to spread his scone. 'Great tea.'

I feigned horror as he put the cream on first. 'Don't do that here! You'll get lynched!'

He looked momentarily stunned. 'That's how the lady in the teashop said it should be done. Cream first, jam on top?'

'A teashop in Plymouth?' In enquired.

'Yes.'

'Ah! They do it the other way around in Cornwall; it's quite the sticking point and wars have been fought over far less.'

He chuckled. 'I did not know that. Let me try one of each.'

I watched him struggle with jam first, making a real mess of it, and smirked.

'Um, I think I prefer the Devon way, sorry.' He bit into it. 'Yes, I definitely prefer the Devon way. Goes on better and tastes better.'

'That's fine; just don't tell anyone here because you *will* be lynched.'

'So, how have you been dad?'

'Very well thanks, son. Living in Salmonweir is an interesting experience.' I poured myself some more tea and offered Paul a top up. 'Though not quite what I expected from my retirement, I must admit!'

He gratefully accepted more tea. 'I can imagine! I suppose you've been reading what the papers say about it?'

'No, I did at the start but now I'm not really interested if I'm honest. I've never read such nonsense and what the papers say is a far cry from the reality of this gorgeous village. We're happy here and getting on well. Oh um, well, most of them are anyway.'

He looked at me curiously.

'We have a medieval monk and a civil war minister who bicker quite a lot, like an old married couple I suppose. A few days ago, a Roman naval officer arrived which annoyed our Celtic warrior queen. Not much fighting between those two yet, but he's kept out of the way mostly. I've only met him twice and should introduce myself properly at some point.'

'Wow, I think it's amazing dad. This is like a real living history village but without the amateur thesps. Have you considered turning this place into a tourist attraction?'

I nodded. 'Funnily enough, yes, we have. In a few weeks' time, we have our first bonfire night spectacular and we're hoping living people will come to see it. That's a tester; we think it'll be a big draw in the long run to meet some ghosts, especially for kids. If that works out, we'll plan a few more.'

'You should have told me, I could have pulled in a few favours or spread the word amongst some of my promo contacts.'

'Then I'm telling you now. We have a bonfire in the park, and we'll have pirates and Romans, Celts and monks, Tudors and pretty much every other time period and what we have over other living history attractions is that this is the real thing.'

'Wonderful. I'll see what I can do when I get back.' He pulled out a notebook and jotted down a few names. In a circle, he wrote FOR DAD 5th NOV before promptly putting the notebook away.

'How are you and your young lady?' I asked when he was finally comfortable.

'Ellie's fine!'

'Set a date yet?'

'It's going to be a long engagement, we think. We're in no rush and we need to save up to get our own place. You know how it is these days.'

'I do indeed. I'll help with the wedding, both me and your mum have money put aside for all three of you. We promised we'd keep that quiet from the solicitors.'

Paul smiled; a few minutes passed before he spoke again.

'How *are* things between you and mum?'

'You've not spoken to her?'

'Of course I have, all the time, but I want to hear it from you. There are always two sides to an argument remember.' He grinned at me.

'Not so bad. I phoned her a couple of days ago. Your sister insisted on it. It was civil enough; we didn't argue which is something, but she's adamant she's staying in Cambridge and I really do not want to leave here. There was no screaming. So, I suppose that is something.'

'That's not all this break up is about though, we all know that.'

'You're right. If either of us were prepared to budge, there would be the remotest sliver of a possibility of a hint of reconciliation, but I think that point alone makes it impossible.' I put my hand gently on his arm.

He rubbed it affectionately. 'She told me what happened the day she left. I think I would have laughed, if I were here, sorry. I don't know how I kept a straight face when she told me about that monk telling her to shut up so he could clear the house of plague and bad smells.'

'I don't know who was the more shocked – me, your mum or Jowan himself. He came back to the house later to apologise for startling her, but she had already gone. I think he partly blamed himself, but the truth is she was already contemplating leaving when he arrived, waving his thurible and telling us all about the plague in the village.'

Paul chuckled. 'Do you know everyone in the village? I saw a man drawing a rag and bone cart on my way into the village and some pirates sword-fighting.'

'Rag and bone man is called Mickey, that's all I know. He spends all day of every day pulling that cart along the street and back again. I never got more than a "good morning" out of him.'

'What about the man with the book?'

'Man with the book?'

'Yes,' Paul cleared his throat, 'he wore modern clothing, 1990s I'd say. That's what made him stand out from the others. But he also held an attractive leather-bound book. I saw him on a bench about half a mile out the village.'

'Don't know, but if he had modern clothes, he's either new or not a ghost at all. I'll bet it's another bloody reporter.'

Paul nodded thoughtfully. 'He looked up at me and back down again when I drove past.'

'I don't suppose you noticed the title of the book?' I offered him the plate of scones.

He refused the scones. 'No, sorry, I was too far away.'

'Not to worry. I'm sure I'll bump into him at some point.'

There was a firm and urgent knock on the door.

'Oh, who might that be?' I rose to answer it, Paul was curious enough to follow me. On opening the door, I was surprised to see Dora Wilson; she looked concerned.

'Hello Dora, how wonderful to see you!'

She smiled nervously at me and then at my son, offering him a quick and formal, 'good morning sir.'

'Dora, this is Paul, my son.'

Paul waved cautiously and frowned at our visitor, calculating, examining her.

'He is as handsome as his father. Sorry to bother you gentlemen, I'm sure father and son have much to talk about, but I heard the most awful noise earlier. It was like a ship's horn and it came from here?'

It took us both a couple of minutes to realise what she had meant.

'Sorry for startling you, Mrs Wilson,' said Paul, 'that was probably my car horn, nothing to worry about. I used it to let my father know I'd arrived. Would you like to come in and share some tea and scones with us?'

She smiled and shook her head, 'Thank you for your hospitality, but I must politely decline the kind offer.'

'No, thank you for visiting. You know you are welcome here any time Dora,' I explained.

She smiled at us both and walked off down the garden path; I closed the door behind her.

'Wow,' said Paul. 'Just, wow. Seriously – wow!'

'I agree, she is beautiful although I didn't think she was your type. But she's also dead and you're spoken for. I'm not sure a relationship between you two would work in those circumstances.'

'That's not what I meant, dad. *That* was Dora Wilson.'

'Yes.'

'That was *Dora Wilson.*'

'Yes son, that *was* Dora Wilson,' I repeated the sentence a third time so the word "was" didn't feel left out and end up developing self-esteem issues.

'She's in the village, *this* village,' he trailed off as made our way back through the house and returned to our breakfast bar.

'Why are you so interested in her? We have a pirate, a warrior queen, a Roman, a Viking and a medieval monk and you're interested in a woman who died some 35 years before you were born? If you want to hear war stories, your two living grandparents have enough of them.'

'Dad, what do you really know about any of these ghost people of Salmonweir?'

'A lot, I interact with them every day, so I've got to know them quite well.'

'What about,' he paused, and adopted a cautious note, 'how they *died*?'

'I don't ask if they won't tell. Some have told me, but others have chosen not to discuss it; it's rather impolite to talk about one's demise I think, and I haven't been researching them either. I'd rather not know if they don't want to talk about it.'

'You were a detective and you've never heard of Dora Wilson?'

'No, sorry. Is she famous?'

He rubbed his finger across his lip and leaned back in his chair. 'You might want to look it up if you've worked out how to use the tinterwebs.'

'I have you cheeky so and so, now tell me *how you know Dora Wilson?*'

'One of the last women in the country to have been hanged. Not the last one, because everyone knows her case. But, Dora Wilson? With her, it created an outcry within the legal community but barely made it in the media who wouldn't have touched the story, After all, this was war,' he put on his best upper-class officer voice. 'We did what we had to do. Dig for Britain and all that, old chap!'

Paul cleared his throat. 'Some legal historians think it was the ammunition the abolitionists needed to push it through parliament.'

'What did she do?' I pressed impatiently.

He shrugged his shoulders. 'She drowned her two children.'

'She did *what?'*

'Oh yeah, a real-life *Tess of the D'Urbervilles* that one. She was from a country farming family, married a low-level navy officer from Plymouth – above her station, many thought. They married, had two kids, he went away to war and died fighting at sea.

'*HMS Hood,* she told me.'

Paul nodded. 'When she learnt of his death, she fell into a depression and became a recluse. She killed both her children a few months after the ship sank and they hanged her for it. Even the judge who passed sentence didn't want to do it but was constricted by the law. He retired and called into question the value of capital punishment in killing people overwhelmed with grief, war or no war.'

113

I looked on stunned as my son just came out with all this information about a woman I thought I knew. 'How do you know all this?'

'I did Legal History at A-Level, remember, and hated it. She was one of the case studies we worked through. I knew she was from Cornwall but didn't know she settled here. I was shocked to see her if I'm honest.'

'Wow.'

'Sorry dad, I didn't mean to startle you.' He touched my shoulder in comfort.

'No, it's alright. It shouldn't surprise me. So many in this village died from tragedy, so why I thought she might have lived to an old age I don't know. It does seem now that they must have *all* returned at the age they were when they died. I suppose I always knew that, deep down.'

'It would also explain why she has never mixed with the other ghosts and refuses to come to the house for tea. I put it down to her being prim and proper, but she must isolate herself because she's ashamed of what she did.' I put my head in my hands. 'That poor woman.'

'Well, sorry again.' He reached out and touched my shoulder before changing the subject. 'Hmm, that was good tea! Why don't you give me a tour of the village and then I think it's lunch o'clock? My treat, of course.'

We passed Dora on the way down. We smiled; she smiled and bid us a good day. No words passed between us.

In the pub, some pirates challenged my son to a rum drinking contest and he was subjected to some awful poetry. Although the ghosts could eat and drink, they can't get drunk or put on weight – I hastily had to explain that to Paul to avoid his total embarrassment. Next, we decided to take a walk through the park so I could show Paul the progress on setting up the bonfire and display.

The weather was unusually mild again and my son asked if it was always this warm. I burst his bubble in pointing out that the Cornish weather was erratic, warm one day and wet the next, although warmer on average than the rest of the country, hence the succulents and palm trees.

The display was taking shape, slowly but surely. The bunting was already going up and some of the local children were hard at work clearing the leaves, twigs and tidying up the park. It had been left alone and neglected since the last of the living residents left, but it was starting to look like itself again.

'Wow, look at this. It's going to look great, dad! I really hope people come.' He had just stopped admiring the flags on the bandstand (which had received a new lick of paint) when we caught sight of Ebrel and Philip walking hand in hand along the path. After a brief exchange, they made their way towards us.

Ebrel offered my son the "butter wouldn't melt" smile she had given her father just the other day and – get this – she followed that up with a curtsy. 'And who might you be, good sir?' she said.

'Miss Ebrel, Philip, good afternoon to you both. This is my son, Paul.'

'As handsome as his father!' she said, repeating Dora Wilson's sentiment.

Philip shot her a jealous look, so I quickly went on. 'Paul was on business in Plymouth and decided to come to Salmonweir to have a look around and tell me about his recent betrothal to an eligible young lady.'

Ebrel's face immediately straightened, adopting a formal tone. 'Delighted to meet you, your young lady should consider herself fortunate becoming a part of your esteemed family. Your father has been like an uncle to me

116

– a good friend and confidante. How fortunate you must feel to have him as a father?'

'Indeed,' Paul said, slapping me on the back. 'He's a diamond.'

The expression elicited curious looks from both Ebrel and Philip.

'Is there news of Eddie, perchance?' Ebrel asked me with genuine concern.

I had to stifle a chuckle at her continued efforts to impress my son and shook my head. 'Nobody knows where he is. Thanks for your help the other day, both of you, but this will remain a mystery for now.' Nobody except Harry presently knew about the knife damage and asked him not to say anything.

'If there is anything else we can do to help, sir, please ask?' Philip pressed. 'When he comes back, I will make amends for my own actions. I hope we can meet for a beer and talk. No malice intended.'

'Very gracious, Philip. I hope you get that opportunity. I will, however, need to talk to you about your whereabouts on the night of Eddie's disappearance.'

His face slumped. 'I know my behaviour was not becoming of my position.' He sighed. 'I went home. I was back by 10:30.'

'I see. Can anyone verify this?'

'When I arrived home, Richard, Barnaby and Clement were awake, practising at music. Barnaby commented that it was early and noted the time. That's how I know exactly what time it was. We remained up for some hours discussing music, amongst other things. We all go to bed, but we cannot sleep. We just-'

'I understand, Harry told me that he and his men go to bed and go through the motions of going to sleep without actually sleeping. I imagine this is what you do too?'

'That's right, sir,' Philip replied. 'I go to the bed, lie there thinking about my existence, engaging in private prayer or reading a book. Writing, sonnets about love-,' he looked at Ebrel and went pink. 'Writing, I like writing and I sometimes stay up just writing. You can ask any of the other gentlemen. They will tell you the same thing.'

Satisfied with this, I nodded. 'Thank you, Philip. I will verify that with your friends. May I ask what you two have been up to today in this lovely weather?'

'We were doing nothing wrong, just walking around the park.' Ebrel blurted out, turning bright red.

'None of my business,' I smiled. 'I trust the both of you will be here for the bonfire and fireworks? They can be quite romantic.'

'We will,' said Ebrel, 'Father is looking forward to seeing them. He always enjoyed community festivities.'

'Wonderful. I'm not sure I've seen your father leave the shop in all the time he's been here. It may be a good opportunity to introduce your father to Philip, formally.'

Philip nodded. 'I hope so. Mister Blackman, we found something in the bushes while we were, uh, walking.'

'What did you find?'

'A most curious thing indeed,' said Philip, 'a blanket just over there in the thicket. It's like somebody was stabbing through it. Quite a shame, it looks like a good quality blanket too.'

'Can you show me?'

Chapter 7

By the time we arrived at the shrub where Philip and Ebrel found the blanket, we had acquired another interested observer. The Roman officer Cato, who had been putting up a banner outside the garden's northern gate, noticed the two young lovers exit the trees. He went over to speak to them only to spot the blanket lying on the ground.

'Good afternoon, Cato. I see you've found yourself a new job already?' I said, pointing to his handiwork.

'Oh,' he replied, 'this is just a small favour for Kensa as appreciation for her hospitality and help so far. She's been most accommodating so far. A rather pleasant woman indeed with many Roman virtues.'

I looked at Cato, narrowing my eyes but his expression was unreadable. 'Kensa is our Iron Age Warrior Queen,' I explained to Paul.

'A bit like Boudicca?' Paul offered, helpfully.

'Do us both a favour. Please, please, please do not mention that name to Kensa if you meet her. I've never heard her utter so many expletives in a single sentence. Something about a horse's rectum and somebody's head forcibly inserted into one. I don't know whether that was an indication of what actually took place or what Kensa would have done to the queen of the Iceni given half the chance.'

'I am getting the impression that they didn't like each other?'

I shook my head vigorously and turned to the Roman officer. 'I'm pleased you two are getting along so well, Cato. I thought we mind end up with another situation like Eli and Jowan.'

'Oh no, Kensa is a charming woman!' Cato exclaimed, 'Not what I had come to expect of the Dumnonii. She would have made a great vassal ruler under Rome. I can see why her people loved and cherished her so. I'm pleased to have found such a great acquaintance.'

I nodded. 'I am pleased! When you were alive, you would undoubtedly have been enemies.'

'You never know. We have much in common. Just yesterday, she showed me how to defend myself against a larger assailant when unarmed. I admire her a great deal.' The Roman flushed, realising he was running away with himself.

'Of course, we lived around the same time so naturally I already value her counsel more than that of Jowan. A pleasant man, but he does drone on about his god a bit too much.'

'How is her armour reproduction hobby coming along?'

'Now you've reminded me. Kensa can tell you all about it tomorrow. We would like to host a lunch for you DI Blackman. And perhaps your son, if you are still here?' he gave my son a hopeful look.

'Thank you kindly,' replied Paul, 'but I'm leaving later today. A shame, I think I'd like to meet this Kensa.'

'Unfortunate. Perhaps next time?'

Paul nodded.

'Right, let's take a look at this blanket, shall we?'

I counted some thirty cuts through the blanket, most concentrated in the upper-central area. It's more than likely that – had a person been lying on it – most of the strikes would have hit the area of their chest, arms and upper belly.

My son gave me a knowing glance but kept quiet.

I made my excuses, thanked all concerned for their help, and left the gardens. I didn't want to alarm Harry and his crew, so I first went to the shop to see Corin Penrose.

I handed over the blanket and asked if he recognised it.

'Yes, that looks like one I sold.' He said, coming out from behind the counter. 'The only person who bought a blanket from me was that boy you keep asking about, Eddie. I can't say for certain whether it is the one, but it certainly looks like it. Of course, it'll be no good to him now in that state, though will it?'

'There's a high chance it's his, as far as you are concerned?' I turned the blanket over in my hands and tried folding it.

'I couldn't swear on the Holy Bible, but it certainly looks like the one to me. I've no reason to believe it's not.'

'Thank you, Corin. I need to see Harry and give him the bad news. This is getting more concerning by the minute. How do you kill a dead person, and why?'

He shrugged. 'You're the gentleman of law, I'm just a shopkeeper.'

'Another of Salmonweir's little mysteries. Add it to the list.'

Corin nodded. 'Have you seen my daughter recently?' he enquired.

'I have. Ebrel showed me this blanket. She's down at the dock now with Philip. They're finally taking the tour of the ship.'

'A sailing ship is no place for a woman,' he protested. 'I do *not* understand what she hopes to get out of visiting a ship full of ruffians or how such an invitation should come about. I hope she was not drinking with some of the crew.'

He was still unaware of the reason why the offer was made in the first place. There was no reason to tell him yet, if ever, but I realised now that in light of new information about Harry, he may find out or I may have to tell him. 'She's a curious young lady, and Philip was keen to see what, to him, is future technology. They are young and want to learn as much of the world as they can. Alas, my only regret is that I could not go with them. I'd love to see a genuine tall ship as it appeared back then.'

'That's fine, so long as I know where she is. I contend she acquired that curiosity from her mother,' Corin retreated back behind his counter.

'Do you mind me asking. What happened to her, and your sons?'

A dark look passed across his face and I regretted asking. 'All I know is that Ebrel and I died within a few days of each other. My sons and wife were alive at the time of my death, though my youngest son was ill.' His expression changed from darkness to a brief flicker of pain before righting itself. The stoic Corin Penrose was before me once again. 'How old they were when they died, and if I met my sons and wife on the other side, I have no memory of it now. Perhaps that is part of the condition of our return?'

'I am truly sorry for asking.' I said quickly. 'Was Ebrel close to her mother?'

He gave a barely perceptible nod. 'That they were. I suspect it's from Tegen that Ebrel also gets her strong-mindedness. Ebrel was never like that in life so only God himself only knows why she has chosen to express that now. She was a quiet child, sweet and unassuming with impeccable manners.'

He cleared his throat and changed the subject quickly. 'Speaking of children, I hear your son is in the village? Has he now left?'

I dropped the line of questioning. Stoic he was, but unfeeling he clearly was not. 'No, he's still here. He had a phone call from his mother just now and I didn't wish to snoop. He's just outside but will be in in a moment.'

As if on cue, the door opened with the tinkling of the bell and Paul stepped in behind me, giving both me and Corin a broad smile.

'Hello sir, can I help you? I'm Corin Penrose, owner of this shop.'

'Delighted to meet you, Mister Penrose. You must be Ebrel's father?'

'That's right,' he took a stiff and guarded tone, 'and who might you be?'

'Corin, *this* is my son Paul.' I said.

Corin frowned and looked to both of us in turn, looking surprised and confused in equal measure. 'Oh, I see the resemblance. It's just. You're not what I expected. I saw somebody earlier and assumed *he* was Detective Blackman's son. You look nothing like him. My most humble apologies.'

'That's quite alright. Another new visitor to the village?' Paul asked.

'Yes, this man's fashion was not dissimilar to your own attire and he held a book, a leather-bound book.'

Paul and I exchanged glances. 'Where was he?' I asked.

'He sat on the edge of the wall just outside there,' Corin pointed to the front of the shop.' Then he took out his book and started reading. When I asked him what he wanted, he just stood up, turned his back on me and walked away. It was quite rude if I do say so myself to not even acknowledge my presence.'

'That certainly wasn't me. I am partial to reading the occasional book, but I don't have one with me today and I certainly don't own any leather-bound books. I saw the same man earlier on the road into the village. Dad didn't know who he was.'

'Another mystery beckons,' I said, 'Another batch of new arrivals may make this interesting. I'm sure we'll cross paths with this mystery book-carrying man soon enough. If you see him again, you know what to do.'

'Of course I will, DI Blackman, we know the routine by now.'

We bade Corin farewell and once we got outside the shop Paul told me it was time for him to leave. After Valarie called, Paul's cancelled client called too wanting to rearrange their consultancy for early the following day and wondered if Paul could reschedule. With a near 3hr drive back to Plymouth, we both thought it wise to leave to get ahead of the rush hour traffic (yes, Cornwall has one!)

As I closed the front door, I noticed a slip of paper poking out of the letterbox. I still received snail mail; after all, I still had bills to pay. Thankfully, circulars and junk mail had reduced to almost nothing. This was a slip of paper and not a letter. I hadn't noticed it against the white of the PVC door and all that poked through was the corner. I pulled it out of the letterbox. It was cheap paper, not writing paper, but the rough-edged type typically torn out of a spiral notepad. It read:

Edy is ded.
Hes not comming back this tym.
I know hoo did it and I no wy, man
B more care full wen u aR out in the vilag
"Frend"

The handwriting was like that of a child and written in red ink; oh, how cliché to sign it "from a friend"! That sort of thing rarely happened to me in real life, of course, and it's probably that this person has become a little too obsessed with detective novels and films. Still, it added another complication to this mysterious series of events.

I folded the note out and left it face up on the breakfast bar while I put the kettle on and prepared another cup of tea, pondering the tone and content of the note. It concerned me that there was someone in the village toying with me like this. In real life, witnesses went to the police unless their life was in danger. Otherwise, it was a suspect, but this did not feel like the words of a suspect.

The second conundrum was, of course, the notion that somebody who was already dead (undead?) could be murdered. If I phoned Devon & Cornwall Police, the conversation would probably go something like this:

"Yes, hi. This is Detective Inspector, retired by the way, Karl Blackman of Salmonweir. I wish to report a murder."

"I see DI Blackman, what can you tell me about the victim?"

"A young boy, perhaps fifteen or sixteen years old."

"How long ago did he die?"

"I'm not sure, but I think around 1716."

"Quarter past five yesterday evening? Is that when the alleged murder took place?"

"No, he died in the year *1716. But that's not when he was murdered. I think somebody killed him again five nights ago."*

Everybody knows about Salmonweir by now so the worst I could hope for is that they'd hang up on me after threatening to arrest me for wasting their time. The best is that they would have a good laugh – partly at my expense and partly at the sheer daftness of the situation in Salmonweir – and *then* hang up on me. Ultimately, neither would get me far; I was on my own with this one unless I could call in a favour or promise to offer my services in future.

I tapped lightly upon the door to the house now serving as Cato's home. It was a small bungalow on top of the hill near the church with a nice view over the bay – he said he liked to look out at sea as often as he could.

When Cato first stepped through the door just a few days before, he was surprised to see that he would have the house to himself – explaining it was the size of a small barrack block and he expected to share it with at least half a cohort, by my reckoning about 40 people.

Kensa answered the door and she offered me a beaming smile. 'Detective Blackman, so pleased to see you! Please, come in from the rain.'

A bland blanket of grey had settled over the village when I left the house and a fine mist of rain moved sideways off the coast as I made my way up the slope. The shelter of Cato's warm home was not before time. Gratefully, I stepped through the doorway and closed it quickly behind me, shutting out the cold and the wet.

'May I get you something to drink?' she asked, taking my coat and hanging it on a hook behind her.

'Do you have coffee?'

Her face screwed up slightly at the suggestion.

'Is that ok?' I asked, slightly taken aback. 'If you don't have any, tea will be fine.'

'Oh we, ah, *Cato* has some. I just don't like the drink and don't understand how anybody could. How do you like it?'

'Milk and one sugar, brown sugar if you have it but white is fine if you don't.'

I followed Kensa through to the kitchen to see a table piled up with metal. One end had a neatly stacked

131

pile of metal strips while the other had a mess of metal of all shapes. Between, an open toolbox displayed an array of hammers of different sizes.

'This looks like Roman armour. Is this yours, Cato?' I asked the Roman who held a kettle in one hand and the electric cable in the other. Positioning the device and lead close to his head, I watched amused as he gradually and slowly put them together. As they get close, he pulled them apart again.

He replied without turning to look at me. 'No, that's Kensa's. She's designing Roman armour.'

Curiously, I watched Cato repeat his strange pattern three times before deciding to ask the obvious question. 'Cato, dear friend, what in Jupiter's name *are* you doing?'

'I am trying to understand.' He did not shift his gaze from the kettle and the electric cable, repeating the strange process for a fourth time.

'Understand *what* exactly?'

'To understand and see how the fire from this,' he waved the cable towards me, 'gets into this to heat the water.' He shook the kettle; there came the familiar sound of sloshing water.

'I presume you know to connect the cable to the kettle and switch it on at the wall?'

'I know,' he came back quickly, 'I want to understand *how* it works. Where does the fire come from? When does the fire start?'

I stood up from my chair and moved to his side. 't's not *actually* fire, my friend.'

'But the water is cold at the beginning and hot at the end,' still he did not turn his gaze to me, 'and I want to see how it is heated. If it's not fire, is it pitch or oil? Maybe coal? If so, where are these fuels lit?'

I removed the cable from his hand. 'I'm afraid you cannot see electricity. It's an invisible force that activates inside the kettle when it connects.'

'Rather like magic?' Finally, he put the kettle down and turned to me. I plugged the cable in and switched the mains on. It fired up within seconds, beginning that familiar low grumbling.

'Not magic, we know how it works; we just can't see it.'

He nodded thoughtfully. 'Thank you.' There is something else I would like to discuss with you about the entertainments available.'

'What entertainment?'

'I believe Kensa calls it a "television"? Could you perhaps enlighten me?'

'I will do my best. I'm not the greatest fan of the television.' I let Cato pour us both a coffee. Cato took a thoughtful sip. After a few such silent sips, he began his interrogation of this brave new world.

'Kensa has shown me how to *record* programmes for later viewing.' He led us into the small living room. A delightful looking spread was already on the table – bread, cheese, fruit and some cold meat.

'This looks impressive!' I commented genuinely.

'Thank you. This is what I prepared but it's nothing special – the best I can do under the circumstances. Some of it is what I ate while in barracks. Kensa just finishing off her ideas.'

'I'm touched you went to this much effort for me, really you shouldn't have.'

'It's nothing, really. I wish we could have come up with something more imaginative. I *am* amazed how much of this Corin Penrose could order. Take these olives from Iberia. Did he import them himself? Did he travel to

Iberia? If so, how did he incur such little expense to charge so little for them?'

'No, we have a food market that covers the world now. Anybody can buy almost anything from anywhere.'

'I suspected as much. I assumed that this global market is thanks to the Roman Empire? Has it really endured so long?'

I let out a sigh. 'I am not the right person to ask, but The Roman Empire as you would understand it ended about 400 years after your death. A lot has happened in that time. I will seek, oh, actually – can you read? English, I mean?'

'Kensa is teaching me this also,' he flushed.

'When I am next in Penzance or Truro, I will get you some books that might help you understand.'

'Lunch is served!' exclaimed Kensa, walking through the door carrying a plate full of, well I'm not quite sure what it was but they looked like birds that were decoratively dressed with seasonal berries. She placed them on the table quickly and went straight back into the kitchen while Cato poured the three of us white wine and topped it up with warm water and honey. This was about as authentic as it was going to get.

'Do you like Calda?' He gestured at the glass.

'I've have never tried it,' I tentatively lifted the glass, sipped at it, and nodded my approval. 'I could get used to it.'

Cato looked amused. 'This is simple food. It is the sort of thing that the lower classes, soldiers and gladiators ate. I only wish I had greater resources with which to honour my guest.'

'Cato, really. This is wonderful!' I don't think I'd eaten quite so well in so long, my Doctor would be pleased if this became my regular diet.

Kensa returned with two more plates of poultry – there must have been seven or eight roasted birds on the platters. It was clearly too much food for the three of us, at least for one meal. Had they intended me to stay a few days to help them finish it all off?

'Please sit and help yourself!' Kensa sat down and grabbed a leg of bird, immediately tearing into it. This was the first time I'd witnessed her eating and it was amusing to see manners that today would seem unladylike but, in her time, would have been normal.

There was a distinct lack of cutlery on the table but there *was* a napkin; not wishing to offend my guests, I tore off a leg and tucked in. It was rather tasty – dry but flavoursome. Taking Kensa's lead, I popped some berries in my mouth with the next bite.

'Kensa, what is this meat? It's nice and succulent.'

'Herring gull,' came her short reply.

Chapter 8

I stopped chewing and raised my eyebrows. 'It's gull? As in the loud white creatures that steal your chips, feast on rotting food and drink sewage?'

'The same. Tasty are they not, considering they only seem to eat what we throw away?'

'Mmm,' Cato agreed.

I suddenly didn't want to eat any more and imagined a pool of raw sewage swilling around in my stomach. My next thought was the summer I moved here.

On my first visit to Penzance, a big mean looking herring gull stole an ice cream out of my hand before shrieking triumphantly as he shot off across the beach and found himself chased by three or four others wanting a bite of the chocolate flake. I love salted caramel ice cream and had been enjoying it.

I could have shot him then, and all the others. I almost kicked one later that day when, sat eating a tuna baguette at St Michael's Mount, another tried to steal it from my plate.

'There's hundreds of them around here,' Kensa went on, talking while chewing, 'so I thought "why not"? and killed a few today.' She stopped to take a gulp of wine. 'They're no good to anyone and just get in the way. You're always saying how they wake you up too early in the summer.'

'Oh, I see.' I looked down at the bird wing clasped firmly between my fingers and suddenly didn't want to eat it. 'Of course.'

I'm not sure which of them started first, but soon they were both in uproarious laughter. It took mere seconds for the penny to drop. 'Oh great, a joke at my expense!' I beamed, 'so come on, what is it, really?'

Kensa pointed to one plate. 'Pheasant,' then to the second, 'quail,' then the third, 'and that's duck. Corin Penrose got them from a local butcher. I asked him to get something wild and tasty.'

'You knew Kensa was going to do this?' I asked, turning to Cato.

'Of course!' He poured himself another drink; in contrast, I had barely touched mine. 'Can you now tell me about this "television"? I understand that it can be a library, a theatre and an arena. I understand that. There is one aspect of this *television* I do not understand. Two, actually.'

'Please, ask away.' Kensa watched us both curiously. Of all the times I had visited her in her own home, she had not once shown any interest in the enormous Idiot Box hanging on the wall.

'Yesterday morning, I saw a curious display. Two gentlemen seated on a theatre stage. Well, there were actually three gentlemen, but I believe the third must have been a judge or referee to make sure these other gentlemen abided by the rules and didn't end up killing one another. It occurred to me afterwards that this theatre presentation was named in honour of this third gentleman.'

'I see. What happened?'

'I thought the two men would play music, perform a play or dance. But a woman came out onto the stage. It seemed both men laid a claim of betrothal on this woman; both wished to marry her and sire children with her. Only Jupiter knows why because she was certainly no Helen of Troy. Mind you, neither man could be compared to Adonis or Hercules for that matter, and would no doubt cry like babies if they were presented with a sword. They looked as though they'd cry like babies if asked to sing or perform too.'

He paused to take a breath. 'It appears this woman had two children by the first man. The second man laid claim to fatherhood of a third child. A disagreeable discussion followed because the first man believed the child was his. I found it all rather strange that such a private matter should be considered valuable knowledge or entertainment. To me, it was neither. Could they not have at performed some Aristophanes to entertain the masses?'

I nodded courteously as he explained the outcome of this story. He went silent for a few minutes afterwards; I was about to cut in and explain that I can't understand why anyone would watch it when he started telling me about something else.

'Later on, there was a debate of some sort – rather like when groups of officers like me get together to discuss tactics, or philosophy. Only, the debate, such as it was, featured a group of older ladies. The subject of debate on this show concerned the male anatomy and to illustrate the debate, a succession of men came out.'

'I do not recall how the debate concluded, but I did not feel entertained, nor did I feel I learnt anything from it merely that these ladies had quite different ideas on what they thought was the ideal male bodily form.'

I said nothing. Poor Cato had just discovered daytime television and his life would never be the same again.

'I must admit, they would all have served well in the legions, such were their muscular statures.'

He took another sip of drink.

'I have one final question – we Romans and the Greeks before us gave so much to literature, poetry and the arts. In this world in which you live, have playwrights and games organisers simply run out of ideas? Did Rome use them all up that we have to resort to such... trivialities and nonsense?'

'Some believe so, Cato!' I raised my glass to him. 'I do not indulge much in television if I'm honest and I'm not sure what to recommend to you.'

'So far, it's been hideous! I would happily see out the eternity of my existence not experiencing another minute of it.'

Kensa nodded in agreement.

'Perhaps modern sport might be more to your liking. Have you heard of football?'

'Yes as a matter of fact! Just the other night I watched something called *Weekend Sporting Highlights* and I wanted to ask you, what happens to the losing team?'

'How do you mean?'

'At what point are they executed to the gods? It does not appear to take place in public. Most strange.'

'Oh, they play again the following week against somebody else. It's like an ongoing saga. For some fans, more like a trial of the gods.' I used the opportunity to change the subject. 'Thanks again for this wonderful meal. Kensa, I couldn't help noticing the scrap metal on the kitchen bar earlier on. Cato says you are designing armour now?'

Her freckled face beamed at me. 'Yes! I have been spending some time on the, ah, *internet*? I wanted to see if I could get some real armour to sell to people at the Bonfire Night event.'

'I believe you mentioned this before. Glad to see it's going well.'

She nodded. 'I hope you don't mind me saying, but the situation is worse than I first thought. You people have little idea how to make proper armour from my lifetime. Cato also finds reproduction armour awful.'

143

She shook her head furiously. 'So, I thought I would attempt to make some. I was not a great armourer in life, and I had some superb blacksmiths to make mine.'

'I'm sorry I still know so little about you compared to,' I went to say her name but caught myself in time, 'so many other people from your era. Can you tell me about your life? How did you become queen?'

'I was not supposed to rise to chieftain, but my uncle died without an heir and his companion swordsmen – I guess you might call them knights – voted me his replacement. I was thirteen years old and already the finest warrior in the clan.' She took another bite of meat, once again speaking while she chewed away, and nodded profusely.

'They felt my father was too ill and my brother too young. The Romans came in my tenth year as queen.' She remembered Cato in the room. 'But, what was I saying? This armour, it's poor and would not survive in battle. I wondered, if I cannot be a chieftain again because this world won't allow it, perhaps I can be an armourer and sell it on this *internet* as others do?'

It was dark by the time I left Cato's house and I once again cursed the poor lighting of the village. There had always been poor illumination with the only streetlights on the main road leading to the dock and the beach, following the main road for about a hundred yards.

I noticed it more at this time of year and with the clocks set to go back in just a couple of weeks, it would only get worse. It was especially bad here on top of the hill as the mound of the churchyard blocked what little light came from below.

I made my way precariously towards the church, guided as much by memory of the pattern of steps as by the tiny amount of light from the stars and from below. I cursed my stupidity for not bringing a torch but made it to the main path next to the churchyard without injury. I stopped to admire the view; the ocean seemed little more than an endless black with the occasional flicker of light from a passing boat or ship. A cool wind passed over me, reminding me how quickly the temperature can drop at this time of year if I dawdled too long. It also reminded me that it would get colder in the coming weeks.

As I reached the path, I began my descent, looking for signs of life in the church. It was dark so likely that neither Jowan nor Eli were in there tonight.

Their respective homes were (naturally) almost as far apart as they could get – Jowan lived a few houses down from Cato, and Eli chose his home closer on the west side, near my house. As I've probably already said, this was on the hill the other side of the harbour – the symbolism of his choice not going above my head.

As I turned back to the path to resume my journey, something caught my eye. Behind a gravestone, I saw a dark shadow rise and then dip. I stopped, froze to the spot, and stared at the grave marker.

Only the smallest amount of light from the streetlights below reflected in the glass windows of the church, but it was enough to catch the shimmer of movement in the dark.

I held my breath and stood still, holding my position for at least a minute. I contemplated going over to investigate but in the dark with my dodgy eyes and the assumption that I was probably being paranoid, turned and made my way slowly down the hill.

I continued to get that tingling at the back of my neck though, the way the hairs stand to attention and the ears pull back slightly when you think somebody or something is close behind you.

Short, agonising, precarious steps and I couldn't shake the notion that somebody or something watched – or worse, followed – with every footfall.

My mind started working overtime; it seemed there was a killer on the loose in the village, though I'd not yet had 100% confirmation of it. I imagined somebody or something creeping up on me, waiting, watching, moving silently with each step as I made my way precariously down the hill.

My paranoia grew with each step, imagining that when I reached the part of the path where it got too close to the cliff, whomever followed me would rush out and push me over the edge before I had the time to react. I tried to force these thoughts from my mind, to push them away.

How do I know I wasn't a target for simply trying to find out what happened to Eddie? I didn't, I concluded, and as I reached the bottom of the hill and stepped onto the tarmac, I breathed a sigh of relief. I casually walked down the road, rounded the dock, and made my way to the road on the other side towards the adjoining footpath leading up the other hill and to the safety of home.

Reaching *The Lady Catherine's* bow, I turned around quickly but saw nothing there. I wasn't surprised as there was nowhere for any potential stalker to hide here.

The sound of singing pirates, not to mention the large crowd on deck dancing and drinking rum, would no doubt put off stalkers for the time being – alive or dead.

I took comfort in the closeness of *The Lady Catherine* then, even though it was unlikely any soul aboard could see me in the darkness. I turned right up the path and made my way towards home.

The sound of singing subsided as I pushed through the kissing gate and climbed the steepest part of the hill. I relaxed long enough only to have my senses stirred again with the feeling of somebody behind me. My feeling was confirmed when I heard the kissing gate open and close.

Finally, I had had enough. 'Who is there? Show yourself, *now*.'

'Mister Blackman, there's no need for that tone of voice!' I relaxed again as Dora Wilson appeared on the path behind me. 'If I didn't recognise your voice, you would have given me quite the *fright*, sir!'

I sighed in relief. 'Sorry, Dora. I left Cato's a little while ago and thought somebody followed me from the churchyard.'

I moved out of the way so she could sit on "her" bench; I hadn't realised I stood right next to it.

'I was up there just a few minutes ago,' she said, 'I didn't see no one.'

I sat next to her on the bench. 'Maybe it was you? I saw a figure on the south side, near the war memorial. I thought I saw a head poke out from behind one of the gravestones and disappear again.'

'That weren't me. I were on the other side tending a couple of graves there.'

'Oh, I see. Whose graves? Didn't know you knew anyone buried there?'

Even in the dark, I could see the solemn expression on her face. 'DI Blackman, you know whose graves I visited. There's no need to act all innocent with me just to be all gentlemanly about it. You know what I done because your son told you.'

For a moment, neither of us said anything.

'I could see in his eyes right away. He *knew* what I done. I was at my children's graves, the children what I killed.'

'I won't do you the disrespect of lying. I know and yes, he did tell me. I'm not judging you – either as a police officer or as a human being. I don't know what happened. Out of respect to you, I haven't read up on it.'

'Thank you.' Her tone was difficult to read. 'But I shan't blame you if you don't want to know me no more for what I done.'

'My opinion of you has not changed. You are a good woman, Dora Wilson, a kind and gentle soul. In these times, you would have got the help you needed and deserved beforehand and afterwards too.'

'Don't change what I did though, Mister Blackman. My children are still dead at their mother's hand. I should have been strong for 'em after their dad died. It's what we did then. It's what millions of women done when they lost their husbands in the fighting. It was expected of us. While they was fighting for us, we had to fight at home for what was left.'

To that, I did not have an answer. 'Would you like to come and join me for a cup of tea?' I asked for maybe the fiftieth time. On reflection, it was all I could say.

'Thank you, Mister Blackman, but not tonight. Perhaps another time, though.' That, at least, was progress.

'I'd like that very much.' I bade her good evening and made my way back up the hill to my home. I no longer had the feeling that somebody was watching or following me. If it wasn't paranoia, my pursuer had likely given up.

Once inside, I was grateful for having got back into the warm, fired up the central heating and prepared for an evening of reading. After rifling through about three pages of my book, curiosity got the better of me and I switched on my aging computer.

I hadn't wanted to do this before, but Paul's revelation piqued my curiosity, even though I still felt uncomfortable about the invasion of privacy. I found a website called *The British Crimepedia* and went to its page on the Dora Wilson (nee Jenkins) case.

It told me little beyond the limited information that Paul had already given me – she was a farm girl who captured the attention of an junior naval officer who, in the early years of the Second World War, was assigned to *HMS Hood*.

They married in 1935 and their children were born in 1936 and 1939 respectively – aged five (the boy, named Thomas) and aged two (the girl, named Olive) at their deaths.

Following the sinking of the ship in May, Dora Wilson had indeed fallen into a depression that lasted several months. She eventually became a recluse, pushing away both sets of grandparents and all medical help for melancholy the military health network – such as it was then – offered her.

She killed her children on 12th October 1941, went to trial a month later almost to the day – the 11th November 1941 and hanged on the morning of Monday 1st December 1941 after several calls for Parliamentary intervention were rejected amid mass protests across Cornwall and in London. I checked the calendar; that was why she had been at the graveyard, today was the anniversary of the death of both children.

With that question satisfied, the question I then asked myself was "do I or don't I" for some of the other people with whom I now share the village. It's unlikely they'd have much information about the earlier ghosts so that wouldn't be worth the bother. The more recent (anything since the start of the British Empire) would certainly be worth checking. There's nothing like governmental bureaucracy for maintaining historical records.

As I have already said, I felt it was an invasion of privacy. I still felt that way which was why I chose then to look up what happened to *The Lady Catherine* and her crew, specifically to see if there was any information on Little Eddie.

I visited a popular web encyclopaedia and found out that the ship attacked a Royal Navy convoy ship off South Carolina destined for British colonists in the Yamassee War.

It proved a stupid move as they were close to the colony and the Royal Navy scrambled three frigates to defend the supplies; Harry was vastly outgunned and outmanned but the ship and crew may have used speed to its advantage and escaped had it not been for a fire breaking out in the hold that set alight the gunpowder stored inside it.

Then I saw it, that final clinching paragraph that read: *The dead body of the Captain – Harry George Chillcott (commonly known as "Hook Hand Harry") was pulled from the water and displayed as a warning at the Charles Town colony [74]. Just one survivor was pulled from the water – identified only as The Cabin Boy "Eddie".*

The 15-year-old boy was believed to be the son of a freed slave who once served as one of Harry's inner circle. What the role of the freed slave was has been subject to much debate but the consensus is that he was third in command of The Lady Catherine *for a short period before his death in 1715 [31].*

We do not know what happened to Eddie after his arrest and transport to the Charles Town colony with speculation ranging from suggestions that he was sold back into slavery, adopted by a wealthy family, and becoming a cabin boy aboard one of the Royal Navy frigates that sank The Lady Catherine *[75].*

The picture, the sketch, was most definitely not the Eddie I knew. "Little Eddie" was small, slim, a bit wiry, dark haired and tanned with a hangdog look, but most *definitely* of European descent and white skinned.

The Eddie in the woodcut picture was still small for a 15-year-old boy, but he was unmistakeably black – not even of mixed race, but clearly of immediate and direct West African blood.

'Oh shit,' I muttered. 'Why aren't these things ever easy?'

The missing boy, whoever he was, was not the same cabin boy *The Lady Catherine* had the day she sank off the coast of Charles Town. Why had Harry, or any of the crew for that matter, kept this from me?

I opened the file containing the photographs that Harry had taken for me on that morning after "Eddie" (or whoever he really was) had gone missing. I had already pored over these twenty times and didn't expect to find anything new today. Harry had done a thorough job just as I had asked.

'Sleeping space one, sleeping space two, sleeping space three, overhead sleeping space one,' I muttered as each photo came up in turn. It's not technical to give them names like that but what the hell, I didn't have a regulator and I wasn't officially in CID anymore so I can call them what I liked.

I spent an hour carefully going over all the photos, but I did spot something; it was gone ten though, the pirates were likely in full party mode and I had to get ready for bed. Feeling exhausted and knowing there was nothing else I could do, I retired to read. I now had two reasons to confront Harry in the morning and I needed sleep.

After fidgeting and going over everything in my mind – Eddie, the other Eddie, the anomaly in the photograph, being followed, I settled into a restless sleep.

Chapter 9

The following morning, I went straight to *The Lady Catherine* to speak with Harry and Benjamin again. For privacy's sake, I recommended we went to the pub. It was open, but there was rarely anyone in before 10am, today was no exception.

When flesh and blood people staffed it just six months ago, it opened at 9am, serving breakfasts and hot and cold drinks. That proved popular with the early risers and backpackers heading to and from Land's End. We've easy access to the South West Coast Path, our only concession to the tourism industry.

Morwenna opened up because there was no reason not to do so and because the pub was one of the best local meeting places for Salmonweir residents.

'Here again, Karl?' quipped Morwenna. 'It's a bit early for you to be drinking. What'll it be?' She'd lined up a row of glasses along the bar ready for polishing and place back in the overhead racking.

'You're right, it is too early. Just a coffee for me, please. Lads?' We were the only people in the bar.

'Rum,' said Harry and Benjamin in unison.

'Diversifying?' I asked Morwenna, pointing to the barista machine behind her.

She turned to look as if forgetting it was there. 'Ah yes! We thought I best get used to using it if we have lots of people in here on Bonfire Night looking for warm drinks. It does hot chocolate too.' She beamed.

'it was a real luxury back in my day and my husband managed to get a small sample for our wedding day, probably the first and last time he bothered with romance. Talking of the Bonfire Night, you haven't forgotten about the meeting this evening, have you Karl?'

'Actually, yes I *had* forgotten but I will make sure I'm there. This is the last one before Bonfire Night?'

She nodded. 'It is. No excuses permitted for this meeting barring death, and seeing as most of us are already dead, even that is no excuse.'

'Where is Babajide?' I peered behind the bar and into the back room, unable to see the young man.

'He's setting up the function room for tonight. He's also reading the instructions for this.' She tapped the barista machine. 'Please take a seat and I'll bring the drinks over when they're ready.'

We sat in the far corner away from prying eyes and ears, but we needn't have bothered as there was still nobody else around. Not a word passed between us until the drinks arrived. Morwenna placed them on the table and lingered a little too long for my liking. Then I cleared my throat and she scuttled off.

'I don't know if you recognise what I'm about to show you,' I said, removing the pile of printed photographs from the folder, 'but my instinct tells me it shouldn't be there.'

I showed them a photograph of "Eddie's" sleeping space just as they had photographed it last week.

'That be where Eddie sleeps,' Harry rightfully pointed out. 'Right there! See Benjamin? That's them photo things I took.'

'I've asked you two to come today because I have to show you something. Two things, actually.' I pointed to the place on the photo where I had circled the strange object. 'Firstly, do you know what that is?'

They moved their heads close to the photograph and peered closely.

'That red thing? Looks like a circle to me?' asked Benjamin.

My heart sank. 'No, that's the mark I've used to show you where it is. I mean the thing *inside* the red circle.'

'Little shiny thing,' said Harry.

'Yes, that's right the little shiny thing. I understand you've cleared the area and moved Eddie's stuff into storage for now. Who did it?'

'That were me,' said Benjamin, 'on myself.'

'Do you remember picking anything up that looked unusual? Especially, this item… whatever it is?'

He put his head on his chin and leaned forward again to stare at the photograph intently. 'I dunno what that is and I don't remember nothing like that.'

'Are you quite sure? It could be important to the investigation.'

'Yeah, I'm sure. There were bits of metal or something,' he paused, thinking for a moment.

'Actually, Karl. Yeah, there *were* something there, but I didn't think nothing of him. It were like a metal tube or something, like a bit of pipe. It didn't look like nothing I recognised and I didn't think it were Eddie's. Just a bit of pipe,' he thumped the photograph for effect and then crossed his arms.

Finally, I let out a sigh of relief. 'It does look like a short tube, I agree. What is it, what happened to it and did you recognise it at the time you cleared Eddie's stuff into storage?'

'No, I didn't know what it was and I threw it over the side of the ship. It weren't no good to me.' He shrugged and turned to his Captain who nodded in agreement.

'That's a shame, I would have preferred that you brought it to my attention, but it's gone now. If you find anything else unusual on the ship, please let me know?'

'Aye,' Harry answered.

'Secondly, I want to show you a note that somebody put through my door.' I know that you can read and write, Harry, but can you Benjamin?'

His mouth twitched. 'Little bit, not much. Captain Harry done all that an' we didn't need to. What's the matter?'

'Oh, nothing. I know there are few in this village who can, I just wanted to check.' I unfolded the note and presented it to them.

'He says "Eddie's gone",' Harry informed his First Mate, 'n' he's not coming back.'

'Do you know who wrote this letter, either of you? Do you recognise the handwriting or the language?'

'It's English,' said Harry without a drop of irony. 'awful English, but it is English.'

'Thank you, Harry, but what I meant was – do you know anyone who writes in this style, with these spellings and in that handwriting?'

'No,' said Benjamin. 'Not me and I don't know no one what does.'

'Nor me,' said Harry, 'but I'd like to know how 'e or she knows Eddie is gone. I'd very much like to know how they know if you get my meaning.'

'Thank you, gentlemen. Benjamin, I have no more questions for you, but I would like to talk to Harry about something else, in private.'

'S'alright Benjamin. Go back to the ship. Me n' Karl got Captain things to talk about.'

The First Mate nodded at me, more relieved than offended at having been asked to leave. 'Righto. Captain, see you back at the ship!' Benjamin finished his rum in a single chug and left the pub.

Now it was just the two of us, and Morwenna – who had started unnecessarily cleaning tables closer and closer to our position, clearly trying to listen in on our conversation. 'Another coffee please, Morwenna!' I signalled. 'And maybe a slice of hevva cake?'

She disappeared behind the bar. Satisfied she was out of earshot, I wasted no time in enquiring about Eddie – both of them. 'Who was Eddie?'

'You know who he is. Son of my old First Mate.'

'Are you sure about that? Because there's a lot of information about you and your crew that I have taken at your word, Harry. I like you and I consider you one of the closest friends I have here. I want and need to know all about Eddie if I'm going to find him.'

He spread his arms wide. 'Why all the questions about Eddie *now*? Haven't we talked about this enough. And why does it matter?'

'This is why.' I placed before him the print off, the one of the woodcut of the other Eddie – the black one, the son of the former First Mate, the only survivor of *The Lady Catherine* about whom until yesterday I had not known a single thing. 'Who is he?'

'Oh shit,' it was all Harry could say.

'If Eddie was the boy who went missing, then who is this? If this is Eddie, who was the boy – the pale-skinned, dark-haired British boy who went missing last week?'

Of all reactions I expected from Hook Hand Harry, seeing him break down in floods of tears was the one I least expected. He covered his face with his hands and sobbed. If I could have given him a man hug then, I would have done so.

'Harry, are you all right?' I enquired.

Harry stood up, almost knocking the stool over, and stormed out of the pub, slamming the door behind him, leaving me dumbstruck and Morwenna aghast holding my coffee and hevva cake. 'What did you just say to that poor man?'

'I can't say, sorry.'

'Well whatever it is, *I've* never seen him like that.' Her tone was sharp and accusatory.

'Me neither,' I felt my cheeks flush. 'I think I just made a stupid mistake.'

'Then please don't go after Harry and hound him. He was clearly upset and that's the last thing this village needs right now.' She slammed the coffee and cake on the table.

'No, I won't.' I sipped the coffee and took a much-needed bite of the cake. 'I think this has all a bit much for him.'

'Who is that boy?' she asked, peering curiously at the printout.

I hastily removed the print from the table. 'That's what I'm trying to find out. Do me a favour though, if you heard anything just now, don't repeat it. It's important to everyone that you don't.'

She nodded an affirmative. 'I won't say anything. I wouldn't put any of this in jeopardy. Is it anything to do with Eddie?'

I took a long sip of the coffee. 'It might be and that's something else I need to find out. Promise me, Morwenna.'

'I promise I won't say anything,' she blurted out and quickly followed it up with another question. 'Did he kill Eddie?'

'Morwenna!' I really couldn't do with all these questions but held my tongue back; she didn't mean any harm. 'Sorry, but I don't know and we don't even know if

Eddie is, erm, dead again. I can't really say anything else I'm afraid until Harry has calmed down – out of respect for him and for not getting too many people tangled in my investigation.'

Morwenna smiled apologetically. 'Sorry, I don't mean to pry. I'm sure Harry will talk to you when ready.'

I sat there in contemplation for a few minutes, wondering when (and whether) to talk to Harry again. Morwenna was right, I should leave him alone, but I had to get to the bottom of this if we were ever to find Eddie again.

As I drank the last dregs of the coffee, the pub door opened. Half expecting to see Harry or Benjamin, I was quite surprised to see a group of walkers – human ones! Actual living, breathing human beings walking into the pub. They were two women and one man – all aged in their mid to late fifties at a guess, wearing matching red rain macs and dressed like they were out for a long walk.

They came in, stopped about a metre beyond the door, looked around nervously but did not move.

'Good morning!' called Morwenna cheerfully from behind the bar, 'what can I get you?'

They noticed me and cautiously made their way to the bar to place their orders. I gave them a friendly wave, stood up and took my mug back to the bar.

'I can certainly recommend the fruitcake,' I said to the group, 'it goes best with the farmhouse dry if you like cider.' I pointed to the relevant pump.

'Oh, thank you,' said the man, 'I think we have all our provisions for the walk though.' He gestured at his rucksack. I took a brief moment to study him. He had a grey-white beard and a rugged look that suggested he was used to long walks on this sort of terrain.

'Walkers. Where are you off to?' I asked.

'We're taking the coast path to Land's End,' piped up one of the women, offering me a warm smile. She looked to be the youngest of the group but not by much – she was short and dumpy.

The other woman was average height and willowy. 'We're staying in Mousehole.' She got the pronunciation right – Mow-zul – though in my experience, anybody who pronounced it "Mouse Hole" was often quickly corrected by a local.

'We're expecting to take the bus back to Penzance from there,' said the third woman, 'assuming they are running today?'

'Lovely day for it,' I commented, 'but you should be careful on the coast path. The weather can turn nasty quickly, especially at this time of year. They should be running as it's mild today. They only cancel if the weather makes going treacherous.'

'Thank you,' said the man,' it's our first visit to Cornwall in a long time.'

'Welcome back to Cornwall and welcome to Salmonweir.' I offered him my hand.

He shook it and then stepped back in surprise. 'Oh, I can touch you?'

It took just a second to realise what he meant. 'Ah, I'm not dead. I'm Salmonweir's resident human pet. DI, retired, Karl Blackman. I'm sure you've read in the papers that I run the village as a slave economy with me as its god-king.'

'Oh, my apologies! I should have recognised you from your photo in the papers.' He laughed. 'I haven't heard your described like that *yet.* For the record, we are *not* reporters.'

I eased off a bit. The thought *had* crossed my mind. As mentioned, I'd never had much respect for the tabloids, but it had gone from merely awful to outrageously awful since Salmonweir had become centre of the universe.

'I'm Eric Nugent, this is my wife Margaret,' he gestured to the shorter woman and then the willowy woman, 'and my sister Heidi.'

I shook both of their hands in turn. I noticed that Heidi had a pale band on her finger where a wedding ring once had pride of place. 'That's quite alright. It's natural to assume everyone you meet here is dead but there is one who is still flesh and blood – just me.'

'Yes, I read about it all in the papers,' Eric repeated, 'I suppose the penny simply never dropped when I saw you. Are you acquainted with everyone here in Salmonweir?'

'I know most by name though there are some I've never shared more than about five words. Some I count as friends and see every day. Some never leave their houses and some seem to enjoy their new life. Like any other village really except they no longer have functioning physical bodies.'

'We all have days like that.' He chuckled and rubbed his beard thoughtfully. 'We were taking the coast path and decided to look around when we realised where we were. I hope you don't mind our curiosity, but we wanted to see if some of the tabloid stories were true.'

'What stories? Actually no, I don't want to know and can only imagine. I stopped reading after the first few days and don't imagine they have got any better.'

'Not really,' he said before an awkward silence passed between us. I got the impression he wanted to explain. Maybe they were now claiming that the ghosts were flooding Cornwall to steal our benefits.

'May I interrupt your conversation, ladies and gentlemen?' Morwenna piped up from behind the bar, thrusting a flyer under Eric's nose.

Eric leaned back as is the custom with short-sighted people when having reading material held a bit too close to their faces to read properly. He blinked twice and carefully took it from Morwenna. 'Bonfire Night!' He exclaimed, 'how lovely!' before showing it to his companions.

'We all hope it'll bring people to Salmonweir, for tourism, so they can see there is nothing to fear from us.' Morwenna went on. 'We might be dead, but we're not scary! Not all of us, anyway.'

The man smiled and nodded at Morwenna. 'Do you mind if I keep this?' he gestured at the flier.

'No, please do and take some more.' She tapped the pile on the bar and then pushed a few more leaflets towards him. Eric collected a small handful, stuffing them inside his coat.

'Will you still be in Cornwall on Bonfire Night?' I asked the group, eagerly.

'No,' replied Heidi, her face dropping, 'but this looks like it could be fun! We might come back, right?' she asked her two companions who both nodded in agreement.

'We hope so too,' I went on, there is far more going on than a bonfire and fireworks, there's lots of other things too so bring any kids you might know. We'll have a Guy competition and some genuine historical food.' I looked at Eric, 'if you like craft beer or cider, we have an open-air bar.'

His face lit up.

'Well thank you DI Blackman, we will certainly think about it!' said Margaret.

'Karl, please.'

They finished their drinks and made their excuses, thanking Morwenna for her hospitality and the leaflets. I walked out of the pub with them, pleased to have seen living people to help, equally pleased that their interest in our Bonfire Night Spectacular was genuine. As I waved them goodbye after directing them back to the coast path, I heard an inhuman roar from the pub roof, something dropped to the floor, and then I heard a huge thud followed by a shout.

It had come from around the side of the pub. I quickly made my way to the other side of the building to investigate the disturbance.

The terrifying roar I initially presumed to be an escaped lion belonged to Kensa. The thought that such a wild and deep roar could come from such a small set of lungs was surprising. What was even more surprising was that this pint-sized woman had, at sword point, a man who looked as if he could easily overpower her, should he have chosen to do so. The fact that she was touching him suggested he too was a ghost.

She yanked the man to his feet, grabbing him by the scruff of the collar of his jacket. His clothes looked a bit 1990s. 'He was watching you from around the side of the building,' Kensa growled, pushing him at me.

The man stumbled towards me. Instinctively I put my arms out to catch him, but he passed right through me. He'd been clutching a folder. That too passed through me and fell to the floor.

'He followed you and Harry to the pub and waited until you came out. I had to be sure that's what he was doing.'

'Hello,' I waved at the man more apologetically than I might ordinarily have done under the circumstances.

He scrambled to his feet, looking embarrassed from Kensa to me and back again.

'Is it true you've been following me?'

He gave Kensa a shifty look. All of three seconds passed before she put her hand back on her sword.

'Yes,' he snapped his answer. 'I need to talk to you. Well, all of you eventually. About an important matter.'

'Well?' I challenged.

He picked up his folder, open to the first page and began reading. 'Dear customer slash future customer of Afterlife P-L-C. Following on from the announcement of our company's winning bid for the franchise, we want you to know that we take our new role in the delivery of your afterlife service very seriously.

He paused, letting the information sink in.

'As custodians of this prestigious brand, we wish to continue to deliver the superior service you have already come to expect from the afterlife, but also present you some exciting and significant improvements on your existing service package. Over the coming weeks, we will announce a range of upgrades for our existing customers that we will roll out to our future customers.'

'Hang on, wait a minute. You've been following me so you can deliver a *sales pitch*?'

He nodded and went on. 'We have made significant improvements across the service area. As your new provider, we want to give you the afterlife you deserve and make you proud to be one of our customers – we want you to say: "Yes, this is a brand I love!"

'What are these words?' growled Kensa. 'It sounds like evil and trickery, sorcery that no druid of mine would ever understand!'

But the man went on. 'Your satisfaction is our aim in what is the biggest overhaul in the two-hundred-and-fifty-thousand-year history of human existence. This will not be easy, but we are ready for the challenge and there are exciting times ahead for all of us. For a limited time, we wish to offer you our premium service at a significantly discounted introductory cost. The first three months will cost-'

I turned to Kensa. 'Alas, Kensa my dear, welcome to the inane piffle that we in the 21st century call "Marketing Speak".' I turned to the man. 'Listen you cheeky sod, I'm not dead and I don't expect to be any time soon, so you're wasting your time cold-calling me.'

'But sir, I just wish to take a few moments of your time to answer a few questions about your needs.' He closed his book. 'Your feedback is important to delivering the improvements we seek to implement across our range of services.'

I put my hand to my head. If a day would come that listening to jargon was ever going to give me a migraine, this was likely the day. 'No thank you, but I'm surprised somebody decided to privatise the afterlife of all things,' I said, amused. 'One question – why?'

'It's simple,' the man said, 'the old bureaucratic system had become too large that it no longer functioned to the satisfaction levels that our customers expected. With the delivery package that Afterlife PLC offer to you today-.'

I raised my hand and cut him off again, 'if it's your intention to drive me to suicide through inane delivery of meaningless sales speak, then you are going about it the right way. Please, for the sake of my sanity, no more.'

'Certainly sir, but we implore you to consider one of our amazing offers. We offer tailored packages to all four hundred thousand deities and will-'

I put my hand up again. 'Wait – there are four hundred thousand gods now?'

He nodded enthusiastically. 'We're adding more every day to improve customer choice.'

'So, what are you, an angel?'

'Oh, good heavens sir, no. The angels – sorry, the Afterlife Executive Board of Directors – don't do this sort of thing anymore. I'm just a normal human being; dead, but human nonetheless. About a year ago, I found myself bored with the loneliness of eternal existence and decided to look for work. Afterlife PLC offered me a job as a Customer Service Outreach Officer. They promised benefits of a fast track to the Gold Customer Package and a few other perks. It was all rather agreeable.'

'What's your name riddle-speaker?' I'd watched Kensa throughout the conversation and she seemed no clearer on what we were talking about than she was at the beginning.

'Tobin.'

'Well Tobin, what brings you to Salmonweir?' I asked.

'Opportunity!' and then he put his hands up and slowly move them apart like the kind of motivational speaker who people pay to watch them stand on stage and throw around words they just made up.

'500 departed souls have made a new life here. Rather than focusing on those hanging around the waiting rooms like the rest of the Sales Team, approaching those who have yet to come to terms with their new situation, I thought I might be able to entice some back!'

He wasn't wrong. I could already think of a few.

'I mean, people who have already been there and wish to make a wiser choice the second time around. There's a planet full of ghosts – some of them must be bored haunting the same boring places, scaring people in the same way. It must get rather tedious for them.'

'I don't think you'll find many people in Salmonweir willing to take you up on your offer, some, but not many. I suggest you speak to Brother Jowan, the monk, and Eli, our Puritan Minister. They may be able to point you towards congregation members who no longer wish to be here.'

'Wonderful! I presume it was one of those esteemed clerics who helped the first returnee find his way back?'

My heart sank; I knew what he was going to say before I ever asked the question, but I asked it anyway. 'Who?'

'The young boy, the pirate. He came back about a week ago. That's what gave me the idea to come to Salmonweir, to see if anybody else wanted to return upstairs.'

Chapter 10

I'm not a churchgoer (I'm a lapsed Catholic, had I mentioned?) but the next day was Sunday morning and I decided to go after both services were finished; I sometimes felt the need to "check in" with the man upstairs.

The system of when each preacher held his service worked surprisingly well. As an early riser, Jowan preferred to deliver his service to the Catholic element of the village first so they could share in the glory of creation of the morning. This suited Pastor Eli who preferred to address his congregation with a full belly and fully awake so he could remind them of the glory of God with a clear head and mindful of the sumptuous breakfasts they'd just eaten.

That's not to say there was no conflict over the use of the church. Eli hated Jowan's incense and would open all doors on his arrival – and leave it open during the service – to get rid of the smell. He also methodically went around snuffing out the candles then closing and locking the side chapel Jowan used for private chantry.

For his part, Jowan, who had promised he would snuff out all the candles and remove catholic paraphernalia from the church during the break between services, nearly always left *something* behind. One of his vestments, a relic – usually something simple enough that he could say he forgot such a trivial thing, but something blatantly Catholic that it enraged Eli and start his service on a bad footing.

All was quiet in the church when I arrived. Incense lingered in the air and Eli had cleared away his tools of the trade. I wasn't alone though; Harry occupied one of the front pews.

'If you're here for a service, you've missed it,' I said to the pirate captain. 'How are you, my friend?'

'I know that,' he said softly, 'I'm a god-fearing man but not like any of them lot. You can't sail the seas facing death every day – from other pirates, Royal Navy, Spanish convoys, waterspouts, storms, whales, sharks and rogue waves without putting y'faith in the almighty.'

'I imagine not,' I said and took a seat next to him.

'I don't hold with the realms of men like Jowan and Eli, no sir. They don't have true faith like what a man of the sea does. They don't see God. They don't live with the danger.'

I nodded. 'I understand you, Harry. I'm a Catholic but I haven't been to a service in at least a decade. I'd be intrigued to see Jowan deliver a service if only out of historical interest.'

He sighed deeply. 'I came here to pay my last respects to Eddie.'

My heart skipped when I heard that name. 'You know then.'

'Aye, He ain't coming back, I know that now. That man Tobin told me.' He pointed skyward. 'I suppose he don't matter much to this world no more, and I needs to tell you what's what.'

It seemed Tobin had already introduced himself to most of the village. Of course he had; a salesman never misses an opportunity to get ahead of the competition. I'd rather he'd waited a while and talked on a personal level with some of the village residents rather than seeing them first as potential bonuses. I expected no less under the circumstances. My only hope is that he'd also considered sticking around and come to like it in Salmonweir.

'He does matter, Harry. You don't have to tell me his story until you feel ready to tell it. He's not coming back, true, and I'm no longer sure what knowing about him would accomplish.'

'It matters to you and it matters to me.' Harry turned to me. There was a single tear in his eye.

'That boy, the African one. He was the son of my former first mate. I promised the lad and his dad I'd protect him, but I couldn't. His dad were arrested in the colonies and executed. It were his dying wish that I become the boy's guardian.'

'What happened to him after, after *you* died?'

'You know I can't remember much of the afterlife? Even if I did, I couldn't be allowed to tell ya. Well, I can tell ya this. That boy, he lived a long and a good life. They saw his seamanship skills and he eventually joined up with the Royal Navy. Little bastard, I'd have killed him if I were still alive to see him get his commission!'

Harry laughed proudly and then looked at me. 'He were Eddie. We called him Eddie because we couldn't any of us pronounce his proper African name. No matter how hard we tried, we all make us selves look stupid, you get me? So, he became Eddie and he liked it that way and we liked it that way.'

I simply nodded.

'The other boy. The Eddie you know. He were the son of another first mate, a much earlier one. I promised to look after that lad the day my old first mate died of sickness and I did my best when I was alive, didn't I? We all did.'

'You were a great guardian from what I could see, Harry.' I'm not sure if my words were reassuring, but it felt the only natural thing to say under the circumstances. 'He clearly liked you as much as he looked up to you.'

He flinched but went on. 'Only he weren't aboard *The Lady Catherine* for long before he ran away. I were upset, cos I made a promise didn't I? And him getting away like that, it was like I broke my promise to me old First Mate. And I couldn't have that because Captain Harry always kept his promises, didn't he?'

'You can't watch kids all of the time especially with the lifestyle you had.'

I remember a time Valarie phoned her mother for two minutes to ask if she was on the way. When she returned to the kitchen, there was an overwhelming scent of gas and baby Claire playing around with the knob.

'You made a promise to his dad, but you shouldn't blame yourself for the kid absconding.'

Harry said nothing for about a minute. 'And I never found him again, never knew what happened to him, see. That was until the day we got back here. His name were also Eddie and I was so happy that this Eddie were back

182

because it meant we could finally all be together. Course, he must have died a few years after me because he were younger than that the last time I saw him but he were still a young lad, see.'

'What happened to his mother?' I asked.

Harry's head dropped. 'I just told you, she died of sickness.'

I blinked, confused. 'But you said the first mate... oh!' As one penny dropped, a second rolled into place. 'Who was the father?'

'That be me. I were Eddie's dad.'

'Did the lads know? Do they know now?'

'Ah no, my Rose went away when she discovered she stopped bleeding like the ladies do. She were sure by that point that she were with child. The excuse we used was that the First Mate got a ship and went away.'

'She came back after she had him, claiming the crew mutinied and she came back to my ship, all the time still pretending to be a fella. Eddie stayed with her family and he'd be there until she were ready to have him aboard as her cabin boy. Luck be that she never got pregnant again. He were nine when she died and he were with me three year before he ran away.'

'The crew *still* don't know he is your son?'

'No, they think Rose – or Robbie Redsword as they knew her – was the father and the mother some tavern wench he was sweet on. I'd appreciate it staying that way Mister Blackman?' He looked at me with sincerity and placed his hand on his heart. 'Swear to me.'

'Your secret is safe with me, Harry. Thank you for telling me.' I placed my hand on my own heart to reiterate my promise.

'They won't be upset so much that Rose weren't a Robert, though some will be angry at following a woman. More anger would be for me that I wasn't honest, that I lied. Cap'n loses the trust of his men and afore you know it, you got yourself a mutiny. You hearing me?'

'Of course, Harry. I won't tell anyone.'

'Thank you, kind sir.'

I bade Harry good day and left him to his thoughts.

Just off the north transept was a side door leading to the two rooms serving as the preparation area for services. When the last human minister was here, he occasionally took people in there for a private chat. I had only been in there once, but was surprised at how attractive it was. It had, according to the information leaflet, once been the entrance lobby to a small crypt that collapsed 20 years after the church's foundation. Floodwater undermined the structure one autumn and the underground structure collapsed. Residents bricked up the crypt and converted the lobby to other uses.

I could hear two distinct voices from the prep room as I passed the door. They belonged to Jowan and Eli. They had never been (to my knowledge) in the church together at the same time after the day Eli arrived. What didn't surprise me is that they were arguing again.

'Silence Jowan!' I heard as I pushed the door open.

The two men squared up in the centre of the room. Eli held a knife firmly in his hand, pointing in threateningly at Jowan. He dropped the blade to his side on seeing me.

Jowan had never cowered before Eli even when the puritan was at his most aggressive. However, I never expected to see the monk squaring up like this. He was more like a drunken thug. The only thing missing was a broken beer bottle.

'What *the hell* is going on?' I asked both men.

'Nothing,' said Eli.

'Nothing,' repeated Jowan.

'It doesn't look like "nothing" to *me* gentlemen!'

Eli threw thee knife to the floor and popped from the room, leaving me and Jowan alone.

'This can't carry on, Jowan. I don't care who started it this time. You are both as bad as each other.'

He opened his mouth to plead but I waved him down. 'I don't want to hear your excuses again, Jowan. You're *not* innocent either and this needs to end for the good of the village,' I reiterated, 'preferably before Bonfire Night. The last thing we need is you two fighting in public. What do you think the newspapers will make of that?'

'Yes, you're right. Somebody needs to end this,' his growling tone had me taken aback. Jowan wasn't just angry, he was out for blood. 'Now leave Mister Blackman, *now*!'

I did so, not because I felt threatened by the monk, but because I thought The Man Upstairs would let me off this once considering the mental state of his representatives in the village.

I exited the church to a welcome cool sea wind and a clear day overlooking the village. The harbour beneath me thronged with people on the east side, perhaps 150 people. They seemed to group around a single figure standing on the dock.

Still, *The Lady Catherine* was the only ship on the other side of the harbour. Even from this distance on the hillside above, I could see a few men on the top deck and a couple of the rigging turning towards the figure at dockside.

To my left, and overlooking the sea from her usual spot, I could clearly make out the black-clad figure of Dora Wilson.

This is my favourite view of the village. I particularly love the way the houses blend into the hillside. There is no uniformity to the pattern. To an outside observer, it probably looks chaotic, a bit like somebody dropped a handful of Monopoly houses into a valley, correcting the position of those that had not landed upright but otherwise made no attempt to make them a uniform direction.

You can also see the gouge in the valley that used to be the river but is now the route of the main road as the stream from the east fed alongside it and meandered down towards the harbour.

I made my way down Church Hill. I had to be careful with my footing as the tarmac here is smooth and slippery when wet. That's not good on this sort of gradient, but I managed to make my way down without any trouble.

I crossed the open space and joined the back of the crowd. I could see through the gaps that Tobin was at the head of the rally. I could make out the occasional word, enough to understand that this was a mass, public sales pitch.

'Karl, what are you doing here? Looking to leave us early?' I turned to face Ebrel smiling up at me nervously.

'Hello Ebrel, no I was just coming back from the church when I saw the meeting. I didn't know it was Tobin until I got here. I could ask the same of you?' I lowered my voice, not wanting to annoy others by talking all over Tobin's sales pitch.

We stepped back a few paces and let some of the crowd fill our gap from behind.

'Oh, I'm just here to see what is on offer. I'm not planning on going back or anything like that.' She looked down at her feet.

There was a sadness in her eyes and I pressed her to explain. 'Have you had a fight with Philip?'

She looked at me quizzically. 'We did, over that boy, but we're fine. No, I-' she turned away.

'Is it your father? Ebrel, my dear. Would you like to go somewhere quiet to talk?'

She gestured to the low wall lining the harbour. We were out of earshot here. She sidled up next to me and looked straight down at her feet. This move alone made me realise how sheltered she had been in life compared to modern 19-year-old girls.

Right now, this undead young woman looked more like a child than she ever had in my presence. Here, out of her depth, trying hard to fit in while her father did what he could to resist doing the same, was obviously going to take its toll.

'No, it's not father,' she said eventually. 'It's everyone. Perhaps it's the stress of the Bonfire Night thing, but so many people are being rude at the moment. It's not nice.'

'Like who?' It was moments like this I wished I could give the poor girl a hug.

'That woman in the pub.'

'Morwenna?'

'Yes. I was in there with Philip this morning but there was nobody in the bar,' she explained. 'I went around the back behind the bar to find someone. As I

189

reached for the door, it opened and she came out. All I did was smile at her and ask her for two hot chocolates, but she shouted at me, quite unreasonably. Philip was disgusted and we left without buying a drink.'

Ah, the fragility of youth. 'She's quite hot tempered, I wouldn't worry about her.'

'Normally I wouldn't,' she went on, 'but she called me stupid and disrespectful and said to keep my nose out of where it wasn't wanted. I told her I wasn't snooping but she wouldn't listen, just kept shouting at me.'

'That's not on. Did you tell your father?'

'Yes. He went to the pub and Morwenna told him I called her a horrible name. But I didn't, she's a liar! He took Morwenna's side and told me not to talk to my elders like that again.' She shrugged her shoulders. 'He won't believe me.'

'You said "everyone" – who else has upset you?' I pressed.

'The two church men.' She nodded up the path towards the church. 'Usually they're both friendly and nice to me. I think they want me to start going to church. I bid Jowan good morning and he, what's the expression I heard you use? "Looked along his nose at me"?'

'*Down* his nose,' I corrected.

'Right, that. About an hour ago, I saw the other one, Eli.'

My heart sunk at remembering the altercation I had just broken up.

'He called me a "stupid girl" when I asked how his morning is.' She put her face in her hands and again I wished I could comfort her. 'I asked him if the morning was pleasant. That's all! Everyone is being so horrible.'

'Oh Ebrel,' I commiserated. 'I wouldn't concern yourself with those two. I just had to break up an argument between them. Eli went at Jowan with a knife if you can believe that.'

She looked up sharply at me. 'A knife?'

'Yes! I don't think those two will ever see eye to eye, but I never imagined it would come to that. I still don't know what happened between them. Eli popped away and Jowan just shouted for me to leave.'

She looked relieved at this. 'I thought they were angry with me about what happened with that boy, Eddie. I worry they think *I* did it.'

'Absolutely not!' I protested. 'It wasn't your fault he ran away. I believe you and Philip didn't hurt him. Jowan and Eli are sulky and bad tempered and always angry with each other. You're more of an adult than the pair of them put together.'

She nodded thoughtfully and chuckled at my last comment. After a brief pause she spoke again. 'I miss my mother. I need mum.' I was suddenly struck by the difficulties Valarie and I were placing upon our children and felt a moment of fleeting guilt.

'It's not right that I should come back and not her or any of my brothers.' She removed her face from her hands and looked at me, pleading with me to know the answer.

All I could do was shake my head. 'I can't explain any of this, Ebrel. I'm so sorry. I can no more explain why you and your father came back than I can explain why your brothers and mother did not.'

'I feel so alone without them.' She continued to sob. 'Philip's nice, of course he is, but I don't like most of the other residents and I wish they would all just go away.' She paused and then hastily added. 'Not you though.'

'That's why you wanted the phone, to see if you can meet other people in your position? To see if any other places in the world are experiencing this?'

She nodded. 'Dad won't let me have one though.'

'Why don't you come over to my house later. Your dad said you wanted an internet phone. I don't know if I have one, but I'll show you how to use the computer. Would you like that?'

She nodded, wiping away her tears. 'Yes. Thank you.'

'Perhaps you should speak to Tobin now he has finished? He might be able to tell you something about your mum or your brothers.' Tobin had finished his speech and the crowd was dispersing. A few lingered nearby, waiting to have a private word with the sales rep.

'I did, earlier,' she said, 'but he couldn't tell me anything.' She stood up and rubbed her eyes. 'Sorry to detain you, Karl. I should probably go. Father will need me back at the shop.'

'Ebrel, if you want to sit and talk for a while, I am in no hurry to get back home.'

She shook her head profusely. 'No, it's quite alright; I don't want to upset dad any more than I already have. Thank you for listening Karl, you're a good friend to me and I will never forget that.'

I gave her a sweet smile and bid her good day, happy to see her leave in a better mood.

Threading my way through the dispersing group of people on the dockside, I went straight to Tobin who, by now, had a crowd numbering just three people. I was on first name terms with them but our relationships in terms of wordage barely broke double figures.

There was a woman who looked like Queen Victoria and apparently died one year to the day before that particular monarch. The other two were children, twins no less. They were plague victims and Jowan once told me he'd been the one to give the boys their last rites. As I approached, all three peeled away in different directions. By the time I reached him, he was alone. 'Hello Tobin!'

'Mister Blackman, how are you this fine morning?'

'I'm very well, just catching up on the morning's news. You seem to have had a substantial crowd?'

He beamed at me. 'Indeed! I think I've made a rather shrewd decision to come here. I only hope nobody *else* comes to steal my patch. Had to chase one away already.'

I looked at him impressed. 'Oh yes? I guess great minds think alike.'

He nodded sharply. 'I didn't know him. He certainly wasn't part of my sales team, but the cheeky blighter denied that's why he was here.'

'I guess he's gone now.' I urged. 'You have Salmonweir all to yourself?'

'Yes, but if he comes back, will you please tell me as soon as possible?'

'Of course,' I agreed. 'What does he look like?'

'Modern clothing like mine.' He gestured the flat of his hand to around my height. 'About so tall. Slightly chunky. Oh, and he carried a leather-bound book. Have you seen him?'

Somehow, I knew he was going to say that.

Chapter 11

It was the morning of Bonfire Night and I was somewhere I didn't want to be – at Eli's. He called me in a distressed state, insisting I join him right away, which I did. 'It's insanity! Insanity I say!' complained the preacher, waving the telephone handset under my nose.

Several weeks passed since the fracas with Brother Jowan. Neither man wanted to talk about the incident. Subsequently and naturally, neither man was prepared to talk to each other. This made making final preparations for Bonfire Night difficult. That wasn't the end of the matter, I would get to the bottom of it when the time was right.

'Who are you trying to phone?' I asked.

'That man, Tobin.' He shook the handset at me again for added effect as though I could do anything to speed up the call centre.

'He was in the pub about half an hour ago. I saw him go in with a large wad of leaflets. Probably organising another sales presentation so he might still be there?' I pointed to the door and turned towards it. 'I'll go with you if you like and we can talk to him together?'

'No, it's not him I want. I don't believe he can help me. I asked him lots of questions, but he recommended I phone this number. I want to talk to them about something.' Then he passed me a business card. 'Could you contact them?' he pleaded.

I looked down at the piece of card. It read:

AFTERLIFE PLC

For All Your Post-Life Needs.

Every Belief System Catered For!

"Your Death, Is Our Life"

Call: 0899 412 768 3476

'Of course I will.' I picked up the receiver and dialled the number. After a few rings, the predictable recorded message kicked in.

'They all speak in meaningless tongues!' Eli said, 'and I don't understand a word of it. I would declare it devilry if I could even make sense of the words. I'm not sure Satan himself could unpick their meaning!'

'*Welcome to the Afterlife customer support line. If you are calling about our new range of platinum packages, please be advised that we have a dedicated line included in your information pack. Please hang up now and call the alternate line. If you are calling about Rebirth5000, our range of reincarnation packages available in the Asian subcontinent, we have identified the source of the problem and will be offering replacement bodies to anybody presently enrolled on the platinum and gold packages in the next few weeks. We apologise for any inconvenience this may have caused. For silver and bronze package customers, this process may take a little longer. We will contact you in due course.*

For our flexible bargain budget package – also known as "Bamboo" – we are very sorry, but your package excludes compensation for this particular problem. You will get a body at the first available opportunity. Present waiting time for Bamboo Customers is approximately eight years and six months. In that time, you have full access to our executive suites. Please note that if you are calling outside of Asia, we are sorry but during our trial period, geographical limits presently apply to Rebirth5000. We hope to extend this option globally in future. If your call is about anything else, please listen to the following options.'

I sighed audibly.

'Congratulations,' said Eli, 'I think you've already lasted longer than I did the first time. You have to press some numbers soon.'

'For sales, press 1. For billing enquiries, press 2. To update your account information, press 3. For...'

I covered the speaker. 'What do you want to talk to them about?'

'Uh, I need to speak to Tobin's people, his masters.' He answered back quickly.

'Manager,' I corrected. 'Yes, you've already told me that but what about? I can't make sure we're talking to the right people unless you tell me what it is.'

'...Press 5. To hear these options again, press 0. For all other enquiries, please hold the line and we will pass you through to a customer advisor.'

'If you don't want to tell me, you have a potentially long wait with the call centre,' I pressed Eli, but all he did was agonisingly shift from foot to foot and look all about him. He would not look me in the eye. The more I glared, the more he looked away.

The line went silent for a moment before some music kicked in and my heart sank. 'Why am I not surprised it's Greensleeves?'

After a few minutes of an awful tinny version of the Elizabethan classic, it stopped. I thought my luck was in, but the pause was for another recorded message.

'Welcome to the Afterlife PLC customer information desk. Your call is important to us! Please hold the line and continue to be patient at this busy time and a customer advisor will answer your call as soon as possible.'

That voice went silent and another cut in. *'You are in a call queueing system. Your place in the queue is presently nine million, two hundred and sixty one thousand, eight hundred and sixty three.'*

I covered the mouthpiece again. 'Eli, are you sure you want to do this? We could be here a while? There's millions of people in front of us.'

He nodded. 'Yes, please. It's important.'

'Please tell me what it's about? It's the only way I can help you. It's the only way *they* will be able to help you.' Under my breath I vowed to slam the phone down if he continued to mess me around.

Thankfully, he bit this time. He hesitated a moment. 'A member of my congregation wishes to return and would like to discuss their options. They would like to speak to Tobin's superiors in person about personal complications.'

'Complications?' I turned the business card over, hoping that Tobin would have put a personal office phone contact or at least a mobile number on the back, but no such luck. If it came to it, I would drag Eli down to the pub and get Tobin to call his boss.

The electronic voice informed me that a "mere" five thousand calls had been handled in those few minutes. Realising we could be there several hours just waiting to get through, I put the kettle on and made tea.

It was a little blustery outside and I hoped the weather would pick up for the evening. If it didn't, there was a strong chance the fire wouldn't be lit – and though that wouldn't be disastrous, it would put a dampener on the evening for our inaugural tourist event.

I checked the clock; it was 11am and events were supposed to start at 5:30pm with enough activities to keep the crowds entertained and occupied. We had no idea how many people to expect. I must admit to being impressed with the creativity and input from all involved.

Fed up with having the phone clasped to my face, I placed the handset on the table and put the speakerphone on so we could both hear the slow progress. With Eli here, this was the ideal time to probe him with a few questions about the knife incident.

The weeks had passed but my curiosity had not. The presence of the knife made the incident even more disturbing considering it was the most likely method by which Eddie left our world for a second time. I simply could not ignore that even though I doubted Eli was a killer. Most of his anger was directed at Jowan. I'd never yet seen him lose it with anyone else, although I was reminded how he'd call Ebrel "a stupid girl" that day.

Eli sipped tentatively at the tea, made an approving face, and placed his cup and saucer on the table before leaning forward and pressing his hands together. 'I get the impression you wish to as me a question, DI Blackman. If it's about the incident in the church, then I am not prepared to talk about it. It was weeks ago I know, but I'm not ready to discuss it. Anything else, please ask away.'

In the background, Greensleeves was back on the speakerphone. A few more thousand had been shaved off the queue – great.

'I know. You're right, there is something I want to talk to you about, but it isn't that incident, at least not yet anyway. What I do want to hear from you on that matter, and I already have Jowan's word, that it will not come between you two tonight. Either work together or keep out of each other's way. Your squabble, whoever is right and whoever is wrong, and no matter which of you started it or what it's about, it *must not* ruin this evening for the rest of us. Is that clear?'

'I agree. My personal preference is to avoid each other. If I encounter him tonight, I will not impede him. However, I will not work with him so please do not ask. Is that clear?'

'I agree,' I touched my teacup to his. 'You have different tasks tonight and shouldn't encounter each other.'

Eli nodded thoughtfully. 'What else did you want to talk to me about?'

'I need to know your movements and actions on the night of Eddie's disappearance.' I carefully placed the teacup on the table.

He looked startled and his face flushed. 'I'm sorry Mister Blackman but I would like to know the meaning of this? When did you begin to suspect me?' His tone and his pose became suddenly defensive.

'I don't suspect you of anything. In light of the knife incident in the church, I need to know what you were doing the night Eddie disappeared. I don't recall seeing you in the pub?'

He cleared his throat and looked at me suspiciously. 'I was in the church reading some literature. History books about the church and its hierarchy and about what happened in the years after my death.'

'I'm glad you're putting your time to good use.'

'I can't say I agree with it all,' he went on, 'but the more benign message does seem to be popular with the younger generation here. Without reform and change, my church would never have existed would it not? That's what I have to remember.'

'I quite agree, and I must say you surprise me.' I shifted in my seat. 'But back to that night. Did you spend all night in the church?'

'Yes,' he looked to the sky, pondering. 'I left at midnight. Yes, that sounds about right.'

'Were you alone? Either in the church, on the route home or at home?'

'No.'

I paused, waiting for an explanation but he didn't elaborate. 'Who were you with?'

'I cannot say, but with God as my witness, we were together all night and left together and-' he flushed.

'And what?'

'We spent the night together, here.'

This small admission surprised me; what didn't surprise me was his desire to protect the other person. Frustrating, but I no reason to suspect him. It had to be another mystery on the tangled web of Salmonweir and of Eddie's disappearance. 'Whatever you want to tell me, you have my confidence. Whatever you tell me does not leave this room.'

'I know.' A dark shadow passed across his face and he picked up his tea.

'Eli, my friend, you are a man of a great many mysteries. If ever you want to tell me-'

'Not yet,' he insisted.

'Hello, Afterlife PLC Customer Care Line. This is Brigida speaking, how may I help you?'

I raced to the phone and snatched it up just as she finished her salutation. 'Hello, my name is Karl Blackman. We have had a Sales Rep in our village for the last few weeks by the name of Tobin. We have a group of people wishing to discuss their packages with a Senior Sales Advisor? We have some queries with our contracts.'

All the while I was talking, I could hear Brigida talking 'uh-huh, hmm, yes, right, ok, yes.' When she finally realised I'd stopped talking, she spoke in a German accent. 'Oh, sir I am sorry, you have the Customer Care Line. For upgrades, you still need the sales line. I will put you through to the call queue for sales.'

Before I had a chance to protest, I was back to Greensleeves and information that I was only fiftieth in the queue. The universal law is that no matter where you are in the world, and with all things being equal and relative, your wait on a sales line is infinitely shorter than the wait on a customer support line. I think just four seconds passed before the call was answered.

'Hello, this is Maria. Afterlife PLC Sales. How may I help you today?'

I repeated my spiel about wanting to talk to Tobin's supervisor about a potential sales deal for him.

'Oh, I'm sorry. You need Sales Support if you want to talk about a pending application or to talk to a specific sales team. This is the sales line.'

'Oh, I think we've just come from there?'

I heard her typing. 'No, you came from Customer Support. I'll put you through to Sales Support now.'

And with that it was back to Greensleeves – again.

'What's going on?' asked Eli anxiously.

'I'm being passed from department to department.' Sales Support was also lightning fast in responding to my call. Just as the young lady was about to put me through again, I halted her. 'Please, no more Greensleeves. I've already heard it enough for a lifetime and two Afterlife PLC service packages. Can't you just put me straight through to Tobin's supervisor?

'I'm afraid that particular individual is out of the office today. Can I instead put you through to Tobin?'

'No, apparently he can't help-'

But she cut me off. 'Thank you, I will just connect that call for you.'

Silence passed for a few seconds. I thought she had cut me off for my pleading and mild rebuke, but she quickly came back. 'I have located that Sales Advisor and will put you through to his direct line sir. Thank you for your patience.'

I started to protest again but she had already gone. In her place was an answerphone. *Hello this is Tobin. I'm probably on a sales visit at the moment so if you would like to leave a message after the funerary bell, I will get back to you as soon as I can. Your Death is Our Life.*

'Tobin, it's DI Blackman. Firstly, we hope you'll be here for the Bonfire Night Spectacular in Salmonweir. Secondly, some people from Eli's congregation wish to discuss a return upstairs with you. I believe you've already put Eli onto your sales line but nobody there can help. There's a potential lucrative sale for you here if you can organise this for us, my friend! See you this afternoon.' I put the phone down.

Tobin was the first person through the gates for the Bonfire Night Spectacular; in fact, he turned up earlier than expected and entered the park to a round of applause from the team putting on the last-minute touches. Eli, who was mixing up the mulled wine, made a beeline for the man. He quickly slunk back to the table when he saw Wilhelmina Yorke co-opting the young man to listen to her introductory speech.

His face remained a calm expression throughout which meant one of two things – it wasn't as awful as we'd all feared, or Tobin was a world champion liar. When finished, he came straight towards me. He didn't get far.

Seeing him stand, Eli left the table, once again making a beeline for Tobin but had to retreat a second time when the young man was interrupted, no, actually grabbed by the arm, by Harry, who wanted to show off his swordsmanship.

'Ye see, what it is,' Harry said while Tobin looked at me with an expression that could only have meant "help me!", 'I don't know nothing about how Kensa would've fought back in her day. Perhaps you can gimme a few tips? Like, based on what you seen up there?'

'Sorry to disappoint, my friend,' said Tobin, clapping Harry on the shoulder. 'I don't know anything about it. I've not seen much sword fighting. Just remember, it doesn't matter who wins. Have fun and learn something from each other.'

He hastened a retreat again and with long strides made his way to me. 'Detective Blackman, thanks for your call. I was intending to come as I need to talk to you about an urgent matter.'

Over his shoulder, Eli was making his way towards us once more. Only this time, he clearly did not intend to let anyone interrupt him.

'Oh really?'

'Yes, it's about another former resident of Salmonweir. I had to check before coming to you, but-'

Eli grabbed him by the arm and looked at me apologetically. 'Sorry Detective, I need to talk to this young man. You know I've been waiting a while now?'

I waved them both off. 'That's quite alright, Eli. Tobin, I will catch up with you later? I'm crowd control tonight. I don't expect trouble, so I'll be standing around looking bored and not much else. Please, come and see me whenever you like.'

The place was buzzing; hell, I was buzzing. Everything looked and felt great. All I needed was for tonight to go swimmingly and the village could become the non-living history capital of the world. "Salmonweird" would be a badge of pride for Cornwall and no longer a tabloid slur.

I was looking forward to Harry and Kensa's swordfight. I was looking forward to Wilhelmina's speeches (yes, really!) I was looking forward to Morwenna and Babajide's open air bar complete with specially selected local beers and ciders. I was looking forward to seeing actual humans mingling with actual ghosts and getting on with each other.

Somebody had other ideas and that was about to ruin our evening.

Chapter 12

They arrived in the hour after the sun set on Salmonweir. I counted around three hundred people – actual living breathing humans. They queued patiently outside the gates of our village and, when the gaslights came on, opened up with a collective "ooh" and a round of applause. Taller heads stretched to see the stands, the stalls and the bright colourful decorations and lights.

They filtered through the gates of the village park for the first (hopefully annual) Salmonweir Bonfire Night Spectacular. I started to worry whether we'd be able to fit more in, but the end of the queue seemed to be about the limit.

It may not seem like a lot to the sort of people who go to these things all the time and feel like sardines cramped onto a village green but considering that we *expected* a grand total of zero, it was already shaping up to be a rip-roaring success.

'Roll up, roll up!' declared the booming voice of Wilhelmina Yorke. While she had no panache for poetry, she had a commanding voice with which to deliver speeches. 'Hear ye, hear ye. Ladies, knights and gentles,

Salmonweir Tourist Board proudly presents to you the first ever annual Salmonweir Bonfire Night Spectacular.'

At Wilhelmina's insistence, people eagerly crowded around the roped off area to see precisely what the Tudor woman was about to introduce. They gladly accepted the free mulled wine the local children passed around.

'To open the evening, in just a few minutes you will see the most extraordinary sword play between the village's greatest son and its greatest daughter – two *monoliths* of village history, two *titans* of its warring past, two *beasts* of the Cornish South Coast.' She bowed and they applauded.

'First, we have the legendary pirate captain of the fastest ship ever to have been built on this peninsula, Scourge of the South Seas, the Terror of Virginia, The Beast Who Slayed a Hundred smugglers of Penzance and sacked the fort at Bermuda twice! There is a statue dedicated to him at the dockside. The village is proud that he put Salmonweir on the map during the Golden Age of Piracy. The one, the only – Hook Hand Harry!'

Harry made his way out of the shadows and into the fire-lit circle. A wave of cheers, shrieks and whoops went up from the crowd. Harry bathed in their adulation with a bow and some showmanship of swordplay. It excited the crowd no end.

'Aaaand his opponent. She fought off twenty-five Roman legionaries single-handed. She burned twenty of their ships with little more than five flaming arrows and all before a breakfast of venison and wild berries, washed down with the finest mead. Her ferocity was so well known that the Romans halted all advances into Dumnonia as a modern land full of ferocious savages who could never be Romanised.'

The crowd oohed at this.

'They thought her Diana reborn. It is a nothing short of a travesty today that you would not know her name from the history books that speak openly of a woman named Boudicca who achieved far less. I present to you, the one, the only, Kensa the Celtic Queen!'

Though I didn't doubt the accomplishments of Kensa or Harry, I am pretty sure there was more than a *little* embellishment in those introductions. But what the hell, it was all good fun and it *was* a travesty that Kensa wasn't as famous as Boudicca or Cartimandua. Eh, listen to me showing off my history!

Harry naturally chose his First Mate Benjamin as his second. An excellent swordsman himself, I had seen the pair sparring and even teaming up in recent days against the other warriors of the village. I was not surprised to see

Cato at Kensa's side as her second. The two offered tips and words of encouragement to their respective fighters.

'Ladies and gentlemen, please give your support to these two fine swordsmen of this village. May the best historical corporeal being win!'

A round of applause rose and then died as the two warriors first selected and then tested their weapons by swishing them through the air. Harry chose a cutlass, a weapon with which he was no doubt familiar. Light and cutting, he favoured speed over strength.

Kensa, equally unsurprisingly, chose a long sword that to my untrained eye looked like a claymore. Impressively heavy and sturdy, she held it with two hands and a whole lot of menace.

'Good lady,' Harry began with the insults that were probably not customary at any point in history but would entertain the crowd no end, 'I thought we were to fight, yet you come here and wield a toothpick before me?'

'Good sir, *this* is a fine sword,' Kensa fired back, 'though I fear you have chosen the wrong weapon. It looks the sort of thing children and Romans might train with. I fear for you that my victory will be both swift and thorough.' She turned and gave an apologetic smile to

Cato who shrugged his shoulders and laughed along with the crowd.

They crossed swords, nodded, and the battle commenced.

I had been to battle re-enactments before and found them good fun, but this was something else. After ten minutes of some impressive swordplay, traded insults and much showmanship, Harry had the edge.

He took advantage of Kensa missing a swing and losing her footing at the same time – a moment of bad luck. Harry took that moment to strike a killer blow. Well, I say killer, but all he did was trip her up and hold the tip of his sword to Kensa's throat while declaring victory.

'The winner!' declared our poet, stepping into the ring. 'Hook Hand Harry! Congratulations, Harry.'

The crowd erupted into applause in which, once again, Harry bathed while he helped Kensa to her feet. 'And acting with supreme gentlemanly grace in victory. Will you, later this night, give the good lady the chance to win back her honour?'

'That I will!' The pair shook hands and left the field. 'A word of warning, ladies, gentles and children. Both Kensa and Harry are expert sword masters. Please do not try any of their tricks yourself. They are good friends and

216

practice together all the time. Plus, as they are both ghosts, they cannot harm each other or be harmed by these weapons.'

'If only you knew,' I muttered.

'What was that?' asked Morwenna who I hadn't realised had been standing there; she made me jump.

'Oh nothing, just thinking aloud,' I said. 'I didn't hear you sneak up?'

'I'm silent but deadly as all innkeepers should be. Suitable for taking glasses from your table without you noticing,' she grinned. 'I'm keen to see what Babajide is going to do with the cider and beer tasting. I think he's also organising cocktail competition, but I've been too busy to check on him. It should be good for business.'

'Wonderful. Where is the stall? I should go and sample.'

She gestured beyond the clump of trees. 'Up on the band stand, next to the bar. It's the only area stable enough to hold all those bottles.'

I was supposed to be on crowd control and hadn't been to that part of the garden yet. Morwenna and I went in different directions. She accosted two children, pointing them in the direction of the mulled wine supply.

There was already a prominent crowd around the band stand and I could make out Babajide doing his best. I threaded my way through the crowd and passed by the bar. I raised my hand to the young barman, but he didn't see me. It was dark in the shade and he looked as though he had too much on his hands already. I didn't want to disturb him so moved on.

A group of pirates were already in full swing and song on the main path. Their tune was yet another about a woman called Sally Brown. I had no idea who she was, but as she featured in at least three different songs I'd heard them singing; she must have made quite the impression with sailors in her day.

What an atmosphere this was. There was a distinct chill in the air; my breath billowed out in puffs, dancing, exploding and then curling back on itself. The light wind brought the temperature down, but it seemed only to spur people on to enjoy it. More chatter filled the air, carrying over me and through me.

The sound of a mechanical pipe organ firing into life startled me back to the present. Where it had come from I do not know, but it's possible it popped onto the green opposite the bandstand. 'Roll up, roll up!' called a young couple dressed as chimney sweeps. 'Gather 'round people! Come and see the marvellous machine.'

I confess to liking the sound of pipe organs and stopped a few moments to listen. Who should join me then, but Cato. He gave the same look to the mechanical organ that he gave the kettle, the oven, and the microwave when he first arrived – curiosity. He didn't just want to know how they worked as a general principle, but also how each part created each effect. To my shame, I could not explain that either.

'Such contraptions we never had in Rome.' He rubbed his stubble thoughtfully. 'Yet we failed to find an opponent as advanced as us. We thought we never would and now I see this.' He shook his head thoughtfully.

'Don't feel bad. This thing was invented about 17 centuries after your death. By today's standards, it is ancient technology. That doesn't mean it isn't fascinating or pleasant though.'

'I find the technology astounding. What Rome could have achieved had it survived so long as to experience such wonders?'

'How are you getting on with the books?' I'd made good on my promise and hired some famous volumes on the rise and fall of Rome so that Cato could catch up.

He shot me a quick glance. 'Oh, I have just reached the section about an Emperor named Hadrian. Claudius was Emperor at my death. I thought he achieved much but Hadrian seems a man so much greater than I could have imagined. I fail to see how the empire could do so badly with such men in Rome, especially after learning the lessons of Nero's errors.'

I looked at him glumly. 'I'll let you be the judge of the direction the empire took, my friend. You'll come to see eventually how and why it all goes so wrong.'

He jolted, suddenly remembering something. 'Oh Jupiter, how forgetful! Eli was looking for you. He asked if you could go and see him by the bonfire? He said he's doing the final checks before lighting it and can't really leave.'

'That's quite alright, thanks Cato.'

I followed the main path down the gentle slope that led to the south of the park. The trees gave way to what was normally open space but for this evening was an avenue leading to the fireworks display area. By the moonlight, I saw the stacked firewood that would later become the bonfire.

I saw movement around the firewood. Convinced it was Eli performing his final checks, I hastened my step.

The sound of the organ music faded into the background and the light flickered and paled to almost nothing. I moved quickly down the processional way towards the bonfire.

The figure moved about the stack. 'Eli, is that you?' I called out.

The figure didn't change its movement, it still appeared to float and dance around a small section of the wooden pile.

'Eli!' I called again. 'What did you want to see me about?'

The closer I looked, the closer I got, the more it seemed that the person wasn't at the bonfire, but inside it, behind several large planks and piles of wood and trying to push their way out.

My heart started racing and I cursed under my breath, hoping I was wrong as I hastened towards the unlit bonfire. There was a spark of orange; I couldn't tell where it came from, but it dropped from a short height, hit the floor and then appeared to grow at the feet of the figure.

I stopped walking and ran, raced towards the engulfing pile as fast as my nearly six-decade-old legs would take me. I was now convinced that there was somebody inside the fire, trapped, and it was about to go up in smoke.

I didn't see the barrier. I was so focused on the figure inside the fire pleading for my help that I fell into and then over the safety fence. The full heat of the fire hit my face. I looked up and saw a man pleading for his life from behind burning logs of wood, a spreading inferno engulfing everything in its path behind him.

You never get over seeing something like that and the first time I attended a fatal road traffic accident as a uniform copper, I puked all over the side of the road. I puked at the next five or six too. After a while, you develop a kind of immunity on the outside. You never get over watching a human being die before your eyes though; you just learn to cope with it. You never learn to cope with the helplessness.

I could now see it was Tobin and as quickly as the fire had started, he was gone, disappearing into the ether, spreading out in a thin blue mist that faded into the smoke and dissipating on the wind.

The crowd must have seen the fire start as another round of applause went up. In the background, I heard the voice of Wilhelmina Yorke over the PA system 'Well, it seems the fire has started early ladies and gentlemen. Please help yourselves to more complimentary mulled wine and soak up the atmosphere on this wonderful evening.'

Two figures appeared at the beginning of the processional way and began systematically lighting the lamps leading towards the fire, towards me, towards the scene of the crime.

I felt numb. I had just watched a man die. Granted, he had been dead about 20 years. As far as I knew he could come back any time, but it was still horrific to watch a man plead for his life as he burnt to a second death, unable to escape it.

'What's going on?' It was Ebrel's voice.

By the glowing light, I could see the other person lighting the lamps was Philip. 'I thought there was another hour to go yet?' he asked nonchalantly. 'Has there been a change of plan?'

'It looks like it.'

'Is everything alright?' Ebrel asked. 'You look deathly pale.'

'Yes, all's well. Let's focus on making this a good one? Great job, both of you, the park looks remarkable.'

Ebrel blinked at me suspiciously. 'You don't sound or look as though "all is well", Karl.'

'I'm *fine* Ebrel, really.' I turned my back on the lovebirds and marched back towards the fire as though nothing was amiss – but there was. Our killer had just claimed a second victim.

I forced a smile and welcomed the descending crowd warmly. 'Welcome, everyone! There was some suggestion the weather might change a little later, the wind might pick up, so we've decided to light the bonfire early. The fireworks will go ahead on schedule though.'

As the crowd fanned out into the open space around the fire, I caught sight of the combatants and their seconds lurking at the back. If I could declare anybody's innocence this evening, purely out of a lack of opportunity, it was Kensa, Cato, Harry and Benjamin. I hailed them over.

'A private word with the four of you, now, please?' I gabbled the words out with all the urgency I could muster.

'Of course,' said Kensa, smiling at me warmly. 'Did you like the fight?'

'It was great, thanks. But I-'

She went on. 'We are just getting ready for the second, actually. Benjamin suggested something called a "tag team" battle. I rather like the-'

'Sorry to interrupt you, Kensa. There is a more urgent matter, let's go somewhere quieter to talk.' I led them back along the processional way and recounted the story as exactly as I could recall it. 'Sorry, I didn't really know who else to tell.'

'We have a killer in Salmonweir,' said Cato.

'We still don't know what happened to Eddy and now they've definitely killed one of us, maybe even two.' Harry concurred.

'Without a motive for killing Eddie and now Tobin, and nothing to link them, I can't rule out another killing tonight. So, I'm asking you four to watch for anything suspicious and report back to me. Anything out of the ordinary, no matter how insignificant, could be important. I fear our only evidence just went up in smoke.'

'Why didn't he just walk through the wood?' asked Benjamin.

'Maybe he couldn't? He can come and go as he pleases and the rest of you can't, maybe he's not fully part of either world. Maybe the angels gave him special powers or loaned him a physical body. Maybe they only let him come back once. I don't know. I'm not sure anyone could answer that question properly for us except Tobin himself – if he ever returned. What is important is that somebody *knew* they could trap him in that fire and use it to – for want of a better world – *murder* him.'

I had two other people I needed to talk to, and both for different reasons.

I left the four of them to plan their patrols and went to the cordoned area where Eli should have been preparing the fireworks.

Hopping over the fence, I was grateful for the light from the fire as I wound my way through the rows of fireworks all neatly placed, ready to be set off. Eli was not at the safety area and he hadn't been at the fire so where the hell was he? And who was looking after the fireworks? We'd agreed somebody would be present right throughout the evening, but the area was vacant.

I hopped back over the fence and worked my way back into the crowd. That's when I saw the other person I wanted to talk to – Brother Jowan. I took him aside, leading him away from the crowd until we were completely clear of it.

'Whatever is wrong?' he asked. 'You look upset, Karl.'

Once again, I recounted the story of Tobin's demise. 'Do you know where Eli is? Have you seen him at all tonight?'

'As if I would! We've not spoken in weeks as you well know. I have no intention of speaking to *that man* again. Vile creature. If I had my way, he'd be expunged from this village for what he did. How such a man could ever become a man of the cloth I do not know.'

'I am aware of your latest altercation and I need to know why. What was it all about? Why was he threatening you with that knife? What would have happened if I hadn't stopped him?'

Jowan shook his head vigorously. 'You will need to talk to him about that. I can't even bring myself to tell you of his sins. They are for him and him alone to confess and renounce.'

'I have and he's not talking. So, I am asking you because it could be crucial to what happened to Tobin.'

A dark shadow passed over his face. 'You think he killed Tobin?'

'I can't rule anything out. He wasn't at the fire and should have been. He isn't at the fireworks area now and ought to be. If you know anything, you need to tell me. Jowan, this is important.'

Jowan sighed. 'He may be at the church, but he will most likely not be alone.'

'Oh I see, delivering a homily to some visitors?'

He screwed his nose up. 'Oh no. It will be Eli and one other. You should, perhaps, see for yourself and then maybe you will understand. What was your other question?'

'Both you and Eli had many conversations with Tobin during his visits here. Can you imagine why he may not have been able to break out of the pile of wood?'

'Interesting,' he turned to look back at the fire, 'he told me that he is neither alive nor dead. I can only assume he exists between the physical and the spiritual planes and able to come and go at leisure. That is all I know.'

'Thanks, Jowan. Sorry, one last thing I've just remembered. Tobin told me about a new visitor to the village, another former resident. I've not met this person, but have you? You're usually first port of call for most.'

'No Detective Blackman, I know not of any new arrivals though I keep hearing about a man with a leather-bound book and dressed in clothes similar to those you wear, though I have not yet met this man. Perhaps that is the man to whom Tobin referred?'

'Yes, perhaps.' I scratched my chin. 'Tobin's already mentioned him once though. If that's him, he's proving rather elusive. Thanks Jowan. I'll go to the church and find out what Eli is up to.'

Chapter 13

I didn't get as far as the church; I barely made it to the garden gates before Eli hastened through and almost passed right through me. 'I'm sorry Mister Blackman!' he exclaimed. 'I hadn't realised the time. They'll be wanting the fireworks soon.'

'Where have you been?!' I demanded to know, almost growling.

He turned around and looked at me, flabbergasted. 'Well sir, I was at the church in prayer, my presence was requested. And there is no need to take that tone with a man of the cloth.'

I glared back at him, meeting his words with silence.

'I realise it was my task to oversee the bonfire and the fireworks but I *am* here now and we can get started right away, can we not?' He turned on his heel and began marching towards the crowd.

I spotted Cato and Kensa coming towards me and waved for their attention, gesturing at Eli. They upped their pace and closed in on him, blocking his way through to the fire. 'Move out of the way, both of you. This is no time for silly games!' he snapped but they would not move.

Instead, at my insistence, they stood with arms crossed, mirroring each other.

He turned back to me. 'What are they doing? What is the meaning of this?'

'Eli,' there we go, that copper voice again, 'I need to ask you a few questions. A man was killed tonight and I need to know exactly where you have been, with whom and for how long.'

'A murder, here? But whom? And why?'

'It was Tobin.'

'Who would want to kill such an agreeable fellow?' Cato and Kensa closed in on the preacher.

'At the moment, you're my only suspect.'

'Don't be so stupid, Karl. You think me a murderer because I was not at the fire?' He shook his head and turned away from me, addressing Kensa and Cato. 'Move aside or I'll just Pop past you, and I would rather not be so rude in front of a lady and an officer of fighting men.'

'Eli,' I said again, 'if you do not come quietly, I am going to have to arrest you and I'm sure a man of your integrity will not want that. I know you've been anxious to meet with Tobin. I need to know why.'

He turned to face me again. 'You can't detain me; I've done nothing wrong!' he pleaded.

'Then you need to talk to me about where you've been and what you've been doing.'

Eli regained his composure. 'Not now, not here. I have a fireworks display to organise.'

'I've left Philip and Ebrel in charge of that now. They know what to do. Now, come with me.' I stepped forward; Cato and Kensa stepped forward. Had he a physical body, we'd have all been inside his personal space.

He ignored my insistent tone, approached Kensa and Cato fearlessly and in a split second, Popped through to the other side.

I'd had enough. He was my only suspect and I couldn't let him go. I instructed the Roman and the Warrior Queen to take Eli, which they did with efficiency. Thankfully, all those present, alive and ghost, were too busy enjoying the festivities to notice or care.

Eli could have Popped away again but must have thought better of doing so a second time. Perhaps he hadn't taken me seriously or perhaps incredulity of the situation and anger had finally given way to reason. Either way, he stopped protesting. 'You are making a big mistake, Karl. It will be difficult to ever forgive you for this.'

'I'm sorry Eli, but you have left me no choice. You have two options. House arrest in your own home – and I will have to ask myself whether I trust you enough not to Pop in and out at will, or I can ask Harry to put you in the brig and ask the crew to keep an eye on you until I can ascertain your guilt or innocence. That's your only choice, my friend.'

His head dropped but he answered quickly. 'Home. I won't cause you any trouble and I promise to almighty God that I will not leave until we've had the chance to discuss this properly.'

'I realise your vow to God is important. But please give *me* your word too?' I pressed.

'I believe this is what you do to make a solemn promise.' He put his hand on his heart. 'As God is my witness, I will not leave my home without your permission or prior knowledge.'

Just thirty minutes passed since Kensa and Cato escorted Eli from the park. I tried to mix again, but I couldn't help thinking of poor Tobin and simply had to talk to Eli tonight. I made some excuses, thanked some random people for coming, and then gracefully bowed out as host.

The silence in Eli's living room was eerie compared to the vibrant autumn buzz outside. The only noise was the faint ticking of the grandfather clock in the hallway and the occasional floorboard creaking above my head.

After his first altercation with Brother Jowan on the day of his arrival, I walked Eli to the place on the hill where he said his house had been in life. Disappointed that his old house no longer stood, he chose to live in the modern dwelling.

This was only my third visit to the house and I was pleased and surprised to see what he had done with it.

His first venture out into the village was to introduce himself to the other ghostly residents, practically interrogating them on their knowledge of The Bible and demanding to know whether they had "papist" sympathies. I went to the house at the insistence of pretty much everybody to ask him to curb his activities to avoid upsetting people. He was conciliatory and though he made it clear that he did not like Catholics or anyone else he felt were not doing Christianity properly, he promised to keep most of his thoughts to himself. Then, he moved onto another subject.

Of all things since his arrival back to Salmonweir, Eli acquired a taste for what to him would be futuristic gadgets and he spent the next 15 minutes explaining his newfound passion. I watched as this grown man, sorry, *dead* grown man stood mesmerised by the craftwork and inner workings of a grandfather clock.

I'm not expert, but it didn't look either high quality or in good condition, but a new imitation of something much older. I left him to it then, hoping it would dampen his zealotry.

The following day I witnessed him going house to house again. My heart sank at thinking this was another recruitment drive for his puritan mission.

When I challenged him on the matter, he said he had put all that aside, would allow people to come to God in their own time and way, and was seeking unwanted clocks. If the house had one and the residents didn't want them, would they be prepared to hand them over or trade for something they did require? I offered to help in what was quite possibly the strangest house move I'd ever taken part in, but it was enjoyable.

On the table before us was a small carriage clock. When I say it *was* a small carriage clock, I mean that quite literally – the pile of parts is not doubt what it used to be before Eli deconstructed it.

He noticed my curiosity. 'I know what you're thinking, but no I did not break it in anger. I've decided to take it apart to see how it works and to see if I can put it back together again.'

I nodded. 'When did you decide this?'

'Oh, weeks ago. It is only tonight I've decided to begin piecing it back together. My incarceration here has given me need for distraction to calm my mind. Prayer is not always enough.' He did not once look up at me.

'You get angry easily, don't you Eli?'

He nodded. 'I freely admit that wrath is my downfall more often than I'd' like. It is not something about which I am particularly proud. It harmed me in life and now in this strange afterlife we have here in Salmonweir, I often find it harder to control.'

'Why did you kill Tobin? Was it a fit of rage? Did he antagonise you and you saw red and killed him? Was it, in fact, planned? You urgently wanted to talk to him.'

Still, he didn't avert his gaze from the deconstructed clock parts scattered across the table. The more I looked at it, the more I realised he'd carefully set out the various parts into loose groups as though classifying them by function and form. 'I didn't,' he said croakily.

'Then who did?'

He placed the pieces calmly on the table and folded his hands together. I had never known his voice so calm. 'How should I know? I wanted to talk to the man. It serves me no purpose to kill him at all, let alone *before* receiving an answer to the question I posed him.'

'You lash out, we both know that, and you just admitted to having a temper. It might have been an accident. Was it an accident?' I pressed.

'I did *not* kill him,' he said, his voice still silent and slow.

I must confess to being surprised at Eli's remarkable calm in the face of my antagonism. 'What question?'

'It is unimportant now, Karl. Tobin is gone and I am far from being happy about it.'

'Help me out here, Eli. You were anxious to talk to Tobin, you've been anxious to talk to him all day. I doubt anything that happened tonight is unimportant. You need to tell me everything, start at the beginning. Give me something to work with, I want to help you.' The floorboard went again.

'You saw me before the sun went down,' he started. 'You know I spent most of this evening preparing the fire and doing the final safety checks for the fireworks.' As if on cue, they started up again. I noticed Eli smile and I smiled with him.

Coming back to reality, I gave him a serious nod. 'Yes, I remember. I'm more concerned about what happened after I left you there. Instead of staying at your post, you went to the church.'

He took a deep breath, or what would have been a breath had he had a body. 'I left the bonfire and the fireworks after my checks, feeling safe that nobody would interfere with them. I went back to the crowd, to try to engage with some of the public. That's when I spotted Tobin talking to that Roman soldier and the noble savage woman.'

I cleared my throat. 'Kensa? If she heard you calling her that she would gut you, slowly.'

'It was nonsense talk, mostly, so I left them to it. I waited in the processional way until I saw them pass. That was when I saw fit to impose myself on Tobin and ask him the question, I had been meaning to ask of him day. He knew why I was there; we'd discussed the matter several times already.'

'What matter? What was the question?'

'As I said mere moments ago, it is *not* important. The fact is, I posed my question and he promised to get me an answer within a few days. It was not in my interest to kill him a few hours later, was it, before I had my answer?'

'Perhaps not.' I let the matter go; I would get my answer eventually, one way or another, and though it may be unimportant to the investigation as far as Eli was concerned, especially so if he was innocent, it may not be unimportant to me. 'What happened next?'

'I made my way towards the gathering crowds. I felt elated that so many people were already there to see our display. I spoke briefly to a couple of arrivals, informing them that the fireworks would definitely happen. Everybody seemed in such good spirits.' I could hear the pride in his voice and was struggling to see how he could have murdered somebody on a night that meant so much to me, to him, to all of us. I only nodded.

'Some time after that, I was accosted by a man who told me my presence was required at the church. Naturally, I went immediately.'

'Did he tell you who?'

'No, I just went, just as any good shepherd with a flock would. It was one of my parishioners who had yet to attend the bonfire.'

'Who is this parishioner?'

He looked down at his crumpled hands that he placed firmly in his lap. The man had now shut down, the only visible reaction he had was to the floorboards above us.

After a few moments, I pressed my fingers to my temple. 'If you won't tell me who it is, I can't help you. If you won't tell me who it is, they cannot verify your story, if you won't tell me who this person is, I can only assume your guilt.'

'The slave. The young man who works at the inn.'

I looked at him quizzically. 'Babajide? He's not a slave. He used to be one in life, but he's a free man now like any of us.'

'Apologies. Yes, Babajide. That's correct.'

I placed my hands on the table before me. I'd recalled seeing him at the bandstand. 'Why did you not tell me before? Why the secrecy?'

'I have been offering him spiritual counsel for a few weeks now.'

I narrowed my eyes; it all seemed a bit too convenient. Of course, I would check with Babajide at the first opportunity. 'And you felt I didn't need to know something so innocuous?'

'He wanted to keep it quiet and I am bound by an oath of confidence as to the reasons for it. As for his reason for seeking spiritual counsel, it is anything but innocuous.'

'Thank you, Eli. At the moment I do not know what to believe. I *will* check with Babajide and come back to you.' Another round of fireworks went off above our heads. 'They'll be heading to the pub once this is over and I'm sure he will be there.'

'I know I am under house arrest, but will you at least let me attend church? Could I perhaps go when the party is over? I will gladly go with any escort you determine suitable.'

I nodded. 'I've already said I would allow that under guard. Kensa and Cato have offered to escort you back and forth. I don't believe in removing spiritual privileges from anyone, even when found guilty. I will ask them to come over once the crowd has dispersed.'

'Thank you, Karl. That means much more than you might ever understand.'

As I left Eli's home, I could see that the fireworks had finished and the bonfire dying down. By the remaining light and the ominous moonlight spilling across the rugged Cornish landscape, a stream of people wound through the streets. Though the disappearing car lights along the main road showed that some were leaving, the stream of torches suggested that far more stayed than were leaving.

I made my way back towards the centre of the village. I was exhausted by all this detective work and had really hoped I'd put it behind me when I left Cambridge. No matter where I am, no matter what I'm doing, police work seems to follow me around *everywhere*.

I made my way quickly to the pub. I knew it would be busy, but I didn't quite expect not to be able to move. Human and ghost crowd gave me a round of applause as I entered. I confess to feeling embarrassed. A familiar face approached me and offered his hand. It took me a moment to recognise Eric, the walker from a few weeks ago.

'Oh, you came back?' I shook his hand warmly. 'Did you enjoy the fireworks?'

'Oh yes!' he said, gesturing to his wife and sister parked at a nearby table. 'we came back and we loved the fireworks. Same again next year?'

I chuckled. 'Far too early! But if tonight went as well as we'd hoped then we expect to hold another next year. Also, we have a few ideas for Christmas lined up so stick with Salmonweir for more of the same.'

'Wonderful! Now, can I buy you a drink?' he offered.

I was too busy scanning the bar for Babajide; despite the number of guests, Morwenna seemed to be the only person serving. 'Oh, certainly! I came here looking to speak to the barman, but I think he's indisposed.'

I told Eric what I wanted to drink and joined his wife and sister at the table.

I shook the hands of each woman in turn. 'Are you Margaret?' I enquired.

'Oh yes!' said the shorter woman. 'This is Heidi, Eric's sister.'

'I do remember,' I said, shaking the second woman's hand. 'Have you all come down especially? Where are you staying?'

'At a country spa retreat just a few miles down the road,' said Eric handing me the cider. 'It has a nice big pool, a spa, and at the moment it's offering free massages. Naturally, I was outnumbered two to one and didn't get a say in the choice of accommodation.'

'Oh, give over Eric!' Margaret joked to her husband. 'Making yourself out the henpecked husband. You had a free massage yesterday afternoon when we got there and let's not forget the golf course. He didn't need *much* persuading.'

He rolled his shoulders. 'I *did* enjoy it, took about ten years off me by my reckoning!'

'Is there a Mrs Blackman by any chance?' Margaret asked.

'Margaret, don't be so personal!' said Heidi.

'It's alright,' I said, 'there *is* a Mrs. Blackman, but not for much longer. The divorce is going through. It might take a while.'

'Oh that's a shame,' said Margaret with genuine sadness. 'Do you have kids?'

'We do, a son and two daughters, but they are all grown up and our first one has just got engaged which is good news.'

'Every cloud,' said Heidi and prompted everyone to raise their glasses. 'Congratulations to the father of the...?'

'Groom.'

'Don't know if our boy ever will,' she carried on, 'he never stays in one place long enough. These days, they want to save money for travelling rather than buying a house, don't you find Mister Blackman?'

'Oh yes, that's not such a bad thing. Many of our generation married young and regretted it – too many. Too often I think we all do what we are expected to do rather than what we want to do. What I want right now is here in this lovely little village. I wouldn't have it any other way.'

Babajide did not appear at all that evening. Everyone was having a good time, plenty of offers to buy drinks and I remained at the table with Eric, Heidi and Margaret. We parted promising to do "The Facebook Thing" and confident they'd be back again. When only three people remained in the pub, I approached Morwenna who was at the bar getting ready to call time.

'Ah, Karl!' A great night, wasn't it?'

I grinned. 'We got there in the end.'

'So sorry to hear about Eli. Do you really think he killed Tobin and that cabin boy?' She finished polishing another glass and placed it in the rack above her head.

I frowned. 'How did you know about that?'

She shrugged. 'Word gets around and pubs are gossip sponges.'

'If you ever decide to change the name of the pub, I'm not sure "The Gossip Sponge" will be particularly suitable, even if it is apt and amusing.'

'What can I get you?' She put her hand to the pump of my usual tipple. 'We've plenty of this left.'

I waved her away. 'No more drinks for me, thanks, not tonight. Is Babajide around?'

'He tidied away the pop-up bar and I gave him the rest of the night off; the poor lad was exhausted, but he did a fine job, don't you think? Would you like a coffee?' She gestured at the coffee maker.

I pondered briefly. 'No thanks. Is Babajide upstairs? Can I talk to him?'

'No,' she snapped back quickly. 'He's not up there, I don't know where he is, and it's a bit late anyway. If I see him early tomorrow, I'll send him over to see you.'

'Yes please, although I appreciate it's getting late now. I need to ask you a question about our favourite barman.'

She nodded cautiously.

'Do you know if he has been meeting Eli over the last few weeks?'

'Meeting Eli, for what?' Morwenna's look was one of surprise. 'If he is, he hasn't told me about it.'

'Any unexplained disappearances?'

'You mean like tonight?' she laughed ironically. 'I'm not his mother, he can do what he likes.'

I ignored the slightly sour tone. 'Yes, and any other time.'

'He comes and goes a lot and doesn't tell me where he is going, but then I do the same to him so I can't complain. I've never had reason to quiz him and he gives me no reason to be suspicious. He's a free man now.'

'Yes, I know, I didn't mean.' I cleared my throat. 'Eli told me Babajide visits him several times a week for religious instruction. I wonder if you can confirm or deny it.'

She shook her head slowly. 'As I said, I really do not know. But religious instruction? She patted her silvering hair thoughtfully. 'Sorry Karl. I know nothing of any of it. It's possible he's going to church for individual instruction when he's not working, but it *would* surprise me. He is a Christian man, but he takes it as simply as most of us simple folk.'

'Thanks, Morwenna.'

As I turned away she stopped me in my tracks. 'Or it could be he's tending the... no, he wouldn't without talking to me about it.'

'Can I ask...?' I probed.

She put her hand to her face and shook her head. 'No, it's. I'm sorry Karl. I'm not in a good mood today. I know I've been erratic and it's for good reason. You see, tomorrow. The 6th November. It's the anniversary of my death.'

My face flushed at hearing something so personal. 'Oh, I'm sorry. I did not know. I guess I never really think about that sort of thing.'

A tear rolled down her ghostly face. 'It's all a blur, really. My husband. He, ah.'

'It's all right, you don't have to tell me if you don't want to.'

'I did the worst thing a woman could do to her husband; I took a lover. It was a mistake, one stupid mistake and I paid for it with my life. Babajide- he was- is like a son to me. His heart is so pure that he is probably tending my grave right now.' With that, she wiped a tear from her eye, turned on her heel and marched up to the bar. 'Sorry,' she called back, 'I must go and finish up.'

Chapter 14

The sound of hammering on my door woke me from a groggy sleep. The time on my digital clock said it was just a few minutes to three.

Woken in the early hours in Cambridge, my mind would have worked overtime going through all the possibilities. My first thought would have been an ex-con coming over to take his revenge on the copper who put him away, or a con's girlfriend coming over to exact revenge for putting her fella away.

The third thought might be that there were a couple of uniform officers at the door here to tell me of the death of one of my children in a car accident. Thankfully, I never got any such bang on the door. Those things did go through my head now as the fist thumped heavily against the wooden door once more.

It wasn't likely to be the first *or* the second. It would have taken only the most determined scumbag to trace me down here and go to the effort of travelling the country to face me. The same was true of a partner of a convict. Besides, I was retired long enough for few of them to care, even if they had the resources and the will to find me.

The third was possible but unlikely – I would have heard it from Valarie first. We might be divorcing, but even she would have put that aside to share in our grief together as a family.

I threw on my bathrobe and slippers, stopping briefly to collect the cricket bat from the side of the bed. One of the kids bought it for me as a joke. It had a zombie face and a blood splatter on the blade, and the words *Property of Mortwich Island Cricket Club* on the handle.

Once a paranoid detective, *always* a paranoid detective. Though the site of a zombie-killing cricket bat would more likely make intruders laugh than anything else.

I crept down the stairs; I didn't turn the light on as I didn't want to lose the element of surprise if the visitor had designs on formally introducing my head to something heavy. It's dark at 3am in Salmonweir all the year round, so going was not as quick as I would have liked.

Again, the heavy fist hammered against the door. I still had time, so I slipped into the living room. Faint moonlight fingered its way through the thin curtains.

There was a slight gap between them; I carefully positioned myself to look through without parting the cloth hangings. I could feel a chill coming off the glass and pulled my gown tighter against my body.

I couldn't see anybody at the door. Either they had gone or were pressed right up against it.

That question was answered when a fist slammed against the door once more. Guided more by memory of the layout of my home than by light (Salmonweir only has streetlights at the harbour and along the main road), I swept out of the living room and to the front door. Holding the cricket bat firmly in my right hand, I was surprised at my panther-like speed and agility as I threw open the front door.

Nobody there.

From my position, I should have seen a figure retreating down the path in the thin moonlight had there been one. It was a good view and the main advantage of living on the brow of the hill is that we had a clear view of the village and of people arriving from the docks. Against my better judgement, I stepped out into the cold night.

The chill from the sea immediately attacked my bare legs. Short hairs stood in angry protest. If they could have spoken, they would have screamed for me to get my nearly 60-year-old arse back inside and stand against something hot for the next hour. I ignored their howls of protest and pressed on.

Gravel crunched beneath my slippered feet as I went to the car and circled it. There was no sign anybody had been there. 'If that's you Eli,' I spoke into the ether, my voice quivering, 'then you should know I don't find this in the slightest bit amusing!'

I continued my journey of the car's perimeter and peered over the garden hedge. I looked along the path leading down to the village centre and the docks but could see nothing. I could also hear the waves gently lapping against the rocks of the headland beneath me – and nothing else.

I stood there in silence for another ten seconds. It was bloody freezing and I had no wish to be awake at 3am for any reason. Letting the cricket bat fall by my side I turned back to the house.

The light in my bedroom was on. My heart skipped a beat. I *knew* that *I* hadn't switched it on, I never would have alerted an intruder to my presence. I readied the cricket bat again and stepped in through the door.

Closing it slowly behind me, I held my breath as though that would prevent the hinges squeaking. The sound reminded me that they were long overdue some lubricant. I closed my eyes and mentally imagined myself walking upstairs, trying to work out or remember which of those steps had loose floorboards.

I pictured them in my mind and made a mental note to avoid them.

I glided silently up the stairs, shifting from left to right on those steps as I felt the wood give way beneath me. As I rounded the corner onto the landing, I could see my bedroom door ajar but no sign of movement beyond.

How long did it take me to traverse the landing? It was just nine feet (or thereabouts), but I think it took me a good thirty seconds to cross it. As I reached the door, I threw all caution to the wind, raised the cricket bat and threw it wide open.

The room was empty. The only thing out of place was a small, square, brown box in the middle of the bed. It was about the size of a CD case but twice as thick. I approached it cautiously, placing my cricket bat gently on the bed beside it.

I picked up the box and opened it with a sense of trepidation, my body not wanting to do it but mind willing the thing to just open. I handled it as if it was a bomb. That was unlikely and if I believed for one minute that it *was* a bomb, I'd presently be running down the hill screaming, phone in hand calling the bomb squad.

A folded piece of off-white paper with something shiny beneath menaced me from inside the box. I gingerly removed the note and was surprised to see the shiny thing was a silver bracelet.

Using a tissue, I removed it just as gingerly and turned it over several times. I was half expecting it to explode (which it didn't). It was thin enough to suggest it was for a woman, but plain enough to be the kind of design made with men in mind. It wasn't new either; it had the scuff marks and dull sheen of aged silver. I knew that meant it was high quality, but it had an old feel about it as well as one of quality. This was at least a couple of centuries old. I placed it back in the box, having never touched it with my fingers.

Next I turned my attention to the note, opening it with even more care than I handled the bracelet.

Tobyn ys ded
I tole u 2 bee mor carefull
U ar not beink carful enuff who u talk tu
This brayslet belong tu the killa
Hyde it fr now
I well bee bak

It was the same handwriting as before. After searching the house and finding no trace of anyone, I returned to the bedroom to mull over the note. I stayed awake until the sun came up and *then* fell into a broken sleep.

What is it about the comfort of daylight? Why did I think it was safer sleeping during the day than at night? If one of the residents could come and go as they please and leave me gifts and notes, then the cover of darkness was no advantage and daylight no disadvantage.

I live in a village full of ghosts. If any of them wanted to scare the shit out of me, it wouldn't be that difficult – though in probably 490 of the 499 cases, I would probably just laugh.

I arose early but stayed in until lunchtime and went straight back to the site of the bonfire. I had instructed nobody touch it, but now I was about to give up. Kicking the cold pile of ash in frustration, I turned my back on the cold drizzle of the morning.

I had found nothing inside the remnants of the fire, nor had I expected to do so. I doubted there was anything to find in the first place. 'Nothing?' came the voice of Cato from behind me. I could only shake my head in annoyance.

'Where did Kensa go?'

'To talk to Harry about organising a village patrol. She wants to teach his men some new sword tricks and learn some of theirs in return.'

I nodded. 'A patrol? Kensa thinks Eli is innocent?'

Cato looked at me cautiously. 'Her words were that we can't take the chance in case he is innocent. Until we *know* that Eli is guilty, it is unwise to act as though the killer is not still out there. You believe Eli is guilty?'

'No, Cato, I don't believe he is,' I admitted with a sigh, 'but I have no other suspect. I still don't have a motive for Eli and nothing linking Tobin and Eddie aside from their gender and the fact that they are both dead.'

'I think I should go and find them, Kensa and the pirate crew, see how they are getting on?' He looked out towards the bay. It was clear he no longer wanted to be here, so I waved him off.

My phone rang then; seeing the name *Claire*, I picked it up immediately with a grin. 'Claire, darling! So good to hear from you.'

'Hey dad! How are you?' Her excitable tone began with a babble of incoherence, but she quickly got herself under control. Claire was like that. She was the energetic one of the family, the only one to have run a marathon.

'Oh, I'm fine thanks, love. How are you?'

'Great dad! Just phoned to tell you I got a new job! And ask how you are, of course.' She rolled her Rs and I cringed at the Bristol accent creeping into her voice. She'd lived there for so long that I don't know why it still surprised me.

'Is it gert lush or summut my lover?' I asked, affecting quite possibly the worst West Country accent I could muster. Forgive me, I've only been on the west side of the country for about two years.

'Dad! Don't take the mick.' Then she chose to carry on anyway. 'Arr, it's a proper job, I loves it I does!' she laughed to herself and at herself.

'Fantastic, what is it doing?'

'It's a promotion. I used to be Team Leader, now I'm Department Manager.' I could feel her beaming from the other end of the phone. 'I'm in charge of more people in the main office and now everyone in the second office reports to me too. Well, not yet. I start in two weeks but they're already throwing work at me. Grade 4 work for Grade 5 wages. I should demand a bonus.'

'That's really, really wonderful, Claire. I'm so proud of you.'

'Yeah!' she went on. 'We have a big product launch next year and they think I'm the one who can make it a success, marketing-wise of course.'

'Can you tell me what it is?' I pressed.

'No, sorry. It's a new phone and that's all I can tell you. But, it's going to be biiiiig.'

'Ah well. I'm sure we'll see it in time.'

'But listen, dad, can we video chat tonight? I've got some other important news. Can't stop now as I'm off out with the girls for lunch.'

'Oh ok, of course we can. Speak to you… around eight suit?'

'Brilliant, bye dad! love you! Kiss kiss!' and she was gone. Knowing Claire, she'd intended only to phone me to arrange the video chat but ended up blurting out half of what she was going to tell me during the video chat.

I kicked through the pile of ash once more. As the cloud turned over itself, a dark patch flipped onto the top and fell half back into the pale grey ash. It was only noticeable because the ash from the previous night's wood fire was pale grey, almost white, and this was the colour of charcoal. I'm not a geologist, but it looked like polished granite, a pendant maybe.

Gingerly, I poked my finger into the ash. It was still warm, but not hot. It felt more like warm, dry soil that you tend to get on a hot summer's day, the kind that has you rushing for the watering can. As my fingers touched it, I caught a brief flash of something.

It is Salmonweir, but not the one I know. I'm standing atop the cliff where my house should be but there are no houses here. I turn to the left and see a part of the village that does look familiar. In the Salmonweir dip is the pub and the dock and a few buildings I don't recognise. A couple look Tudor but well-aged.

'Hey!' cried the voice of a child. I turn to look; a boy, perhaps nine years old with a sweet face and happy eyes. He's racing down the track towards the cliff edge where I'm standing steadfast.

He stops before me. 'I have something for you,' comes his nervous and squeaky voice. He smiles at me and my open hand reaches out towards his as he offers me his clenched fist. His eyes are chocolate brown; his clothes mucky but folky, and timeless. I still cannot place a century let alone a year.

I open my hand and let the object he is holding fall into mine. It is the granite pendant.

The whole scene lasted no more than a few seconds before I returned to the real world with a bump and I am DI (retired) Karl Blackman again.

There was nobody else around to share my weird experience. Feeling quite shaken, but calming down quickly, I made my way back to the main path and out towards the garden entrance. I was still mulling over what just happened when who should cross my path, but Babajide.

He gave me a friendly wave as he walked past, no doubt heading to *The King's Head*. I figuratively grabbed him as he passed me by. 'Babajide, I need to talk to you about something.'

'Mister Blackman,' he said, 'Misses Morwenna told me you were looking for me?'

'That's right. It's about Eli. He claims to have an alibi and that you could vouch for him. Can I ask you a few quick questions?'

His brow creased slightly and briefly; he followed it up with a nod.

'Eli told me you two have been meeting for religious instruction. He said you wanted to understand his faith and get closer to God. Is this true?'

'One time.'

'Sorry, one time?' I quizzed.

'After one time, I decided I don't want to do it again. On one time only did I meet to hear about his answer of God.' He smiled nervously.

'I see. This was last night?' I took out my notepad and pen. Even now, retired, I kept one on me at all times.

'A month?'

I let the pen relax in my hand and gave him a quizzical look. 'A month ago?'

He nodded and smiled that nervous grin again. 'It was a Sunday afternoon, I think that it was warm and he-'

I cut him off. 'Ah, thanks Babajide. That bit is not important. Can you confirm, did you or did you not see Eli *last night* for religious instruction?'

'No, I did not last night. One month ago.'

'Did you go anywhere near the church?'

'Not at all.'

'Where were you?'

'I was in the pub before six. That was when Mrs Morwenna told me to move the stuff out for the tasting and cocktails.'

'Ah yes, I remember now. I saw you at the bandstand. You never left?'

'Not until the fireworks. We were so busy.'

'I saw. Thanks, Babajide. And good job on last night.' I tapped the pen against the notepad and put it away, giving him a warm smile. Next, I produced the granite pendant. 'Do you recognise this?'

It was a long shot, so I wasn't surprised when his indifference was accompanied with the affirmation that he had never seen it before. 'I can go now? All is good?'

'Of course, my friend. Have a good day!' He visibly relaxed before carrying on his way. I watched him go and pondered the situation. Eli's only alibi had just collapsed. It was time to have another talk with the preacher.

Eli had another disassembled timepiece spread out on the table when I arrived. At least he was making the most of his house arrest and channelling his time well, I had to remind myself. He must have finished with the carriage clock because this looked like a Victorian pocket watch. Eli had decided to move on to something slightly more complex.

He noticed me looking at the watch. 'I am trying to understand how things work on the inside so I can understand them better and maybe make them work better.' He looked at me soulfully.

I hadn't spoken a word since he let me in, but the look on his face said it all. I sat at the table with my hands pressed together and making it clear that I knew he was lying about his whereabouts. It was time for me to break my silence. 'Are you going to tell me what you were really doing?'

He looked down at the disassembled pieces. 'Flaws in a creation ultimately determine how well it works. No matter how many times you try to make it work, it will still be weaker than it ought. Weaker parts affect the whole, do they not Mister Blackman?' Then he looked me straight in the eye.

The silence broke only by the creaking floorboard I'd heard last night. I wanted to tell him to call in some pest control, but that would take us away from this interesting line of conversation. 'What do you mean?'

'We all have flaws. It's whether we can make them work for the good of all that determines our ultimate use.'

I nodded. 'I won't pretend I don't have them. Yours is your temper, isn't it Eli? You sometimes let it get the better of you.'

He looked down again and his brow creased. 'Yes, I confess I am quick to anger. God knows this and only he will judge me.' He sighed deeply. 'Anger is a personal failing, but it is the least of my sins. Clearly, lying to an officer at law is another.'

'Why don't you tell me where you really were? I will help you if I can and anything you tell me will remain between us.' I still wasn't sure whether I believed he was guilty at this stage, but something drew my attention above our heads – something other than a simple creaking floorboard. 'What was that?'

'What was what?' he shot back nervously.

'Your floorboards are creaking unusually for a mild day, just as it was last night. At first I thought you had rodents. Just now, I don't think that was floorboard that time or mice, was it Eli? It sounded more like footsteps.'

He shook his head a little too vigorously. 'You're imagining things. The stress of this is affecting your judgement.'

'No, I'm not.' I stood up and went to the lounge door leading up the stairs. I pulled it open quickly and charged through. I had made it just halfway up them before Eli popped before me. 'Out of the way, Eli, or I will walk through you.'

'No you won't, you have the manners of a gentleman.'

I raised an eyebrow. 'If you don't *want* me to walk through you, I suggest you move out of the way.'

He didn't move; moments later I passed through him to the other side, took the remaining stairs three at a time and burst through into the main bedroom, panting.

Sat on the bed, looking up at me with abject terror was a man perhaps the same age as Eli; he had light stubble and a curious scar from his left ear, stretching beneath his neck to roughly where his Adam's Apple would be if he had a physical form. His style of clothing was contemporary with that of Eli.

'Hello,' I said, 'I don't believe we have met?'

He stood up and I was quite surprised to see that, despite his scrawny body frame, he towered over me; I am not short.

Eli popped in beside him and took a protective stance. This man was also at least three inches taller than Eli who, until then, I had considered tall by the standards of his own age and would still be in the 21st century.

'Hello sir,' he said in a gentle voice which was distinctly Cornish. 'You must be Detective Karl Blackman?' He offered me his hand and I was surprised to feel the hint of a presence that wasn't flesh and bone but felt physical.

'Oh my, you're *alive*?'

Chapter 15

'Oh no, sir,' he said, 'I am quite dead. I do have more of a physical form than others of our kind, but I am dead and have been for over 350 years of your reckoning.'

'Sorry, I didn't get your name?' I cast a quick glance to Eli. His gaze was directed firmly at the floor.

'It's Jacob, sir.' He stood proudly, raising his chin, drawing attention to that nasty scar. 'And I have heard much about you already. You seem like a mighty fine fellow if you don't mind me saying so.'

'I am delighted to meet you Jacob, but you have me at a disadvantage?'

He glanced at Eli, 'that's what I suspected. I wanted Eli to tell you about me sooner than this. You see, I was straining to hear the conversation from downstairs, sir, as I was last night. I'm sorry f'that as it wasn't my business to know. But I had to – I wanted to know that Eli was all right you see.'

His local accent was a stark contrast from Eli's Home Counties inflection. 'He don't mean no harm, sir. He never means no harm to no one.'

'I'm confused, Jacob. I'm not as young or as sharp as I used to be. Just who are you? Why are you here and why have we never met? You've no reason to be hiding up here.'

Jacob turned to Eli and gently touched him on the arm. 'Eli, you need to tell him now. It can't go on like this. I know you didn't kill that man, and Detective Blackman can help you if you tell him the *truth*.'

He shook his head and sighed deeply, 'I can't. I *still* can't.'

'You have to some time or this good Mister Blackman will think you guilty and the real killer will keep killin', won't they?'

Now it was my turn to sigh. 'Gentlemen, I am *so* confused right now, and I think I will have to go home and lie down soon. But before I do, could somebody *please* explain to me *precisely* what is going on here?'

Jacob lifted his head and pointed to the scar. 'This is what they done to me when they found out what I was. They cut me there because they said I was a pig and deserved to die like one for being what I am. Ask Eli what they done to him when they caught us.'

'There's no need,' I said, waving at both, 'I think I know what is going on. And quite frankly, it doesn't matter to me. The thing that does matter is whether you were the person who requested Eli's presence at the church last night. Are you the person who can provide his alibi?'

He nodded. 'That I was, sir. It were me he came to see at my request. We been praying, see, for forgiveness for those men for what they done to us when we were alive. We been praying every night since we got back that God take mercy on their poor souls.'

I looked to Eli, but he didn't react; his gaze was cast firmly at the floor – in them I read shame, guilt and anger, and more shame.

'You see, me and Eli-' he started.

'Don't tell him!' Eli spat. 'Don't!'

He brushed Eli off then. 'We got to tell someone, Eli! And from what you've said, Mister Blackman seems like a good sort.'

'You see,' he said, turning back to me, 'when we was alive sir, Eli never come to terms with what he was because of his position. But me? I didn't have no one to worry about me like that. I kept meself to meself and as the son of a landowner round these parts, I had certain protections, so to speak. My father, he realised God has his ways and didn't care none much what I did so long as I didn't go telling everyone about it.'

'I think I see now. Jacob, are you and Eli gay?'

'Oh yes, we were so gay together, sir. We had a good life, really, what with the farm and the Cornish weather. Plus, living that near to the sea, what man, woman or child wouldn't be as gay as the day is long?'

I cursed my use – not for the first time – of my anachronistic language. Language that probably seemed like a foreign language to everyone else in the village. 'Sorry, it's a modern word. I mean – are you and Eli lovers, like as a man and wife would be?'

'Yes sir, indeed we are.' Jacob nodded enthusiastically, 'and those boys killed us for it when they found out. And that's what we been praying for, that God forgive them their trespasses like he forgived us our trespasses against him.'

I looked from Eli to Jacob and back again. 'Eli. I understand why you were apprehensive to tell me about this. But telling me could have saved us both so much trouble. You are free to come and go as you please in the future. I will ensure everybody knows.

'In fact, come to the pub this evening. Most people will be there. A public exoneration like this is not how I

271

prefer to do things. I know it's how they do things on TV dramas, but it is the best under the circumstances.'

Jacob looked to Eli and the men nodded at each other. 'That he will, sir. And I will make sure of it. I'll kick him down the street if I must.' Jacob reached out and shook my hand again.

'I have one final question for both of you,' it was another long shot, but I pulled out the pendant once more and handed it to Eli. Just like Babajide, he too accepted it with indifference. He passed it to Jacob who turned it over and passed it back to me.

'As far as I can see,' said Eli, 'it's a normal love pendant. Nothing remarkable about this one. I might have seen hundreds more like it.'

'You know what it is?' I probed Eli.

'Of course,' he threw his arms up, 'a tradition of the time when we lived. Poorer people of Devon and Cornwall who could not afford metal, and especially not gold, would fashion rings, bracelets, pendants, anything they could make from whatever they could get hold of. I'm sure I don't need to tell you granite is the stone of choice here. We wanted to stamp out the tradition, finding it too pagan. Yet it persisted amongst the poorer classes. They did not concern me; I had more pressing matters in Salmonweir.'

My heart skipped a beat. This was my first lead in the case. It didn't seem much, but it was better than nothing.

'Do you recognise this one?'

He shook his head vigorously. 'I wish I could help, but I have already said there is nothing remarkable about it.'

My heart sank then, but now I had a line of enquiry, of a sort.

'Hey dad!' the broken image of Claire's beaming face appeared on my aging laptop screen. Behind her, I could see only a darkened blob that was probably her flat. My laptop is getting on a bit now and probably struggling to cope with images.

'Hey Claire! Always lovely to see your face.' I touched the screen affectionately.

'Dad, you're such a charmer.' She leaned forward and rested her head on her fist. 'How are you holding up?'

'I'm really well, thanks. You know Paul was here a few weeks ago?' I dodged the question. I didn't really feel in the mood to talk about the divorce tonight.

'Yes he told me! We all got together last weekend. Cardiff is only a short trip across the water from Bristol. He said you looked well and told me all about the Bonfire Night thingy.'

'It was only last night but already feels a week ago.'

She nodded and took a sip from a mug with the Cardiff Rugby Club crest. 'It was in some of the papers, apparently. How did it go?'

'Well, of course it was. What was it this time, ghosts stealing British jobs? Draining the NHS?'

She chuckled. 'Nothing like that though one of the right-wing newspapers hoped Princess Di might make an appearance.'

'I can imagine which one.' It was my turn to chuckle and roll my eyes. 'Bonfire Night went well. Really, really well.' Of course, I left out the bit about the murder.

She nodded enthusiastically. 'You need something to keep yourself occupied, dad. I'm glad you found something. Christmas festival planned next? That'll get people down.'

274

'As it happens, I have a bit of something to keep me occupied but not in the way I would have hoped or planned.'

'What's going on?' she asked concerned.

'Well, please don't say anything – to anyone, ever, if you can. I really cannot let this get out into the media. But, I have a case.'

'A case?' she frowned, 'like a criminal case? Dad, you're supposed to have retired! I can't believe the local force is consulting you over their cases!'

I waved her into calm. 'Claire, Claire, Claire. No, you have it all wrong. It's here in Salmonweir. Nothing to do with Devon and Cornwall Police and nothing they would be even remotely interested in for more reasons than I could possibly list in one night.'

'Oh ok,' she paused, 'so what is it?'

'Promise not to tell?'

'Yes dad, of course.' She crossed her heart.

'*We* have a murderer here in Salmonweir.'

She scratched her head. 'A murderer? I thought you were the only living person there?'

'I am. Somebody is killing the other residents.'

She frowned. 'Aren't they already dead? How does that work?'

'I wish I knew, love. All I know is that these people have disappeared in violent conditions. If they've been sent back to their respective afterlife and can't get back, then that qualifies enough as murder for me. We've two dead so far and I can't find anything to link them.'

I didn't mention the notes, the bracelet or the pendant. Claire worries about me more than the twins do, but then the twins are pragmatic, and Claire has empathy in abundance. Since she was old enough to understand the concept of going to work, she always wanted to be a nurse. How she ended up in the cutthroat world of technology marketing I will never understand. I always told myself it was to change it from within.

'Two bodies? Wow.'

'Not even bodies, just signs of a violent struggle and now these two people are gone from Salmonweir and haven't been seen since.'

'Wow. Well, I hope you catch them soon.'

'Thank you. Anyway, I think you said you have two bits of news for me?'

'Yes!' she fist-pumped the air. 'My promotion. We're all going out tomorrow night to celebrate. Massive, massive pay rise. Not that the money matters, but it helps when living in Clifton.'

'Well done. Glad to see your hard work beginning to pay off. I need to come up and see you again, Claire. I realise my fatherly duties are lacking.'

'Oh don't worry, dad. I know you've had a lot on your plate. Have you spoken to mum recently?' There, the question she'd been itching to ask.

'A couple of times, more so through our solicitors than face-to-face. We're keen to get this over with and not let them draw it out for the sake of their own commission.'

She nodded. 'I spoke to mum last night actually. She's being remarkably level-headed about it considering how she's reacted in the past. I don't know whether Paul or Cass have managed to talk some sense into her, but I hope it goes well for both of your sakes. You know where we are if you need us, all three of us.'

'Thank you, sweetheart.' I blew my daughter a kiss.

There was an uncomfortable pause. 'Aside from the divorce, are *you* ok, dad?'

'Of course, I am! I love it down here and do not regret retiring. I think your mum would have been happier if we'd moved somewhere like Truro or Penzance, even Falmouth is a metropolis compared to Salmonweir. She hated the idea of living in the sticks though she never told me *that* until the day she decided to leave.'

While I talked, Claire did little but nod solemnly. 'I think she would have wanted to return to Cambridge eventually and that's the last place I'd want to go, no offence.'

'None taken. I love where we grew up, but when you've made the decision to leave, you *don't* want to go back. I know how it is. And for the record, I think she handled it badly. The more I think about it, the more I realise that mum can be quite selfish sometimes.'

I was slightly hurt by that, but then the truth usually does. Instead, I waved her down. 'Thanks, but I don't want any of you to take sides. I'll always be your dad and she will always be your mum.'

'Come up in a few weekends, dad? Just jump in the car and come tearing up the M5. It's easy to get here. It will be good to see you before Christmas. We can go to the Christmas Market.' Her eyes lit up. 'Or at Christmas! I think Paul and Ellie are coming over for Boxing Day, but

I've made no plans for Christmas Day itself. Mum is going to Uncle-.'

There was a brief flicker and the lights went out. She rolled her eyes. '-she would come here for New Year and have some girly time with me and Cass if she can make it.'

'Sorry love, I lost internet connection. Where did you say your mum was going for Christmas?'

'Uncle Bobby and Aunty Saff. She's not seen them and with Aunty Saff not being well, she thought she ought to soon.'

'What's wrong with Saffron?'

Her face dropped dramatically. 'Mum hasn't told you?'

'No, is it something I should know about?' The lights flickered again but we didn't lose connection this time.

She looked behind her as though expecting her mother to appear there. 'Saff is ill and she won't get better. That's all I can say, really.'

My face dropped. 'Sorry to hear that. If you talk to them, give them my regards and ask if there's anything I can do. Not to sound too blunt, but will she still be around at Christmas?'

'I will tell them, and yes. She has a year at the most and seems pretty – well, relatively – healthy at the moment. She could leave us before then but it's unlikely. There's a slender chance she will get better, but slender is a vast overstatement.'

I nodded sombrely. 'You told me you had some more good news but then we got onto other things?'

'Ah yes. Well. And actually, it's three now. Do you remember Charlie?'

I looked skyward for a second. 'Which Charlie, your ex-boyfriend or your best friend when you were about ten?'

'The second! We recently reconnected and she's moving to Ba-' she stopped and looked over my shoulder. 'Sorry dad, I didn't know you had guests. Want me to go?'

'I don't, I'm here all alone.'

'Oh, maybe it was just my eyes,' she said, not really convinced by her own words and leaving me even less convinced. 'For half a second I thought I saw someone behind you.'

A chill went down my spine, but I brushed it off. 'Some of the residents can pop in and out at random. Probably saw me having private time and went again.' Now it was my turn to fail to convince myself.

Claire just shrugged, unconcerned.

'Was it a man or a woman?'

'I couldn't tell, but big, stocky big, like a rugby player. Not to sound sexist or anything, but I'm assuming it was a man on that alone.'

The only ghosts I knew who could Pop were neither stocky nor big. Eli is tall but thin and almost scrawny. The other three included two women – one plump, one small built, both short. The other was a five-year-old boy. None of them could be described as tall and stocky and none would have the bad manners to turn up unannounced anyway.

A growing sense of unease struck me then in view of the mysterious note and my recent experience with the granite locket.

'Dad, are you all right?'

'Yes. I'll be back in a minute.' It was dark outside, understandable in early November, and all I could see beyond the window was blackness and the occasional twinkling lights from the sea to the south. I closed the curtains and felt only marginally safer.

Something prickled the back of my neck and I turned around quickly. There was nothing there except the chair, table and laptop with Claire's smiling face from the video screen.

'Dad should I go?'

'Can I call you back?'

With a look of concern, she blew me a kiss and closed the connection. The artificial bell sound signed Claire out, leaving me all alone in a quiet house, wind hitting the outside wall. It's amazing what you don't notice when absorbed in technology.

'Whoever you are, this is *not funny*!' I shouted. 'I demand you show yourself.'

Only silence met my defiant yet terrified call, silence, and that November wind. When I was a copper, a local criminal was a known quantity. He or she would give away their position. None of them, to my reckoning, could teleport in and out of buildings or between rooms.

Then I saw it – a scrap of paper that was not mine and wasn't there before. I never left paper on my laptop so that I couldn't type. I approached it as cautiously as I would a bomb, just as I did with the box from last night. Using a pencil, I unwrapped it gingerly. It was a note, nothing more. It was yet another note from the mystery person with poor spelling and worse handwriting.

> **I browt yu the brayslet and I browt yu
> the pendunt. Now yu must fynd the
> ring bye yor selv. Then yu will no who did it
> Hurry, tym is importint now**

I called Claire back. She couldn't come down and help me. She couldn't help if she was only next door, not against a ghost. But I did need the comfort of her voice, her face, her smile, her enthusiasm. Yes, even a hardened copper needs the comfort of his not-so-little-girl-anymore adult daughter sometimes.

'Hello again, dad. You had me worried there for a moment.' She sipped at her hot drink.

'It's alright. Just one of the ghosts up to mischief. I sent him packing, don't worry.'

'Ah that's good. Must be scary enough in a village full of ghosts without them *trying* to scare the shit out of you.' She put her hand to her mouth. 'Ooh, pardon my French.'

'Don't worry, I said far worse to the mischievous git.' I lied, giving Claire a warm smile that barely hid my terror. 'So, the second and third bits of good news?'

'Ah yes. It's Charlie. She's moving to Bath and we're doing lunch this weekend. The other bit of news is that Ellie has asked me to be a bridesmaid.' Claire beamed again.

'How wonderful!' Those were the only words I managed to get out before everything went dark. The lights, the computer, the electronic devices – everything plunged me into the blackness I really could have done without.

Chapter 16

Despite almost needing a change of underwear, the power cut was indeed just that – a problem with the local grid connection.

I saw that as soon as I stepped outside of the house. No streetlights were on and neither were lights on in any of the houses I could see from my house. The only light in the village came from the pub – thank God for backup generators and thank God for the watering holes of Blighty to see us through.

Claire phoned within minutes, checking I was fine. Whoever the earlier interloper was, he or she never came back and never took the opportunity to leave another note. So, no change of underwear needed that night. Power cut or no power cut, I'd promised to meet Eli at the pub and that's where I went next.

The ground was cold, wet and soggy. Dark nights and low light certainly have many charms, but this is one of those occasions where I missed the big city, the bright lights, the paved streets and the endless flow of traffic along the road to see the way.

Because it was so dark, and the pub the only place in the village with lighting not connected to the main grid, the bar was unsurprisingly packed. Eli stood outside waiting for me.

'Hello, Eli. Jacob not coming in with you today?'

He looked down at his feet. 'No. We have decided that the time is still not yet right.'

I was disappointed Jacob wasn't putting in an appearance, but I imagined if he *really* wanted his presence made public, nothing would have stopped the strong-willed young man. 'I understand, my friend. No sense rushing these things, is there? Right then, shall we go in?'

I opened the door and stepped through, finding myself hit immediately with a wall of warmth and light. Gas lighting and fire created a welcome cosiness and goodwill that I hoped had already rubbed off for my announcement in just a few moments.

Salmonweir residents surrounded the bar to three levels deep. Every so often, I could see Babajide's head bob up and down before disappearing behind a sea of people again. I stood in the only open space in the pub, the only place where the ancient oak flooring showed through the enormous congregation of village residents. Eli stood behind me shifting from foot to foot.

'Are you alright friend?' I turned to him. He nodded.

I went to the nearest table and cast quick glances at its two occupants.

The first was Wilhelmina Yorke busily scratching away at a piece of parchment. 'Your legs are like the trunks of trees! No, no, that's not right. Like the solid contours of an old oak. Show me thy rings. Darling, please hold up the branches of me? Hmm, that might work!'

The second person was one of Harry's crew. All his energy appeared directed towards feigning interest in the poetry, offering only the occasional grunt of approval. By now, he'd no doubt learnt not to argue. 'May I borrow your glass?' I asked him.

He looked up at me as though waking from torpor and nodded slowly. I picked up the glass and tapped the bottom against the table.

'My heart shatters like glass without your touch!' exclaimed the poet. 'Oh thank you Karl!' I smiled at her. Sadly, nobody else had heard my banging so I did it again. One by one, the crowd turned their heads towards me. Muttering began and then died.

'Thank you for your attention. I have just lifted Eli's house arrest. The man is innocent. Another party, who shall remain nameless for now,' I cast a quick look at Eli who gave me a quick nod, 'came forward to back up his alibi. He is not the killer. This means that a killer is still on the loose here in Salmonweir.'

The murmurs picked up and died off again quickly. 'In the morning I would like to speak with Harry, Cato and Kensa.' Only Harry's voice called up from the back of the bar. He didn't seem sober. 'Harry, there is no need to feign drunkenness. This can certainly wait until the morning.'

As Harry cackled, the bar launched into raised glasses and muttered apologies towards my companion.

'Eli, I insist you stay and have a drink with me, with us. I am paying of course. What would you like?'

'I assume the establishment serves beer?'

I was quite taken aback. 'Beer? I didn't think you drank alcohol?'

'Alcohol is not against my faith. I simply choose to save it for special occasions such as this and do penance for my pride later. What is it I have heard you say?' he looked at me curiously, 'now seems as good a time to start as any?'

The crowd made way for us, offering smiles and raised glasses for me, and handshakes and apologies for Eli. The crowd around the bar made way, allowing us to queue jump.

I was relieved the crowd accepted it so easily, especially at the unspoken revelation that a killer was still on the loose in the village. Some people find it difficult to accept a person once accused of a crime is innocent of it until the real perpetrator is apprehended. There is always that doubt, a belief of no smoke without fire. It's persistent and nasty, a stain proving not so easy to remove. I admit in my early years I found difficulty letting it go after finding out I'd arrested the wrong person, but you learn to get over it.

Babajide offered us a warm but nervous smile. I could not see Morwenna and enquired about her whereabouts. 'She is, ah, writing her emails to suppliers.'

'This late when there's nobody there and everyone here?'

Babajide shrugged his shoulders. 'She said it was important to do it now.'

I sighed. 'Ok, but you're on your own with all these people?'

'No, not on my own.' He pointed to his right. At that moment, a figure appeared at the counter flap, placed several glasses on the bar and passed through it. 'Please can you help me serve now? It is got so busy.'

'Of course!' came the cheerful reply.

'Ebrel, how wonderful to see you. I didn't know you worked here?'

'Neither did I until about an hour ago,' she beamed. 'I asked Babajide if he would be kind enough to show me how to use these pumps. Apparently, I'm a natural so he offered me a job for the night. I hope it can become permanent?' she looked at him expectantly.

'I sorry Ebrel. That is not my decision to make but we see. Mrs Morwenna will decide soon. Maybe when she see you working the pumps, like ah. What is it you said, "like a boss"? Then she gives you a job maybe, but not *as* boss.' Babajide smiled at her and nodded enthusiastically.

She beamed back at him and flushed.

'That's wonderful. Congratulations on your first job, Ebrel.'

'Dad will be so proud – I think, I hope. What can I get you fine gentlemen?' she asked.

'I would like a pint of Finest Kernow Pale and you Eli?'

'The same please, Miss Ebrel.'

She poured our two pints and handed them over with another beaming smile. We retreated to a table near the door. A few people come over to speak to Eli and ask how he was doing, offering their apologies. The only one I was certain wouldn't come over was Jowan; he didn't disappoint though I'd hoped he would swallow his pride and offer his relief at the man's innocence. I'd noticed him on entry. When he saw me with the preacher, he simply turned away and supped at his wine.

After about an hour, Eli thanked me for the company and the drink and departed. He rebuffed several pleas to drink with others and disappeared into the night. The streetlights came back on outside and that seemed to be the cue for at least half of the patrons to leave. Each of them bade me goodbye and thanked me for keeping the village safe. I confess to feeling a fraud. I'd detained the wrong man and there was still a killer on the loose with no clue as to who had done it or why.

I stood up, the legs of the chair scraping against the wooden floor. With nobody else at the bar, Babajide showed Ebrel how to pour the correct measures for spirits. I hoped her training as a barmaid would give her some direction in this existence after breaking down on my shoulder the other week. She certainly seemed to have perked up tonight.

Jowan had been on his own all night and he was still on his own when I handed my and Eli's glass back to the bar. Ebrel asked if I wanted another drink; I declined, deciding to take the opportunity to speak to Jowan.

'Did you have a good evening?' I asked. When I spoke, his expression changed to that of the old, jolly monk I had known since the beginning. Until that moment, he'd looked lost in his own thoughts, barely acknowledging the other patrons.

'Oh, quite alright thank you!'

'You didn't look it a moment ago?'

'Just contemplating this modern existence and the situation in the village. I spend a lot of time thinking about God's reasons for allowing any of us back to live not alive but not dead either.' He raised his glass.

'Alas, I'm sure you have more insight than I. I'm only an occasional Catholic, Jowan.'

His face dropped. 'We can work on that.' He paused. 'Eli has gone?'

'Yes. I think he had enough.'

Jowan nodded thoughtfully. 'As much as I despise the man, I must confess to being pleased to learn of his innocence.'

'I'm sure he'll appreciate the sentiment.'

'I suspected his innocence, truth be told.' Jowan took another sip of his wine.

I looked at Jowan quizzically. 'Oh really?'

'Oh yes. I know what he does in the church late at night with his "parishioner friend".' Jowan looked at me accusingly. 'I as good as told you on Bonfire Night where he was and what he was doing.'

I thought back, remembering Jowan's words. What he said at the time was ambiguous and confused me a little. He did not want to elaborate at the time but it made much more sense in context now I knew about Jacob.

'You do know what he is, don't you?' Jowan's face twisted.

'Yes.'

'It doesn't concern you?'

'Why would it? Should it?' I crossed my arms.

Jowan shook his head but said nothing more.

I went to say something, to try to reason with Jowan some way but he cut me off. When he cast a look over my shoulder and stood abruptly. 'I should be going. I have some matter to attend. Good evening to you,' he blurted. I watched the monk curiously as he waddled across the pub hastily and left by the far door – the same one through which Eli had left; his wine glass was half-full.

'Are you sure I can't get you another drink, Karl?' Ebrel asked me eagerly. Only around 10 of us were left and I could hear the fruit machine in the corner once more now that the noise had abated. 'Actually, I will have one more please, Ebrel. A half this time. Oh, and a packet of crisps.'

I left the pub around 10pm and went straight home. A cool rather than chilly breeze greeted my exit from the pub. I went straight home, pleased that I could see my route, and humming one of Harry's shanties to myself. For the first time in days, I fell into a deep and unbroken sleep. No notes, no mysterious visitors Popping in and out and definitely no more power cuts.

Three smiling faces greeted me before I'd even had the chance to brew my morning coffee. Nevertheless, I invited them in and offered to share a hearty breakfast. By now, all three had experienced the delights of "A Full English" and it was over this sumptuous feast that we went over what we knew about the victims and their movements.

'The only link I can see between the two victims is that they are both dead. But as that applies to everyone in this village except Karl, not much to go on, is it?' said Harry with a shrug.

'They are also both male,' offered Kensa with an apologetic smile. 'And I doubt that is enough to go on, either.'

I nodded. 'Tobin arrived after Eddie disappeared. I think we can all agree on that too.'

I had to stop my train of thought then because the doorbell rang. Annoyed and apologising to my three unofficial deputies, I went to the door. I was surprised to see Jacob of all people, and he looked more than a little concerned.

'Jacob hello. How are you, please come in!' I ushered him in. He looked inside and then tentatively crossed into my home.

'Mister Blackman, sir. I am sorry to interrupt. I wouldn't be here if it wasn't important.'

'It's quite alright, please come on through. We're just having breakfast.' I led him through to the conservatory with the others.

'Hello sir, madam, sir.' He greeted my three companions in turn. 'I see you're busy so I will just make this quick.'

'Stay as long as you like, really. If you'd like some breakfast, you are welcome. I always make too much scrambled egg. And bacon for that matter. And, I suppose, sausages. And hog's pudding. And fried mushrooms. I seem to have overdone it again so please do tuck in.'

Kensa cocked her head curiously at the man while she chewed on another sausage but said nothing. That woman can really eat; she had put away twice as much as Harry.

'Thank you for your kindness, but perhaps not this time Mister Blackman sir. See, I was wondering if you'd seen Eli.' He scratched the back of his neck nervously.

An impending feeling of dread overtook me. This conversation was already starting to seem familiar. 'Not since last night, I haven't.'

His eyes widened. 'Last night, sir? You was with Eli last night?'

'That's right Jacob. Don't you remember? I took him to the pub to make sure everybody knew he was innocent. He met me there. Eli and I had a few drinks and he left about an hour later.'

'I don't believe we have had the pleasure?' Kensa stood up and offered Jacob her hand.

'This is Jacob, a friend and parishioner of Eli,' I interjected quickly. 'You've not long arrived, have you Jacob?' He reached out and shook Kensa by the hand. As I had, she gave it a curious glance when they broke.

'That's right Mister Blackman sir and Kensa Miss. I've not been formally introduced to no one in the village yet, but I'm sure we all will in good time. You must 'scuse my manners today though my lady, but I really need to find Eli.'

Kensa smiled, nodded and carried on feasting.

'He didn't make it home?' a cold shiver passed down my spine.

'As you say you was with him last night. Well, no, he never came home.' He looked from Kensa to Cato, to Harry and then to me. 'And now I'm worried, Mister Blackman sir. I'm worried that something might have happened to him.'

'Was he upset before he left? Anxious or anything like that?'

'No sir, he was happy as a summer day is long that he was finally going to get his, erm, exoner... exho... something.'

'Exoneration.'

'Yes, sir. That was it. But, I begging your pardon. That Bonfire Night the other night. Like we said, we was at the church together but there is something else.'

I looked at him quizzically.

'It's nothing bad about Eli sir, just in case you're thinking I was lying. No, I told the God's honest truth I swear to that. This is not so much about him as it is about me. You see, he told me to stay home until he was ready. But I couldn't sir, not with everyone having so much fun outside. Before church, I went there and I mixed and nobody challenged me. At one point I saw Eli and had to hide. I saw him with two other people, arguing. I mean like really shouting with them. Eli wanted them to go to the fire so he could see to it and talk to them all proper.'

'And they were?' I pressed. Jacob was quite clearly the talker in the relationship.

'It were the pretty young lass with strawberry blonde hair and a man old enough to be her father. In fact, sir, I think he was her father by the way he spoke to her. No man got no business talking to no young lady like that unless he is her father if you know my meaning. He was really angry and kept saying something that Eli had done wrong.'

'Did you get a name?'

'It sounded like he called her "April" and telling her to get home.'

'Ebrel?'

'Yes sir.'

'Curiouser and curiouser. Another thing for my to-do list, talk to Ebrel and Corin Penrose. You three, we need to adjourn this meeting and start looking for Eli.' Each put their food down and stood up. What should happen then, but my phone rang. It startled Jacob who no doubt had not yet seen a mobile phone. I quickly grabbed it and read the display. It was Paul.'

'Dad, hi!'

'Hello son, can I call you back? Sort of in the middle of something.' I garbled the words out. I love talking to my kids, but as any parent knows, they do have a habit of calling at a moment of least convenience.

His voice went silent for a few seconds as he deliberated. 'Uh. Sure. Actually dad. I really need to see you, like now. I'm in Truro and you need to get over here. I have to show you something.'

'Oh, what are you doing down here?'

'I've got a client this afternoon. Well it was supposed to be this morning, but he cancelled and rearranged for about 2:30pm. Can you get here before then?'

I checked my watch: 9.57. 'Yes, I can. I'll get in the car and drive straight up. Should be there by eleven, maybe half past at the latest. How does that sound?'

'Perfect. I'll buy lunch.'

'This really can't wait? We have a crisis here now.'

'It might have something to do with your missing boy. I assume he hasn't come back yet?'

Another shiver passed down my spine. 'No, he hasn't. It seems we have another killing too.'

Paul went silent again. 'Did you look into how any of your residents died in the end?'

I still felt uncomfortable about doing so and I reminded Paul of that fact.

'Not my place to judge but I think this might be important. You've got another killer in Salmonweir. Somebody convicted of a nasty couple of murders when they were alive, I think. I'll know more by the time you get here. I can't send you the details as they haven't set up the digitised files for email yet and I can't download it to my device either.

'That's why you need me to come up and see?' All this time I maintained a neutral expression for the four people in my house. How I managed it, I really didn't know.

'Bingo.'

'Right son. I'll be there by half eleven.'

I turned to Cato, Kensa and Harry. 'I'm sorry, but I will need you three to conduct the search for Eli without me. I'm also going to need one of you to talk to the Penroses. I suggest one of you to go to the shop – Cato, I think you should do that. You're quite well acquainted with them. Kensa and Harry know the village layout better, so I suggest the two of you begin searching. I'm so sorry to have to leave you all to it.'

Then I turned to Jacob and apologised again. 'I have to go but should be back this afternoon. These three capable people will help. Tell them everything you can possibly think of that might help with the search. I trust them more than anyone else in this village.'

Jacob looked downhearted but nodded.

I raced upstairs to get my jacket and, because I was leaving town and didn't want vital evidence going missing, grabbed what Eli called the "Love Pendant". Then I remembered the bracelet that I'd left in the drawer. I picked it up, half-remembering the flashback I had when touching the Love Pendant.

It came as a shock but not entirely unexpected. As my room faded from my vision, I found myself back in Salmonweir of old again.

I am on the same cliff as before, looking down into the valley of Salmonweir. It looks much the same as it did in the other vision but it is not the Salmonweir I know. It is a grey day, but warm. There is no sense that it has rained recently.

I do get the sense that I am not alone, and I turn to my right. There is a teenage boy at my side. He is maybe fourteen or fifteen years old, and I'm certain it is the boy from before – he has those same chocolate brown eyes, but now he has the merest hint of stubble too. Despite the chill on the cliff, I can feel an internal warmth at this boy. It's a feeling that something breached in those six years that shunted two people together, binding their souls for eternity and beyond.

'I have something else for you.' His voice is deeper than before. He steps close to me and I can feel the cool air suddenly warm. 'What is it?' I ask, lifting my chin to face the boy. I don't know why it took so long for the penny to drop, but I realise in these visions that I am a girl.

He smiles at me again. 'Close your eyes.'

'What is it?' I ask with a girly giggle.

'Close your eyes,' he repeats, 'and you will see.'

Everything goes dark and I hold out my hands. Something cold and light drops into it. I open my eyes again. It is the bracelet, looking brand new.

'But-' it's the only word I hear myself speak.

'I won't take no for an answer,' the boy says.

'It's silver!' I exclaim in response. 'How can you afford that?'

The boy nodded. 'It's silver a'right and it's yours. When we're married, you can look at it and remember I gave it you.' He steps closer. I can feel his breath on my forehead, his face moving closer to mine. 'I love you-' and we kiss.

Then I woke up and found myself back in my bedroom, sitting on the bed with four ghosts surrounding me. Kensa knelt before me, reaching for my hand and a look of concern on her face. I snapped out of it quickly and offered her a smile. 'What just happened?'

She quickly looked to the other three – Harry and Cato, and Jacob was still here too. 'You passed out. We found you sat here holding that thing and staring at nothing. You were talking.'

I looked at the Warrior Queen quizzically. 'Talking?'

She nodded slowly. 'Nothing sensible, but speaking nonetheless.'

'Nothing sensible?'

'I heard "Salmonweir" at least three times, sir,' said Jacob.

'And some words that made no sense together,' Harry threw his hands in the air.

'Like what?' Sometimes, Harry beat around the bush a bit too much for a sea dog.

'Oh I can't remember none of them now!' he said. 'But summat about wedding rings and eels.'

I gathered my thoughts and stood up. 'Nothing sensible, as you said.' I checked my watch. 'I need to go to Truro; my son is waiting there. Does anybody else need help on what you need to do while I am gone?'

They responded in the negative, so I went straight to the car and with one final glance at the group of ghosts making their way down the hillside, drove to Cornwall's only city. I spent my journey trying to figure out the identity of the boy in the hallucination but nothing about him was familiar

Chapter 17

It was noticeably cooler when I arrived in Truro. With a population of just under 20,000, this pretty little city is not the largest settlement in Cornwall yet remains the capital. I have a particular fondness for it, especially for the annual Christmas parade (I've been once so far), and it serves to remind me of what I'm missing living right out in the sticks – both good and bad.

Still, the opportunity to see one of the kids is always welcome no matter where we arrange to meet.

It was windy and overcast when I arrived in Truro but felt relatively mild for mid-November. I parked up at the central car park in the city, behind the cinema and a few minutes walk from a boat café moored at Lemon Quay where we'd arranged to meet.

Christmas shopping, decorations and lights were still at least a couple of weeks away, but the midweek crowd didn't seem to realise it. I met Paul at the quay and we agreed on somewhere to eat – a trendy student type bar overlooking the river. Like the shopping centre, it was noisy for a weekday.

We chose seats near the back, firstly because the music was slightly too loud and secondly so we could have some privacy. I ordered pulled pork panini and Paul chose a steak and ale pasty. We both went for soft drinks and tucked in.

Afterwards, we made our way up the hill to the Records Office. The young woman behind the counter remembered Paul from earlier and asked him if he was in Cornwall for long.

'Oh, just a couple of days. I've brought my dad along for some extra help.' Paul clapped me on the back.

The woman looked at me with a hint of recognition but smiled and looked away when she realised her stare lingered a little too long. I offered her a smile as I signed in and left her to figure out precisely why my face looked so familiar. As I turned away from her, I caught her examining my signature more than would be normal for the average visitor.

'She recognised you, didn't she?' Paul chuckled as we climbed the stairs to the newspaper records archive he'd been working in earlier that day. 'You're famous, dad.'

'Quite clearly.' I guess this is something I would have to get used to outside of Salmonweir.

'How does it feel to be a minor celebrity?'

'Considering the stories the newspapers have already published,' I replied, 'it's something I'd rather not have, but it is what it is. Have you heard from any reporters lately?'

'Oh yes, they try every few weeks.' Paul sighed, lowering his voice as we entered the workroom. There was no need as we were the only people in there at the time. 'I usually just hang up. Sometimes I even swear.'

'You have me intrigued,' I said as we found a terminal tucked away enough so our conversation would not be overheard on the off chance. 'What did you find out?'

Paul shook his head. 'I fear I may have you here under false pretences based on what little I could make out, so I apologise in advance. You might be able to figure out more than I could though.' He used the temporary login and we were quickly into the system.

'You said something about a convicted killer?' I watched him work his magic, going back to the files he'd saved earlier.

'Yes, but I can't tell who. I'm sure the person or people who digitised it did the best they could, but the file looks old. I think the copy is too degraded to make it out. I did find out enough to know there were a couple of nasty killings. This person, whoever it was, killed two people and died in Devon. They were convicted posthumously.'

'Man or woman? And when?'

He sighed. 'Dad, the first is so degraded that I can't tell, and the second is little more than a footnote. Two victims – gender unknown for either but one was a teenager and the other middle aged. It might have been pointless you coming here at all. I'm sorry; I should have relayed this to you over the phone.'

I smiled at him and clapped him on the shoulder. 'Nonsense! I get to see my son and you never know what I might spot. Trust me and take nothing for granted. It's amazing how many cases have been solved by figuring out the tiny details. Ever see that telly programme where the detective drops a pen or something and gets ink on his fingers and all over the floor and then figures out not only who, but how the killer did it?'

'*Killed in Kernow* or the other one?' Paul smiled. 'Not there's much difference aside from location. I think most do that.'

'That happens more often than you'd think.'

Paul opened the first file. He was right; the newspaper scan was degraded. It looked as though it may have originally been printed on poor quality paper, the sort of stock that a newspaper with a low circulation used because it was cheap and they didn't have longevity in mind.

Not that the article was a large one. Just as Paul had said, it was about the size of what these days we'd call a footnote. Ever seen a newspaper retraction tabloids post when forced to print a public apology because the person they hounded for weeks and months, and dedicated endless space to hounding them turned out innocent?

'Is this the best quality version there is?'

'Sorry dad, yes. It's the only version of this piece.'

I strained my eyes and peered closer to the screen to make out what few words I could. It read:

Samonweir village: The case of the xxxx xxxxxxx resolved in xxagxxx yesxxxxxy when the xxxx of decxxxxx ixxxxxxex was fxxxx xxxx at a villxxe oxxtsxxx Txvxxxxxk in Dexxn. Morx nexx fxxlxwx. Dxxexxex will xxxxx rexxxx xx Salmxxxxxr for xurxxx soon.

'Ouch,' I said. 'I can't make head nor tail of it. How you managed to tell there were two deaths from that, I don't know?'

Paul shook his head. 'Not from this on its own. This was just a local snippet. The other file is something I found in one of the nationals later. It *seems* to reference this case but without any dates on any of it, it's hard to know for certain. Again, it's just a footnote and doesn't shed much light on what happened.'

He brought up the file and allowed me to read it for myself, all two lines of it.

'Convicted posthumously, the double killer in the Salmonweir murder case was laid to rest today in an unmarked grave in Tavistock. A special service took place this past Sunday at the church in Salmonweir to honour the two victims (aged 19 and 43).' I turned to Paul. 'And this is everything?' I couldn't stop my face sinking, but at least I knew more than I did an hour ago.

'Sorry dad, I really have got you here under false pretences. 'And that is as far as I got this morning,' he said almost apologetically.

'No, this might or might not be a lead, but it's something I should probably investigate anyway.' I checked my watch. 'What time did you say your appointment was?'

'My meeting is at half past two, so I *really* should go.'

'Certainly Paul and thanks so much for this, it's been helpful.' I stood up and gave my son a hug. 'Best of luck with the meeting; I hope it all goes well.'

'Thanks dad and I hope you get something out of this. See you soon and good luck yourself.' With that, Paul was gone, and I was alone in the research room with the extent of my son's morning of research.

'Here we go then, let's see what we can find out.' I'm not technophobic, but I do feel daunted by these places and not knowing where to start.

I heard footsteps gently tap-tapping up the stairs behind me and turned to look. I saw a brief flash of blue round the corner and disappear behind the wall only to appear again a few seconds later.

It was the woman from reception. She smiled at me as she entered the room. I was the only person here (still) so she could only have been coming to see me.

'Is everything alright there, Mister Blackman?' her voice was distinctly Cornish; I felt my face flush at the use of my name. So she *had* recognised me, or had she merely made a note of my name when I signed in.

'I- I think so.' Frowning, I turned back to the screen and clicked the "Home" button.

'The young man who just left said you might need some assistance tracking down some information. May I?' she pointed to a chair.

I nodded in affirmation. 'That was my son and I suppose I do need some assistance. You see, I am researching a rather old crime.' I pointed to the records.

The young woman removed a pair of reading glasses from her blouse pocket and put them on, leaning forward to read. 'Oh my,' she exclaimed, 'what a poor-quality scan!'

'All my son was able to find, I'm afraid. I don't know if it's the newspaper or the scan that's the problem.'

She leaned forward further and frowned. 'It looks to me like a scanning problem. We get that a lot from the first scanners, library staff in the early days not knowing how to use them properly.

My face lit up. 'Is there a chance of a better-quality scan?'

'Maybe, although there could be faults in the paper itself.'

She gave a barely perceptible shrug. 'Possibly, but you may need to spend hours or days looking. You may even need to use subscription services to locate and access them. That can be expensive, and it could involve a trip to London. I'm assuming you won't want to travel?'

'Not especially unless absolutely necessary. Do you know anyone who could do it? I would be willing to pay for a service.'

'We run a research service. We're cheaper than the national network but we don't have access to as many resources as they do. We do it all in-house.'

'So long as I don't have to visit London. How much would that cost me?'

'I'll get you a leaflet,' she said and disappeared from the room before returning with a small, folded piece of paper. 'This is our in-house research services. Most people come to us when they hit a snag but don't want the expense of the national network. It's a great starting point.'

I took the pamphlet from her and opened it out. It listed a number of professional archiving and search services and charges. 'How quickly could this be done? Started I mean.'

'It's newspaper records so it shouldn't take too long. We have access to academic and other research services that the public can't access or would be required to pay an arm and a leg. I don't expect it will take more than a couple of hours to do a cross-search.

'I have no idea what you're saying, but I think it sounds wonderful.'

The young lady smiled. 'I have no major tasks for this afternoon, so if you'd like to proceed, I can make a start almost right away. How long it takes depends on how much there is. I can expect preliminary search results by the end of my shift. Anything more thorough could take a few days.'

'That's fine. I'm looking for newspaper articles – locally and nationally – that give me more detail on this story, anything would be helpful right now.'

She nodded, cautiously. 'We will see what we can do, but newspaper records were not as thorough then as they are now. I shouldn't have trouble finding them, but there might not be much to find in the first place. I'm afraid you *may* be wasting your money.'

Logging off, I followed her down to reception where she provided me with an estimate of services, an estimate of cost and a copy of their terms and conditions to sign and checked, once again, whether I was happy to go ahead with such a strong possibility of finding nothing at all. It all seemed so official (not to mention expensive) but I went ahead anyway and paid my money.

Soon, I was out of Truro and back on the road to Salmonweir. I mentally told myself I would get out of the village more often in the future. Of course, I love being the only human in a quaint village full of ghosts, but I certainly don't want to become isolated.

Valarie will feel smug for hearing me say it, but I do sometimes need the hustle and bustle of urban sprawl.

As I left the A30 at Penzance, my phone buzzed. By the time I found a suitable layby, it had stopped ringing. I picked up the phone and saw I had an answerphone message. Surprisingly, it was the young woman from the Records Office.

Hello Mister Blackman, this is Zofia from the Records Office. I've managed to track down some more stories related to your newspaper article. There's a reference in a small American journal called "Feminist Perspectives on Murder and Other Serious Crimes". Never heard of it, but there is a reference to a double murder case in Salmonweir in a paper written in the early 1970s. I've sent you an email with the abstract. I'm afraid I can't send you the whole paper and it will cost hundreds of pounds to read it. I would normally recommend contacting

the author direct, but I'm afraid she died about 10 years
after writing it.

I heard the rustling of papers.

I also came across a few more newspaper articles
and some names related to the case. There are some dates
for you too. I have to leave it there as I'm due off shift in
about 30 minutes and we've had a group of students turn
up unannounced. Take a look at what I've sent, if you need
any more please call me in the morning. Thanks, my name
is Zofia and the number is...' I cut the message off.

My heart skipped a beat – names and a date. I really
hoped that this was not another wild goose chase as it
had been with Eli. I switched my data on just in case but
was not surprised to see I had no data signal, or at least
not strong enough to check my emails; now, I couldn't
wait to get home to check.

Keeping my excitement under control, I still had
some seven precious miles to go, but there may as well
have been 700. The faster I wanted to go, the slower I had
to go.

A police car with flashing lights pulled up behind me
as I entered the network of busy roads around Penzance.
No matter how often I come to this area, I never fail to be

surprised at how busy it is – so far down country and so close to Salmonweir.

I assumed I had been speeding and pulled into the left lane, preparing to stop while I went over a grovelling apology in my mind. Instead, he shot past me, on through a set of red lights and off into the distance.

My pulse returned to normal and soon I was out on the country roads that would take me home – home to Salmonweir, home to the ghosts with whom I now shared my life and home, hopefully, to catch a killer.

Chapter 18

I had been away only a few hours at that point, but as I passed over the hill and saw the village, the coastline and the valley before me, something felt different. It was ridiculous, but I could not shake the feeling that something had changed in the village in my short absence despite the appearance of calm.

It's like one of those days when a storm is coming but the sky is blue and the wind light and warm, a certain heaviness to the air, but an existential than a barometric heaviness. As the village's familiar landscape opened before me, that feeling only grew heavier.

Perhaps it was because I now felt so close to finding out what happened to Eddie, Tobin, and now Eli, or perhaps it was something different. Perhaps the residents knew that their home was tainted. Perhaps a dark cloud had passed over the village – one that may never be removed.

Or perhaps some critical change happened during my absence?

No, that's nonsense; I had no evidence for believing that beyond my gut feeling. I had no way of knowing or even feeling such a fundamental shift in the world around me in the space of just a few hours, but I could not shake the feeling that this was the climax of my first (and hopefully only) case as an investigator of crimes against disembodied-spirit persons.

I passed the familiar red post box with GR emblazoned on the front. An icon of the village, a few twigs hanging out of the box and a scraping of dirt on the front suggested it saw more birds than letters these days. And then I remembered that my post arrives once a week, handed to me by a nervous postman who no doubt feels threatened by all the ghosts I consider friends.

Next to the post box is the village's only bus stop. No bus had stopped there in months, but I suspected (and hoped) as word got out about the Bonfire Spectacular, that they would do so again.

But first, I had a killer to catch. The constant reminder of why I was now rushing back.

I was so preoccupied with this thought – catching a killer – that I didn't notice Mickey, the Rag and Bone man sitting on his cart in the layby leading to the footpath into the village.

He was seemingly frozen in time, staring towards the rolling grey surf of the sea. It was an eerie sight as I had become so used to seeing him taking his horse and cart along the road, around the mini roundabout (well, the painted white circle) and back up the road again only to repeat the process.

He turned to me as I passed him and, surprisingly, he waved me down. I mentioned before that Mickey was the quiet sort. The only words I ever got out of him were always when I spoke to him first. The rest of the time, he just ignored me. On a good day, he'd wave but not much more than that.

I ground my little car to a halt and reversed up the road. Even though I knew there was and would be no traffic behind me, I checked my mirrors every few inches. I even indicated when turning sharply to get into the layby and pulled up to a slow halt. The ground was sticky and cold under foot and I had to take care not to slip into the shrub. 'Good afternoon Mickey. How are you?'

'Sorry to stop yer,' he said, 'but I wanted to thank yer for everything yer do for the village and wish yer luck for what's to come.'

'Luck for what?' Had news really spread so far and so fast that even the person in the village who'd had no interest in talking to anyone knew about it?

'Finding out what happened. I know yer been away, but a lot can happen in a few hours, can't it?'

'Yes Mickey, it can.' I felt the cold November light wind against my hands and I slipped them into my pocket.

'Hurry home now, lad,' he said, 'they're waiting for yer.'

That comment was particularly odd, but with a quick thanks and a nod, I did just that. The journey back home was slow. I kept noticing things about the village I never noticed before – just how quiet it was, for starters.

I also noticed the number of empty buildings without curtains or blinds, windows leading into vacant rooms. No lighting and with untended and overgrown gardens, this was a ghost village in more ways than one.

Finally, I pulled into the one-way street at the front of my home and switched off the car's engine. I could hear nothing but the ocean and the sound of the occasional shrieking of gulls fighting over morsels.

My heart pounded in my chest. I wanted and needed to go inside, but I could not shake this eerie feeling about the place. I had seen no other resident except Mickey.

Where was everyone? At the very least, I could have expected to see some of the children playing in the street. I should have been able to get the faintest hint of sea shanty coming from *The Lady Catherine* – sounds I had come to associate with my new home.

But there was nothing.

The quietness followed me out of the car and along the gravel track to my front door. I slid the key into the lock with a clunk, clunk, clunk and turned it. Stepping cautiously inside, I got another sudden eerie feeling – that I was not alone in my house.

I was right. There were three ghosts in the living room.

The first was Kensa and she sat in my favourite armchair. She looked up as she saw me and gave me a heavy smile, nodding towards the other two ghosts.

The second was Harry. He sat in the other armchair, the one that Valarie used to favour.

Standing up between them and in front of my fireplace with his back to it, was a man I did not recognise. He wore modern clothing, not dissimilar from my own sense of style.

As I stepped into the room and closed the door, both Kensa and Harry stood to greet me. I had so many questions, but it seemed they were determined to detain the man such was their near-protective positioning before him. As they closed in around him, I saw a brief flash of something. I knew what it was straight away. This was the mysterious man with the leather-bound book.

'Where is Cato?' I asked, remembering I had sent him to the shop.

'I sent him home,' Kensa smiled. 'He acquired the information you needed, and all is now much clearer.'

'Any sign of Eli?' I asked.

She shook her head mournfully. 'No, but this man believes he knows where he might be, assuming he is still with us. He's been quite forthcoming.' She gave the man an appreciative nod.

'Aye,' said Harry, 'lads wanted to look right away but I said we should wait for you in case we disturbed something or got the killer on the run. We both agreed we wanted to do things proper like, with you here.'

Out of the corner of my eye, I saw Kensa nod in agreement. 'We thought you'd know best how to proceed.'

'And who are you, sir?' I addressed the third person.

For his size, he had a gentle voice. 'Sir, Mister Blackman. My name is Branok.' He stepped forward and offered his hand. 'Oh actually, I can't shake hands with you, but the good sentiment is there, sir.'

'It's good to meet you Branok, all the same.' The more I looked, the more I was convinced that this was the man who had been following me around. That night, talking to Claire, my daughter described the flash of a big, burly bear-like figure in the corner of my room.

She couldn't put an age on him then and I couldn't even now he was much clearer. His greying hair suggested middle age, but he had smooth skin for somebody so pale that suggested he was one of those unfortunate people who turned grey when relatively young. That is what happened to my dad's brother. The poor bloke was fully grey before he hit 25, or so I was told.

'You don't know me, but I certainly know you.' I didn't think it was possible, but this big man rose up further in my room, his head almost touching the ceiling.

I nodded cautiously. 'You were in my house a few days ago. You gave me and my daughter quite the fright.'

'That I was sir, and I apologise for my intrusion. I felt it was the only way to talk to you when I thought nobody

325

was watching. I wanted to talk to you desperately, but had to go. I didn't want to put your life in danger.' The man had deep chocolate eyes and the wisdom of years on his face.

'How were you putting my life in danger?' I gestured to the sofa. 'Please take a seat.'

He gratefully accepted. 'Salmonweir has eyes and ears. I couldn't stay, you see. They still don't know I'm here and I would rather it stayed that way. That's why I've tried to be careful, but God knows I've not been as careful as I could have been. I'm not a perfect man and wasn't in life but I did my best sir, I always did my best.'

I gestured to the book still firmly clasped in his hand. 'I'm guessing you are our mysterious book-carrying ghost too?'

'I am indeed. This book is the list of rules of what I can do and can't do. Brought it with me because I want to do things right. I've done what I can to get your attention and I had to check I was allowed to do it. I even approached that salesman to talk to you, but they got to him before he could tell you what was going on. I asked him to set up a meeting, see.'

'Tobin?'

'Yup, that was him. But they got him too.' I thought back to the night of the bonfire. Tobin told me he needed to talk to me "urgently" about another person returned from Salmonweir's history. 'I admit I've been following you for some time. I cannot deny that with God as my witness, but I never intended to do no harm to you. And I certainly never intended to frighten you to an early grave.'

'Have you been leaving me trinkets?'

'Trinkets, sir?' He gave me a blank expression.

'Yes, somebody left me a silver bracelet and a granite pendant along with some notes. I took them with me.' I pulled the envelope from my inside jacket pocket and put it on the coffee table, gingerly opening it to remove the two items and the letters.

His face went cold when he saw them. 'What about a gold ring, it's quite a thick one, have you got that?'

'No, I haven't.'

Harry cleared his throat. 'We found that at the scene of the first, um, incident. Eddie my cabin boy. We found it in his sleeping space after he went missing. We tossed it overboard thinking it were something the lad stole and totally useless to anyone.'

'You know who these belong to?' I gestured to the trinkets.

'Yes sir, that I do,' Branok replied. 'Not only that, I think I know who left them for you looking at these letters. It turns out I was wrong about some things too.'

'Who?'

He shook his head vigorously. 'I can't tell you directly, that's one of the rules. But I can guide you a bit so you can works it out for yourself. I can't tell you *nothing* directly. I will suggest that you find that ring because it will answer any remaining questions you will have spinning around in your head after I'm gone.'

I turned to Harry. 'I have a request to make.'

'You want one of me lads to jump over the side of the ship an find the ring in the water?'

I nodded. 'If it is still there, we need it found. I may also need some of the lads to come and help us find Eli. I realise I am asking a lot, Harry.'

'I'll get the lads on it!' Harry stood and left promptly, leaving myself, Branok and Kensa alone.

After a few minutes of silence, Branok spoke again. 'I'm sorry to say that lad is back on the other side and won't be allowed back no more. Tobin *can* come back, but I don't think he will want to for quite some time. Eli is still around, and I *think* I know where he is. He's safe for now though.'

'How long do we have?' asked Kensa.

'It's important we get to him before nightfall.'

'That's about two hours away. This might sound inappropriate, but I have an email to check before we go anywhere.' I interjected, remembering the information I'd received from the Records Office.

I brought my laptop into the living room, feeling a cold chill hit me. It wasn't actually cold; it was mild. No, the cold I felt was nothing to do with the temperature and everything to do with the current situation and the danger I now felt to my life. Branok said my life was at risk.

My aging laptop took several minutes to fire up, too many minutes – minutes that passed in silence, that heaviness remaining in the air. While it did, the others looked at me expectantly.

There it was **Ref: information about two murders.**

I opened the email and scanned the information. Thankfully, the Archivist had summarised the information in the six attachments she'd also sent, so I didn't need to scan through it all. Three names came up together. That of Branok and two others – both names I recognised. Tentatively, I turned the screen around and showed it to the pair.

Kensa gasped and put her hand to her face. 'Surely not?'

'Branok,' I said, the words weighing heavily on my heart. 'Can you confirm whether you know the two names here. Are you allowed to tell me that?'

He squinted at my screen, partly at the light and partly (perhaps) due to poor general literacy. Nevertheless, he could read well enough to recognise the two names. 'That I do. Both of them, good sir.'

'Can you tell me *how* you know them both.'

He told me. It confirmed what I already knew about those two people.

I looked over the two names, from one to the other and back again several times in succession. 'Which of these people murdered you?'

'Sir, I can't tell you that but, if you ask me another way sir, I think that might be alright.' Branok cleared his throat. 'It has to be a certain way that I can answer, like a yes or no.'

I pointed to one of the names. 'Based on how *they* died, I would guess *this* person murdered you.' I turned to Branok and watched him nod heavily.

Chapter 19

Branok led us to a manhole cover in front of the dock.

I passed over it at least a dozen times every day but never had I once considered its use. It didn't look like a conventional manhole cover. It was too large, for starters. It was also made of a heavy-duty wood rather than the cast iron metal and concrete of today. It looked like oak, and it looked heavy too.

I looked to the shop off to my left, and up the street to the pub, and briefly to some of the houses along the front. Most or all of these would have been occupied on the night Eli disappeared, assuming he disappeared on his route home. Just a stone's throw before me was Harry's ship. I couldn't believe that between all of them, they would have seen nothing.

Kensa went to check on Cato in case we needed help searching other places. Meanwhile, Harry spotted our arrival as we passed the ship and decided to re-join us, leaving his men in Benjamin's hands.

'That looks mighty heavy to me, Karl,' said Harry.

'It is, which is why I would like you to stick your head through the manhole and look down there.'

Harry cocked his head at me. 'Now why the hell would I want to do that?'

'Because I am not going to break my back opening it if Eli isn't down there. You can pass through objects, can't you Harry?' In truth, I had never seen *him* do it – but I could also say that about the majority of the village's residents.

'Oh yes, I can!' the penny finally seemed to drop. 'Never thought of that. Right then, here I go!'

Harry knelt on the ground and moved to all fours before finally, tentatively, sticking his head through the wooden manhole cover and under the ground. He knelt there like that for about a minute.

When he didn't come up, I prompted him. 'Anything?' I asked.

Finally his head appeared from beneath the ground. 'Can't see a damn thing down there,' he growled. 'Too bleddy dark!'

'Don't you have like a ghost ability to see or something?'

'What the hell are you blabbering on about, landlubber? Ghost ability? What do you think we are, magic beings or something?'

My face flushed. 'Sorry, I guess I watch too much Hollywood. I don't know how your powers work.'

'I can walk through walls. Most of us do; bleddy painful though. Some of us can Pop, as you call it. But that's it. We don't have no bleddy ghost abilities! Mister Blackman, I tells you, I think you're the maddest person in this village. Listen to him with his bleddy ghost abilities!' He appealed to Branok who chuckled with him.

'Well, my most humble apologies, Harry. But we need to get that open. If Eli is in there-'

'Yeah, yeah, yeah. Captain Harry knows.'

I knelt next to the manhole cover and examined the lock. It seemed to need a device to open it; the socket didn't look familiar. I contemplated that we may need to destroy a piece of public property, and most likely one with heritage.

I didn't want to waste time looking for a device that probably hadn't existed in centuries, so I immediately went home to retrieve the best shovel I had. The wood was pretty solid, and not half as rotten as I'd hoped – typical. If my shovel had ears and a voice, no doubt I'd have spent the next week apologising and making amends.

All the while, the other two men stood and watched in stone silence. I knew what they were thinking. Although I had only just met Branok, the look in his eyes was heavy. He wanted to find Eli – well, I can't say "alive" can I? He wanted to know that Eli was ok and still in this world. I couldn't imagine why the killer would have taken Eli, let alone kept him "alive" so to speak for as long as this.

The more I thought about it, the more I realised how daft this all seemed and the less sense any of it made.

Finally, something gave way. There may have been no rot on the top, but beneath the top layer of hard wood something soft collapsed beneath my shovel blade and went straight through. I almost toppled over and fell into the manhole cover. I heard cracking wood and managed to stop myself falling.

The cover did not completely collapse. Under my weight it surely would have done. I climbed back to my feet, composed myself, and gingerly slid the shovel beneath the cover. When I was sure I had enough leverage, I pushed the handle towards the ground.

Shaking, shuddering and with great resistance, the cover began to lift. I felt and heard it scrape against the metal frame, but it lifted no more than a few millimetres. I might have broken the underside, but the lock was still clearly intact.

'What is the meaning of this?' Although the wooden manhole cover to which Branok had led us was not on the Penrose' property, that didn't mean he would be happy about the group of us crowding around it not all that far from his shop and creating a disturbance with it.

'Stand back please, Corin.' Authority seemed to be the most effective language when speaking to the shopkeeper. 'This is a serious matter.' I nodded formally yet politely to Ebrel who looked concerned at our antics.

'Fine, but you are duty bound to tell me precisely what is going on.'

'No, I'm not,' my voice softened but remained firm.

His body language became nervous, as did his tone. He looked quickly from me to Harry to Branok and back again – twice over. 'Right. True, Mister Blackman. But is there anything I can do to help in the pursuit of public service?'

'Yes, please don't leave. I'm going to need to talk to both of you shortly. For the moment, I would greatly

336

appreciate if you merely stood out of the way while we investigate.'

'Yes, of course. Would you care for some refreshments?' The jitter in his voice remained.

'That *would* be appreciated.'

He turned to his daughter. 'Ebrel?'

She gave me a sheepish smile before making her way back to the shop.

'Lock's not broken eh?' We could lift that if it was. We could easily get our hands in there and pull it up.' Harry rubbed his beard.

'Harry, great idea. Could you get in there and break the lock? I mean, fiddle around inside the trap and physically manipulate it.'

'Ah, this is another one of them ghost abilities what you think we got right? Ha ha ha!' Harry knelt down. 'I don't know. Can't say I ever tried it before, but I'll give it a go.'

Ebrel returned then with a tray of drinks and set them down on the quayside next to us. 'It's lemonade. Our own recipe. I hope you like it, Karl.'

'Mister Blackman,' muttered her father in resignation rather than annoyance.

I smiled at her as a way of thanks and she beamed back. I was so pleased to see her looking happy. I only prayed we found nothing down there to jolt her back to despair.

I took a sip of the homemade lemonade and raised the glass in appreciation. Turning my attention back to Harry, his face was a mix of confusion and frustration, but his hand was still submerged inside the wooden structure of the manhole cover.

'Ah!' he exclaimed. 'I think I got it Mister Blackman!' Sure enough, there was a clunk as he tugged at it. The door lifted but did not come free. Supernatural writers had a lot to answer for, clearly. 'If I knew how he worked, I might be able to.' Harry paused. 'Oh!' and withdrew his hand. 'I thinks I got it.' Harry threw it open. 'That's my ghost ability right there Mister Blackman!'

'You're never going to let me forget that, are you?'

Harry smiled broadly. 'No!'

He beckoned Branok forwards and together they lifted the now unlocked door off its brackets and broken hinges. It seemed the sheer weight of the thing was the only thing holding it down. The metal of the lock was broken and what Harry had done was twist the metal until it snapped.

At once, I got a faint scent of damp. I don't know why that surprised me so close to the quay. I had to hold my breath; it was salty and rancid with it, as though it was home to generations of rotting seaweed.

'Eli, are you in there?' I called. I could hear nothing except the lapping of the ocean before us. One actual breath and four proverbial breaths held as five faces peered into the darkness. The failing light was sufficient that I could see the floor of a chamber that stood perhaps 30ft deep.

'Corin, do you have a ladder?'

Slack jawed, he nodded at me, but I wasn't certain that he understood a word of it. He remained glued to the spot.

'Corin?'

He turned slowly to face me.

'Corin?' I repeated, frowning in confusion. 'Do you have a ladder?'

Nodding a second time, he ran off to the shop.

The light was failing by the time he got back. Ebrel asked a few tentative questions and I answered them the best I could. I couldn't give away too much and this was still an ongoing investigation. The four of us practically wrestled the metal contraption into the hole, letting it fall to the ground with a bump. Still, there was no sign of Eli below.

We decided everyone except the Penroses would go down while they waited and kept guard.

Hitting the bottom, and even by the failing light, I could see we were in a brick chamber. It was old, looking at the flat brick designs, possibly Tudor or Jacobean. Harry's surprise and wonder suggested he knew little of it, but then as I understood it, he didn't spend much of his life in Salmonweir.

'Eli?' I called, my voice carrying, creating a billow of dust and warm air. It was damned cold in here and I surmised that this was an icehouse.

Harry pointed to a small door in the middle of the wall behind us. It was old and rotten and looked about ready to crumble. I suspected it wouldn't give us as much trouble as getting the manhole open and I was right. It wasn't even on hinges.

Inside this second room, not much bigger than my front yard, we found Eli. He sat slumped against the back wall with his knees pulled up to his chest and his face pressed to his knees.

'Are you going to kill me now? Get it over with. I know nothing, I saw nothing, and I'm tired of your pointless questions.' he said.

'We're, ah, actually here to rescue you, Eli.'

Eli looked up and for the first time, I saw something resembling joy on his face. He leapt to his feet and came marching towards me. If I didn't know Eli any better, I'd have thought the man was about to hug me.

'Detective Blackman?' he exclaimed. 'How did you know?'

I turned to Branok. 'This gentleman suspected you might be here. Actually, he gave us three possible locations. It seems you were in the first we checked.'

Eli gave the man a formal and respectful bow. 'And who might you be, sir?'

'I'm sure Mister Blackman has a dozen or more questions.' Branok explained as briefly as he could precisely who he was and how he suspected Eli's location.

'I am forever in your debt.' And then Eli turned to me. 'Thank you, Karl. I am forever in your debt too. You should probably know who left me here. Luckily, you got to me in time.'

'I know... almost everything. What I don't understand is why you didn't Pop back home or to my place or anywhere out of here? We've all been so worried about you.'

'Ah here we go again,' Harry interjected. 'This is one of them "Ghost Ability" things you was going on about up there. Why don't you just go an ask him why he didn't just grow wings and fly out of here up to the sky, Karl?' He waved his arms to mimic a bird and made a woo-woo sound.

Eli smiled at Harry as he went on mocking me for some minutes. When Harry finally got bored with having a joke at my expense, Eli continued. 'It's simple, Karl. I *couldn't* Pop away.'

'But you can Pop? I've seen you do it.' I frowned.

'That you have, but it doesn't work as you might suspect. In order to Pop somewhere I have to know where I am. I also have to know where I am in relation to where I need to go. If I took you to somewhere in the village, put things in your ears that you could not hear and something over your eyes that you could not see, could you find your way home?'

Sheepishly, I replied in the negative.

'This is similar. I walked around for some time but found only solid rock that way,' he pointed to his left, to his right and then behind him. 'When I found the room over there, I started to worry I would get lost when I hit brick wall that way too.' He pointed to his left again. 'So I came back and waited, and waited, and waited.'

'We need to get you out of here and then I have a killer to apprehend.'

Darkness all but consumed the land when we made our way out of the chamber and back to the quayside. The Penroses returned to their shop. I could see them in animated conversation through the window, just a bare flicker of candlelight illuminating Corin's stocky form. I had my answers. Why they argued that night I was satisfied had no bearing on my case. Clearly a domestic matter, I had no desire to interrupt.

'Go home everybody, please. The best way you can help me now is to go home.'

I walked back to *The Lady Catherine* with Harry, Kensa and Branok, hoping the final artefact would turn up, though what was left to discover was anybody's guess.

343

Still, it would help to confront the killer with all three items, and they'd know the game was over.

Benjamin greeted us on the quayside. In his excited state I finally managed to get out of him that he'd found something of interest. It was the final artefact – that strange shiny object left at the scene of Eddie's disappearance all those weeks ago. They hadn't needed to go looking for it. Of all places, it was not on the bottom of the seabed covered in silt. It appeared back where it started in Eddie's sleeping space.

As Benjamin handed it over, I prepared for what was to come. Like last time, it still came as a shock when the Salmonweir I knew disappeared to be replaced with one of old, one from before I was born.

On the quayside; it's somebody's wedding day. It takes me a moment to realise that this is my wedding day – the white dress is the giveaway. I am wearing the white dress. Branok is before me, smiling. The look in his eyes is adoration and perhaps some pride. I can tell it's him but he looks young, perhaps 25.

Around us, people are cheering and clapping. I turn to face the minister to my right. It is a warm day, the sun is rising in a brilliant and dazzling shade of red. --- Red sky in the morning is the shepherd's warning ---

From the look on his face, I can tell Branok feels he is the luckiest man alive as he moves in for the kiss. He says my name clearly and out loud. 'I will love you until the day I die. Until the day I die, day I die, I die. Die... Die... Die...

The scene fades, like melting paint falling off an easel, dripping and drooling to the floor. Something else replaces it.

Another scene. Branok is on the floor, his eyes stone cold – arms reaching out to grasp at something. He is clearly dead, a look of abject horror on his face, frozen at the moment of his passing into wherever he was to go.

A pool of blood surrounds him and it spreads out across the floor, caking the wooden planking. There is straw and sawdust scattered about the floor; the resulting mush is a sickly pink colour and I do not want to look at it. I feel my left hand rise to meet his face. The ring is on my finger; I look at it and reach for it, taking it off, tugging at it.

I am sobbing, crying, calling out his name. Agonised cries fill the air. The ring comes free and I place it gingerly on his chest. I feel myself fumble around in my pocket for something and pull out two items. One is the granite pendant and the other is the bracelet. 'Branok, please!' I sob. 'I didn't mean- I didn't- but you-'

I hear a voice from behind me, a voice I know. 'No. No! It can't be! This is not right! What do we do now?'

And suddenly, everything becomes clear.

I opened my eyes and turned to my companions. Their look was one of both concern and hope. 'Branok, I have one more favour to ask of you.'

Chapter 20

I knocked heavily on the door. At first, I thought nobody was in, but as I was about to give up and go home, the door opened slowly. A curious face appeared from around the side of the door, thin and spindly fingers clutching at the doorframe silhouetted by the light from behind.

'Mister Blackman.' It seems I was expected this evening.

'May I please come in?'

Babajide cocked his head to one side and reluctantly opened the door. I stepped inside. The bar was eerily quiet as I always imagined they were before opening time, but I never imagined the stillness or the modern musk of polish and dust of old buildings. I never imagined not even hearing the hum of the jukebox.

'Misses Morwenna is preparing for the evening opening; she will be here in a moment.' He turned on his heel to scuttle away but I stopped him with a wave of my hand.

'Actually Babajide, I want to talk to you if that is all right. Please take a seat.' I gestured at the table.

He looked terrified. 'What is this about?' Babajide shifted in his seat and looked nervously over my shoulder.

'Yes,' came the voice from the door behind the bar, 'what is this about?' Morwenna stood behind the bar almost like an indignant soap world landlady ready to kick me out of her pub.

'Hello Morwenna, I will make this quick as I know the pub is about to open for the evening.'

She nodded. 'Yes thank you. Baba, why don't you leave us be?'

'Actually,' I insisted, 'I'd rather he stayed.'

'Why?' Her tone still indignant.

'This concerns both of you.'

She cautiously rounded the bar and approached me but stopped short of showing me anything resembling welcome. 'What is this about? You said you wanted to talk to Baba and now it's both of us?'

I sat down at the round table next to the fireplace. 'Yes, I do want to talk to him but not *only* to him. Will you both please sit down?' I gestured at the two other seats at the bar table.

Babajide shot Morwenna a nervous look but took a seat nonetheless. Prompted by the both of us, Morwenna followed suit.

'Thank you,' I said to them both. 'I am expecting several other visitors and I will need everybody's help on the matter.'

They looked at each other.

'Who is coming? I have to prepare the pub for opening time,' Morwenna repeated.

'And I must count the float and bring barrels up,' said Babajide, nodding profusely.

'It won't take long; our visitors will be here soon, and we'll be all set.'

A heavy hand knocked the door. 'Ah, there we are.'

'I'll get that,' said Morwenna.

As she went to the door, Babajide reached out and placed his hand on my arm – at least he would have done if he was capable of physically touching me. He opened his mouth to tell me something but Morwenna was already returning to the table. Cato whom I had indeed asked to meet me at the pub, accompanied her.

I gave him a friendly grin, but the look he gave me back was one of uncertainty.

He nodded and I nodded back. 'Please sit down, Cato.' I gestured to one of the pub chairs.

He did so; this would have been cosy had it been a leisurely drink on a Sunday afternoon talking about the weather, football, or even which was the best cider the pub served. I couldn't and must not forget that we were here to apprehend a killer and I needed as much help as I could possibly get.

'As you know,' I began, 'I cannot physically interact with ghosts though you can interact with each other. That means I will need help of several spirit persons in the killer's apprehension. When does the pub open, Morwenna?'

'About twenty minutes,' she snapped.

'We have plenty of time, but we'd better get started. As you know, I could not physically see the first crime scene. Harry was kind enough to learn how to use a camera to take pictures for me.' I placed the prints on the table.

'One thing bothered me about the images. I couldn't quite figure out what this was. When I asked Harry to look later, it had gone because they had cleaned the deck of debris. I assumed it had been cleared away, but nobody recalled seeing it. I might never have found out what it was had somebody not later told me.'

'On Bonfire Night, the night Tobin disappeared, he told me he needed to talk about a recent arrival, but the killer got to him before he had the chance to tell me who that was.'

'So far, since all of you arrived here, I have given you all the privacy you deserve. I have not yet researched the methods of your deaths – for those who might have a record, that is. Some have offered this information freely; Morwenna was one of them. When you admitted you'd had an affair and paid for it with your life, I sympathised. Who wouldn't? Of course, affairs are wrong but it's no reason for a wronged partner to murder the person who wronged them.'

I had all three of them transfixed.

'Nobody deserves that,' said Morwenna.

'No.' I agreed.

'I was in Truro earlier today. My son called me there. He seemed to have found a news story about two murders and a suicide, seemingly related. It was a long shot, but I was happy to go with anything, no matter how tentative.'

Babajide and Morwenna both shot me startled looks but I went on, focusing my attention on the Innkeeper and her assistant. 'But what you didn't tell me was the name of the man you had the affair with, Morwenna. When did your husband find out about you two – you and Babajide?'

The look that passed over her face was a mix of relief and sadness. 'Not until the day we left him when he found us in our marital bed. We fled, leaving everything we had not already packed and moved away. I told people I was widowed, and they believed me. We were able to carry on until the day he came looking for us and then he killed us.'

I looked at Babajide, but his gaze was firmly on the floor.

'That's correct, I never told you it was Baba, but is that really important? I wasn't the *only* woman to fornicate with a slave, or any handsome young man from a lower class. Babajide had – has – such humanity. He proved himself bright, willing to learn and a sensitive, caring soul.'

A tear rolled down her cheek. 'It wasn't about the lust; it was about the love. I loved him but I knew nobody would accept us, even as a freedman. It didn't matter in the end because he killed us both.'

She looked at me, pleaded with me to accept her story.

'Except,' I interrupted, 'you were already a widow when you moved to Devon.'

She blinked in confusion. 'That's what I told the people of Tavistock and the village where we lived, yes.'

'No, you *were* a widow. That bit was *not* a lie. Your husband was dead the day you left. They found his body right here in the bar with a stab wound to the heart. The local Watchman presumed one of you two had done it, but they had neither the resources nor the will to find you. If you were out of the village and never coming back, there was nothing for them to worry about.'

She flicked several angry glances at Babajide throughout my accusation.

'Yes, blame the former slave if you were caught. That would have been easy. After all, he was a slave with no legal rights. Everyone would have believed you no matter how outrageous your explanation. You love him and that's why you would have been more than happy for him to take the blame for you; he loved you in return which was why he would have been a willing martyr for you should the law have ever caught up with you.'

'Morwenna, it's over. But I need to know. I need to understand. Why did you kill your husband? Less than a year later, why did you kill Babajide before killing yourself? Why kill Eddie and Tobin? And why let Eli live, what information were you trying to gain from him?'

Morwenna shook her head firmly. 'Karl, where are you getting this information?'

The conversation broke as a heavy fist slammed against the outer door. I glanced over; the silhouette of a heavy-set figure blocked the failing light from outside. 'Do you mind if I get this?' Feet feeling heavy, I went to the door and opened it quickly. The sombre face of Branok nodded and stepped over the threshold with a heavy sigh.

Morwenna caught only the briefest glimpse of her husband before the penny dropped.

Throwing the chair back, she grabbed Cato's military knife from his side, turned around, seized Babajide and held the knife to the lad's throat. 'Get him away from me!' she screamed at Branok and then at me.

'It's over Morwenna, I know everything.'

'Morwenna,' Branok said in a soft and gentle voice. 'I forgive you both for what you did to me, but you can't stay here now. Come back with us.'

'People started talking in Devon. They thought we were lovers. In the end, it became too much to bear.' She turned to the Roman, 'Get away, Cato!' and with her free hand pointed at the bar.

He retreated out of arm's reach but not as far as she demanded. Still he maintained a ready-to-pounce stance.

'Branok didn't kill you, you killed him. Tell me, why did your husband have to die? Tell me the truth. No more lies.'

'He *did* walk in on us in our marriage bed.' She spat at Branok. 'He got angry, grabbed Baba and was going to throw him out of the window but I grabbed a candlestick and he wasn't a threat to us anymore. We dragged him downstairs but when he started groaning, I plunged the knife into his heart.'

'That I did,' said Branok. 'But them's was just words. I wouldn't have done it. I cared for the lad. We were going to adopt him, for the love of God. He was the closest thing I had to a son. We had it all worked out, he would become our legitimate son and inherit everything. You agreed to it all and you *both* betrayed me!' nearly shouting the last sentence.

'You were convicted posthumously, Morwenna. They found out about you in the end.' Out of the corner of my eye, I saw Cato step forward.

'Stop!' she screamed at him; I waved the Roman back. He circled around behind her but again, I held up my hand to stop him reacting.

'And the residents of our village? Did they really need to die a second time?'

'They knew! Both of them knew, they saw us. The cabin boy? He came behind the bar when I told him not to. All he wanted was rum and he died for it. Tobin? That stupid travelling salesman? He *knew*. He had the boldness to challenge Baba about our love.'

'And Eli?'

'He saw us embracing.'

'That was it? He saw you sharing a moment of affection? There was no need for it, Morwenna. I only wanted to help you, to get you to come back with me – both of you.' Branok pleaded with the woman who'd murdered him.

'Most of us had our suspicions about you and Babajide,' I interjected. 'When was it going to end to protect a secret nobody cares about? When you'd

356

emptied the whole village and it was just the two of you left? Does it really matter? What were you going to do when I was the only one left?'

She blinked in confusion, unable to process what I was saying to her, unable to understand she'd taken her paranoia to the extreme with deadly consequences. Cato took the moment to inch forward again. It took all my concentration not too look directly at him and give away his position.

'Please, Morwenna.' Branok pressed. 'Let him go and let's all leave together?'

She shook her head. 'I'm sorry Baba, but I have to kill you all over again.' She pressed the knife to his throat.

As Cato lurched forward to stop her and Branok took a large step forward to help, Babajide threw his body backwards, upending the two of them. I watched helpless as he fell out of his chair and scrambled away from the prone woman.

'Baba?' she said. 'Baba, don't you love me?' climbing to her feet as Cato moved ready to subdue her.

'Get back both of you,' I growled at Cato and Branok. They shrunk away, giving Morwenna and Babajide all the space they needed.

Then I turned to Morwenna. 'Put the knife down,' I said calmly as she took several small steps towards Babajide, the knife falling loosely by her side. 'It's over.'

'Baba,' she repeated, '*don't* you love me?'

He too got to his feet and backed into the corner. 'You know I do, but you gave me no choice. I loved you, but you didn't ask me what I wanted. Stop!'

She froze on the spot; Babajide's firmness surprised me as much as it surprised Morwenna. Cato took the hint and moved away again.

'You didn't ask me if I wanted to go to Devon. You didn't ask me if I wanted to die, you did what you wanted, you always did only what you wanted.' Babajide went on.

'But Baba, we wanted to be together,' she pleaded with him. 'Don't you want to be together anymore?'

'Not like this.' He put his hands together and looked down at his feet. 'I'm sorry.'

Then he turned to me. 'It was me. I left the jewellery. I took them from Mrs Morwenna and left them for you. The memories, so powerful. I thought it would help you find out.'

'But how did you-'

'I can do this.' He disappeared then. One moment, Babajide was before Morwenna, completely at her mercy. The next moment, he was at the other end of the bar. Barely half a second later, he appeared by her side once more.

'Please stop, Morwenna,' Babajide said and put his arm around her. 'It is over. We can do something. We can help. Branok too, if that is alright?' He glanced at his former master.

Branok nodded. 'All three of us, we go together.'

'No,' Morwenna raised the knife, putting it between their bodies.

'Put it down!' Cato commanded, but it was too late.

With a quick flick of the hand, she turned the knife with the hilt towards Babajide and drove the blade into her own stomach.

Both men – Branok and Cato – launched themselves towards her, but by the time they reached her position, she crumpled and became smoke. It lingered in the air, twisting and turning around itself, becoming a column and then dispersed. In the space of a few seconds, our killer was gone.

The pub stayed closed that night as the few of us most involved in the case came together to go over what happened. We decided not to broadcast the news until the following day. That gave us the time to assemble all village residents.

We met in the open space a quick walk from the quayside that used to serve as the car park and would again once the tourists returned. Babajide, Branok, Kensa, Cato and I stood on the quayside with our backs to *The Lady Catherine*. When the murmurs died down, I told them everything – not leaving out that Morwenna killed at least two men in life including her husband and their former slave.

Shocked murmurs passed over the crowd, shock that this woman whom they had come to trust to run their pub, killed two of their number and almost killed a third.

'Where is she now? Where will we imprison her?' The questions came thick and fast. Above the throng, the booming voice of Hook Hand Harry explained that she killed herself rather than allow herself to be taken in.

'Who will run the pub now?' asked Jowan who had made his way to the front of the crowd.

'Branok was once the owner of this prestigious inn. Perhaps he would like to resume that responsibility?

360

Technically it never stopped being yours.' Even before I'd finished my sentence, I could see the big man shaking his head.

'Alas, I cannot. My time here is short. Even if I could stay, I would not wish to do so.

Despite everything that had happened, he put his arm around Babajide. 'There is one who deserves it more. My Babajide, my friend, the man I loved as a son. I believe he has proven himself more than capable.'

'I have no objections. Babajide, do you want it?'

'Yes! I have been practising my modern landlord skills.' He nodded eagerly before clearing his throat. '"Get out of my pub you 'orrible lot!" "We don't serve your kind 'round here!" "What'll it be, my darling?" "If you smash his head through that table, you're paying for the damage sunshine!" 'You're barred!"' He turned to look at me. 'How was that?'

'I suggest you work harder on your mockney accent before letting it out in public again. That was *seriously* awful.'

We dismissed the meeting. Everybody left except Cato and Branok. The latter made quick goodbyes, thanked me for my assistance. I again pointed out he would be welcome to stay. His answer was brief and in the negative. I didn't believe I would ever see the man again.

When it was just Cato and I left, we sat on the edge of the quayside looking out to sea. It was a cool yet bright day, a mix of white and grey clouds hinting of rain to come. A cool wind reminded me that this was still November, mild or not.

Most of the pirates had disembarked and were already heading to the pub so no song came from the ship.

'Poor Babajide,' I commented, watching the pirates go. 'he's going to have a busy time looking after that lot.'

Cato nodded thoughtfully. 'He'll be fine until they taste the rum. So long as he keeps them drinking the cider, he won't have any problems. Besides, I think Miss Ebrel will learn fast how to handle them. How her father reacts to her new job though – I believe she still hasn't told him.'

'What about you?' I asked.

'Me?' he shrugged. 'An officer of the Roman Navy without a ship? I have to find something to do in Salmonweir for as long as I'm here. I've been thinking of joining Harry's crew. He needs a Second Mate and I must say I'm tempted. With Kensa setting up a – what did she call it – a reproduction armoury business, I feel I need to do *something*. I'm afraid I've proven quite useless at the task despite her patience in trying to teach me.'

'You did well earlier. Your first instinct was to protect Babajide and me. You threw yourself at a woman with a knife. She could have killed you.'

He tapped his armour. 'I wore this. It would have protected me.'

'You didn't even think about that; you just did it. So, I was thinking.' I shifted my body to face him. 'I've been this village's only police service for six months. I never expected to have a case, let alone a multiple murder case to investigate.'

'Some retirement, DI Blackman.' The Roman laughed. 'On television the other week, I heard a man, perhaps a retired Police Officer, say "once a copper, always a copper" and I remembered you telling me that "copper" was a term for a Police Officer. Do you agree with that sentiment?'

I nodded thoughtfully. 'You see, Cato, every detective has an assistant to help them share the load. I was wondering whether you would like that job? It's an easy task; we may never have another case for as long as I live. For the most part it's about keeping your ear to the ground for anything amiss.'

He knelt on the floor, knelt down and literally pressed his ear to the ground.

'Sorry, Cato! It's a phrase; it means you need to listen to what is going on around the village. I sometimes forget that I'm the only 21st century man here.'

Slightly embarrassed, he brushed himself off and returned to sitting on the quayside next to me.

'I can't promise you a life at sea and I certainly can't promise you the glories of Rome.'

'Oh no, I never visited Rome in life. I was born in Palmyra to Syrian parents, signed up there, and spent most of my life at sea. Closest I ever got to Rome was Ostia. Never left the town while stationed there.'

I nodded. 'I can't promise you Palmyra, or even Ostia for that matter. I can promise you all the glories of Salmonweir, for what it is worth. This tiny little village where nothing ever happened and now everyone is watching. You might have a lot to do, you might have nothing to do. What do you say?'

He smiled. 'Well, the weather is not as it was in Syria – but that is not all bad.' He sighed deeply. 'I think I quite like the sound of "Detective Cato".' He smiled and then we shook on it.

We will return to the world of Salmonweird in:

Book 2: *A Salmonweird Sleighing*

And

Book 3: *Studio Salmonweird*

Are You Ready to Step into the

Salmonweird Extended Universe?

Turn the page to learn more

Introduction to the Salmonweird Extended Universe

In March 2020, with the worst pandemic in over a century spreading across the world, I asked myself "what would a lockdown in a village with only one live resident look like?"

So I wrote that story and called it "A Salmonweird Lockdown." Several more short stories followed that year including "Sword Crossed Lovers" and "The Crypt" a spooky Christmas short story.

Let's go back to the beginning of this journey and see what happened in Salmonweird when COVID-19 arrived.

A Salmonweird Lockdown

Can you think of a more delightful small pleasure than eating breakfast (pot of tea and toast with locally produced honey) on the patio with the doors wide open?

No?

Me neither.

I switched the heating off last night and today I have all the windows and doors open.

Thank the heavens, spring is finally here!

On the plus side is the glee that comes with knowing the best of spring and summer weather is yet to come. I need to remind myself it's only late March though, so my jumper is strategically placed over the back of the nearest dining chair. No doubt I will be wearing it before sunset.

I'd had a weekend of reading, catching up with the kids lounging in the sun, and not much else planned for the next few days. Bliss.

That was until I heard a heavy fist hit my front door repeatedly.

I placed the mug in direct sunlight (it probably achieves nothing, even on a March day but old habits die hard), lay the tea towel carefully over the toast, and went to answer it.

I admit I was in no rush to get there, even when the knocking became frantic, I maintained my leisurely pace.

I was surprised to see Jowan - the village's resident medieval monk - looking red-faced and anxious.

'Oh Karl!' he said, 'you're here!'

I nodded. 'Where else would I be? The country's on lockdown.'

If he could still breath, I had no doubt I'd struggle to understand the poor chap through the wheezing, but like everyone else in the village bar me, he's a ghost. 'Good, good. I'm sure you're taking every precaution, but you might have been at the pub or the shop or somewhere else around the village and you might have put yourself at risk. You did go to the shop yesterday.'

I blushed. 'I needed honey. I live on the stuff, you know that.'

Despite that I'm the only living person in the village and therefore the only person capable of getting sick, I'm taking the same precautions as everyone else across the country. Yesterday's lapse to go to the shop for a jar of honey was the only time (so far) I'd fallen off the wagon.

Jowan barged past me, almost passing through me, and to the patio where he collected my breakfast paraphernalia and hurried it into the kitchen with a clatter.

'Jowan, please tell me what's going on?'

He closed the patio door, but struggled with the modern contraption until I explained how to do it - not for the first time. 'They're here, Karl,' He proclaimed with a seriousness approaching a Shakespearean tragedy. '*They are* here!'

He gesticulated to the sofa and urged me to sit. Bemused, I complied with his request.

'May I borrow a chair, Karl?'

'Of course? Are you going to tell me what this is about? *Who* are here?'

He dragged one of my dining chairs along the laminate floor. Cringing at the scraping sound, it was just as well that it wasn't actually wood. Before she left, Valarie wanted to replace it with hardwood. So did I in all honestly, but since she left, it only slipped further down my priority list.

Jowan dragged the chair all the way to the front door, climbed it, and tied a bunch of herbs to the hook where I put a sprig of mistletoe at Christmas.

I watched him repeat this process above the patio and then finally to the two small windows on the opposite side of the room. Satisfied, he returned the chair to the dining table and closed the kitchen door. 'There!' Finally, Jowan relaxed.

At no point did I leave the sofa; I let Jowan go about his business and then repeated my questions. 'Jowan, what is this about and *who* are here?'

'Tourists, Karl!' he said, exasperated. 'A group of walkers were trying to get into the inn. I told them it was closed until the evening and living people were forbidden anyway, but they went to the shop. They were touching everything! I tried to stop them, but I couldn't.'

I groaned. 'Some people don't listen, but I don't see what those herbs have to do with anything.'

'Silence, Karl. When you're using detective skills, you're doing your bit for our Salmonweir community. As I believe the young ones of today say, this is where you should "hold my beer".'

I chuckled. 'What do you need me to do?'

'Nothing Karl. Just let me do what I need to do. I would prefer if you remained silent throughout though this is not obligatory. It might help if you closed your eyes.'

I took a deep breath, leaned back into the sofa and closed my eyes.

That's when Jowan started the chanting.

I stifled a laugh but confess to finding it pleasant once I got over the initial surprise.

If Jowan had done this while alive, I must wonder where and when he paused for breath throughout his one-man chantry.

After some minutes, Jowan trailed off to a calm rhythm until finally coming to a stop.

I opened my eyes and was overcome with a wonderful sense of calm as though I'd just had a relaxing professional massage but where no hands went anywhere near my body and I wasn't presented with an eye-watering invoice at the end.

'Thank you, Jowan. I appreciate it. I'm feeling *so* much calmer now.'

Jowan turned to me shocked. 'Oh no, Karl. That was just the opening chant to disperse the miasma. We have much, much more to do.'

'I see. What's next?'

From under his robe, Jowan produced a jar and showed it to me with a smile.

'That smells nice, what is it?'

Jowan lifted it to his face and examined the jar. 'A mix of herbs: mint, some rosemary and honey among other things. I'm afraid I had to make do with what Corin Penrose had in his shop and I'm confident it will do the job.'

'Are we going to eat it?'

He turned to me and smiled. 'No Karl. If you could remove your clothes and lie down on the sofa, that would be grand.'

'What? Why?'

'I need you disrobed while I administer this ointment all over your body.'

'I'm not dying, Jowan!' I laugh-shouted. 'I'm not even sick.'

'Karl, you're *of the faith*, I am required to give you Extreme Unction, sick or not.'

'Can't I do it myself?' I asked weakly. 'Just pop the ointment on the table and I will do it later after my bath.'

Jowan shook his head seriously. 'I *cannot* let you do that. You're not an administered priest; I am. I'm afraid if I permitted you to do this yourself it will not have the desired effect. I might even be excommunicated. Besides, the third and final stage is confession. What use would it be to confess your sins to yourself? No, this is the way it must be.'

No, I didn't want to get undressed in front of Jowan. I had no doubt one day he would administer my last rites and prepare my body for burial, but that day would not be now, not while I was only in my late 50s.

I was trying to come up with an excuse to get Jowan out of my house when I heard a voice call. 'Karl, Karl! You in there? Open up you old landlubber!'

'Oh, what a shame Captain Harry's here for our, um, meeting, chat. Thing. I really must say goodbye Jowan. Can't keep Harry waiting, he's a stickler for timekeeping. Goes with a life on the sea is my guess.'

I leapt from the sofa, raced to the door and threw it open. Harry tumbled in waving a bottle furiously before him. I didn't need to be told it was rum, Captain Harry was rarely without a bottle of the stuff.

Jowan took one look at me, one look at Harry, smiled at us both and to my relief, departed my house.

'Thanks, Harry. If you had left it another minute, I'm not sure what would have happened. He was trying to get me to take my clothes off and rub ointment all over me.'

Harry gave me a quizzical look. 'What goes on inside your ship aint none of my business, Karl. I seen some strange things at sea that nothing shocks me no more.' He tapped the side of his nose. 'Like the time a drunk octopus tried to mate with a bull shark. Didn't end well.'

I cleared my throat. 'What can I do for you, Harry?'

'Nothing much. Me and Queen Kensa was showing each other some sword tricks when we saw Jowan come rushing up here all red faced like. Thought we mighta left it long enough to come rescue you!' Harry laughed.

'Now you're here, you can be my bodyguard until I'm certain he's gone. Would you like some tea?'

He contemplated his rum bottle for a moment, muttered something about it tasting like mermaid snot, and asked if I had coffee.

I didn't, but I knew someone who did. Jowan told me the pub wasn't open, but I phoned through and Babajide answered in three rings.

'This is the King's Head. We don't open until 5pm this evening and living people are banned during the lockdown. Please call back-'

'Babajide, it's me! I need a favour.'

'Oh, Karl. Sorry, what's the favour? You know I can't let you come to the pub.'

'That's fine. I'm not asking to visit. I know the pub has a coffee machine. Could you send up two takeaway coffees if you're not too busy?'

'Just coffee?' he sounded slightly terrified. 'Coffee is all you want, yes? Just coffee. Normal coffee. Like coffee drinkers have when asking for coffee?'

'Yes. What else would I ask for?'

I heard the lad sigh in relief. 'This is fine, Karl. It's good, really. I was worried you were going to ask for a flatty-skinny-latte-machiattaccino or something. The tourists last weekend kept coming in and speaking nonsense at us all. I swear they were making some of those orders up.'

'You're all right, my friend. Just a large coffee with cream if you have it, full fat milk if you don't.'

'Sure, Karl but stay there. Someone will bring them up.' With that he hung up.

Ebrel's beaming smile greeted me at the door 15 minutes later. She handed over the coffee along with a box of complementary pastries which she said were on the house and asked me what Jowan was doing.

'I thought he left. Please don't tell me he's still here?'

Sheepishly, Ebrel pointed to my roof. Following the line of her finger, I saw Jowan crawling about my roof on his hands and knees.

'Jowan, what the hell are you doing up there?'

He stood and glared down at all of us. 'Karl, if you want let me protect you against the plague then I'm afraid I have to take extreme measures.' He wagged his finger at me as though undressing in front him and letting him spread a concoction over my naked body was somehow a perfectly reasonable request.

My eyesight isn't what it used to be, but I could see he'd spread more of his herb bundles around my roof – one on the chimney and three along the dirtiest part of the guttering.

 I need to get back, Karl,' Ebrel said apologetically before disappearing down my driveway.

'Thank you, Ebrel. It was lovely to see you,' I called after her, but she had already gone.

'Come on Mister Jowan! Stop monkeying around up there,' Harry called before laughing at his own joke. 'get it? Monkey! Monk!'

'This is important work!' Jowan called back. 'I need to disperse the miasma and you all must be quiet.'

'Jowan, I'm going inside now. Just do what you need to do.' I turned to Harry. 'Are you coming?'

Harry pulled a face. 'Sorry Karl, you're one your own with this one.' Then he too scuttled off leaving me holding two coffees and the box of pastries.

I slammed the door, then locked and bolted it, falling against it with a huff. I was fully aware that Jowan could just pass through the door or wall any time he wanted if he so desired, but securing it made me feel better all the same.

I placed the coffees and pastries on the breakfast bar and noticed Harry's bottle of rum. He'd barely touched it, probably something to do with tasting like mermaid's snot. I picked it up, turning it over curiously. It had a premium feel about it, emblazoned with a stylised ancient map of Cornwall with the words. *Penryn 800: Pride of Cornwall.*

'Huh? This is an award winner,' I noticed the *Good Tipples: Gold Winner 2018* label and wondered if Harry was finally losing his taste for the good stuff or whether he ever had it.

I poured myself a small glass and had a sip. Rum had never been my thing but with that sliver of a tiny dribble, I could see why it had won an award. Notes of caramel and whiskey and maybe vanilla. It was smooth.

'Mermaid's snot, indeed. It's mine now, Harry!' I put it pride of place alongside my small collection of premium spirits I forbade myself drinking except on special occasions.

I groaned at hearing Jowan clamber around the roof chanting to nobody. I'm sure he would be done in three or four hours with a bit of luck, so I finished my breakfast in silence at the breakfast bar. The tea was cold, so I tipped it away and decided not to waste the coffee.

So much caffeine! It was inevitable I needed the little boy's room after that.

I relieved myself and washed my hands for the mandatory 20 seconds. When I stepped out of the bathroom, I heard Jowan and Harry's voices through the open window; Jowan was now back at ground level. I stopped, held my breath, and eavesdropped.

'Do you think that will work?' Harry asked. 'Will he really stay at home now?'

'I think so,' Jowan replied. 'The idea of me coming back to cleanse the house and threaten to rub ointment over his body every time he goes outside will keep him inside for as long as necessary, I'm sure.'

'It better! That was the best bottle of rum the pub had! You don't know how painful it was to leave it with him, 'e don't even drink rum. Why couldn't I have left something else there?'

'You only drink rum, Harry. Anything else and he would have become suspicious.'

'Yer right but I could cry, Jowan, really I could and if I had a hand to cut off, I'd rather have done that!'

Jowan chuckled and gently touched Harry's shoulder. 'God will honour your sacrifice *and* forgive your mild dishonesty for the greater good. Come along, Harry, let me buy you a drink to make up for it.'

As their footsteps retreated, I let out a chuckle. 'You got me, fellas. You got me good and proper.'

A Salmonweird Sleighing

It's December and for Karl Blackman, the only living person in the Cornish ghost village of Salmonweir, that means unleashing his inner 6-year-old.

But all is not well, when, following the Advent Sunday service, one resident willingly returns to the afterlife with only Karl to witness it.

Did Karl really see something that night or did Harry spike the mulled wine with Cornish moonshine?

Karl must also contend with a TV medium who turns up on his doorstep to help the un-departed re-depart to the afterlife, Babajide continues his war with the coffee machine, while another resident finds a lost love among the new arrivals.

At least Karl's daughter Claire is coming for Christmas. Maybe his other visitor might have gone by then?

A Salmonweird Sleighing, released 4th June 2021: only on Amazon Kindle and Paperback

A note from the author

Hello reader, thank you for buying *Salmonweird: A Cornish Crime Comedy Caper.* I hope you enjoyed it.

May I ask for a minute of your time?

Big name writers can trade on their name alone. Readers often buy new books without a second thought.

For the self-published writer, the reality is very different. For us, it's a constant and unending mission to market ourselves, posting on social media, and engaging with thousands of people every day.

That process is far easier when book lovers like you leave reviews.

We don't expect or need a long thousand-word blog post. Just a few lines will do. Amazon prioritises books with 25 or more reviews and recommends them. The more people recommend a book, the more Amazon will recommend it.

Thanks again for reading *Salmonweird* and please do consider leaving a review and rating. Also, don't forget to keep checking **salmonweird.co.uk** for further news about sequels and spin-offs!